Misfortune Cookie

MICHELE GORMAN

Notting Hill Press
PUBLISHINGS THIRD WAY

All characters and events in this publication, other than those clearly in the public domain, are fictitious and any resemblance to real persons, living or dead, is purely coincidental.

Copyright © 2012 Michele Gorman
Cover illustration Shutterstock

The moral right of the author has been asserted.

All rights reserved. No part of this publication may be reproduced, stored in a retrieval system, or transmitted, in any form or by any means, without the prior permission of the publisher.

ALSO BY MICHELE GORMAN

Single in the City
Twelve Days to Christmas
The Boyfriend Tune-Up
The Curvy Girls Club
The Curvy Girls Baby Club
Perfect Girl
Christmas Carol
Life Change

MICHELE GORMAN

THANK YOU

I'm grateful to so many people. To Andrew, my partner in crime and life, and all my wonderful friends who manage to appear interested when I go on, and on, and on about the books. To my family who, though contractually obliged, seem to be my constant champions by choice. And to all the chick lit writers and bloggers who've been so generous with their support – my wine glass runneth over with love.

Once again my agent, Caroline Hardman at Christopher Little, has proven herself an indispensable professional, and a great friend. Here's to a lifelong partnership. Designer Nellie Ryan, who created the cover for Misfortune Cookie, and Single in the City, was once again a dream, and Lucy York, our editor extraordinaire, was the best grammar task-master one could hope for. She made sure Misfortune Cookie was perfect for publication.

Huge thanks to all the lovely readers who contributed to this, my first interactive writing endeavor: Allison, Beth, Betsy, Brenda, Caroline, Caroline E., Carolyn, Clodagh, Frankie, Gina, Heidi, Jencey, Jonita, Kary, Katrin, Kellie, Krystal, Leah, Lois, Martel, Mary, Michelle, Nadine, Nicola, Nicole, Robyn, Sally, Sari, Tracie, Victoria and the rest of the helpful readers who answered the polls but were too bashful to take credit. And there were even a few boys, whose perspectives were most appreciated: Chris, Paul, Todd and Tony, thank you.

Finally, thank you Hong Kong, and the lovely people there. Some are long-time friends, some new friends, and some, random meetings that gave me incredible insights.

1

'Yarrow nudens?' The squat old woman at my elbow screeches again.

'What?'

'Yarrow nudens?!'

'I'm sorry, I still don't understand.' My pleading look to the Chinese girl sharing my table elicits a hearty smirk as she pretends to ignore me. I wonder if the word for bitch is hard to pronounce in Cantonese.

'Yarrow nudens, yarrow nudens!' She's bobbing with the effort of her exclamations.

'No, no thanks.' What on earth are yarrow nudens?

'No yarrow nudens?' She murmurs in a tiny voice. Clearly I've hurt her with my refusal.

'No,' I say again. 'Just the soup, please.' The last time I let a waitress bully me into an order I was served what looked like brains on a plate. Discretion is the better part of dining in Asia.

She strides to the kitchen to make sure the cook adds a little extra, off-menu flavor to my order. I can hear her in there, shouting in what sounds like tortured cat.

My belly grumbles its greeting upon her return… but there aren't any noodles in my noodle soup. Not a one. Only three sad won tons and a mass of yellowish-pink meat floating in broth. The broth is delicious, if meagre. The meat is as repulsive as it is plentiful – greasy and gamey and unquestionably domesticated. I've just slurped little Tiddles from my spoon.

Undeterred, the squat old shrew redoubles her efforts, this time to make a grab for my bowl. There's at least an inch of broth left. I'm still hungry. I've made my peace with the pet issue, and I'm not giving it up. She's surprisingly strong for a septuagenarian, but desperation to finish my sad supper gives me the upper hand. She tugs. I tug harder. If forks were the cultural norm here I promise I'd use one now in soup-defense. 'No!' I scowl. 'I want to finish this.'

She gives up the fight in a fit of muttering. It's hard to be dignified with the entire restaurant now staring at me. By 'entire restaurant' I mean the five other tables, arranged close enough for the diners to inspect each other's pores. Mustering an upper lip that would have made the Queen Mother proud during the Blitz, I sip my last two mouthfuls and go to the counter to pay. Waiting for the change, my eye falls again on the sparse English menu…

Not yarrow nudens. And the waitress wasn't trying to steal my dinner. She was just trying to give me some *yellow noodles* in my soup.

Welcome to Hong Kong, Hannah.

It's a little different from London. By which I mean that it's alien in every possible way.

Take a city like London or New York, with its mix of architecture old and new. Then raze 99 per cent of the buildings built before the advent of MTV. Pull the rest of them together as you might tug dishes atop a tablecloth, until they stand shoulder to shoulder. Then set them at the foot of the Matterhorn, into which you carve steps instead of roads snaking to the top. This is to save residents from being run down too often by the cab drivers, whose brakes are as weak as their navigational skills. Finally, build high-rise blocks of apartments for seven million people into the mountainside. I've moved to a bustling twenty-first-century ant colony bathed in neon lights.

And now that my suitcases temporarily have a place to call home, this ant is as settled as she can be. It was a gamble to rent an apartment off the internet. I risked topping the StairMaster debacle of 2008 as my most expensive online purchasing mistake. It's one thing to order a wonky jumper off eBay. An unwanted apartment can't be stuffed into the back of the closet. What a relief, then, to see that this 'corporate efficiency apartment' lived up to its photos. And it certainly is efficient. I can watch TV, cook dinner and brush my teeth without leaving my bed. It's like living in a boat on the fourteenth floor. My dinghy in the sky doesn't come cheap though. It's right in the middle of the Mid-levels, which seems to be the Hong Kong equivalent of posh South Ken. Plus, the bank-breaking clue is in the title. Corporations can afford these short-term lets. Girls with modest savings accounts cannot. So unless men here like their hookers with an American accent, I'll have to move out soon. That's where Stacy comes in. My best friend should be here in a few weeks. It's incredible, really. Not only did she finagle a transfer with her bank to join me, but she's even got a housing allowance, so I get to be her unofficial apartment mate.

To say we've travelled along different career paths is an understatement. Her employer bends over backwards for her, where I've generally left my positions at the request of HR. Clearly she's indispensable at the bank, though I still don't know what she does. It seems to involve a lot of meetings, an unintelligible language, and schmoozy client dinners. I can't wait for her to get here. And given the way things are turning out, I'm even more grateful that she's coming.

The enormity of my move generally hits me when I'm dropping off to sleep. Doubt pounds its bony little fists into my chest – a right hook for having no job yet while watching my anemic savings evaporate into the Hong Kong air. Oof! An uppercut for moving to a city that's on the wrong side of the South China Sea from my boyfriend. Youch! Sometimes it's enough to tempt me to search for a cheap one-way fare. Yet even in the midst of this self-doubt, I already know I love this city. I'm excited by my surroundings. I want to sample it in all its guises. There's a feeling of lightness, like I have the freedom to do anything I want here. Which, of course, I do. It's the same feeling I had when I first went away to college, of living my life. It's one of the perks of being a grown-up, along with eating cupcakes for dinner and not making my bed.

The only slight issue is that Sam isn't here. It's not like he had any idea, when he first brought up moving here, that he'd have to be away for work. It's laughable, really. Or it would be, if it didn't make me cry.

2

Our Asian life together was meant to be perfect. What better way to start off than with a fabulous holiday? Bangkok was to be my introduction to life in the East. Sam flew from Hong Kong and, after a twelve-hour flight in which my seatmate's thigh showed no appreciation for boundaries, I arrived from London.

In the airport, I was swept along on a tide of small people. It was hot, despite the air conditioning, and I was bleary-eyed and nervous with anticipation. The whole place was disorientating, at once familiar and alien. Unintelligible announcements bombarded me, and the signs were written in squiggle. I needed an 'Asia 101' sort of city. This looked like a PhD course.

I strained to catch the first glimpse of Sam, but he was lost in the sea of backpackers. People squealed and kissed and hugged all around me as they found their loved ones. Where was mine? It had been a very long two months since we kissed good bye at Heathrow. How ironic that time flew when a term paper or a baby were due, but crawled backwards when waiting for a reunion. Not even the giddy anticipation of living in a new country (read: terrifying second-guessing of decision) sped the days along. Sometimes I had to remind myself that I wasn't dreaming – I really was moving my worldly belongings halfway around the world to start a new life.

'Hannah.'

He saw me first. My heart lodged in my windpipe. In that moment I realized that 'weak in the knees' wasn't just an expression. On over-boiled-spaghetti legs, I went to my boyfriend. We kissed for long minutes while the other passengers streamed past with their families. He felt, smelled, and tasted so good I didn't want to stop. Despite our separation he was completely familiar to me. Who'd have thought that I, Hannah Jane Cumming, could be so happy?

'Good flight?' He clasped my hand like he was afraid I'd disappear. There was little chance of that.

'Wonderful. I was nicely tranquilized.' That was an understatement. I could have taken out my own appendix.

'Han, I'm so glad you're here. God I've missed you! You look beautiful.'

I knew for a fact that I did not look beautiful. I'm not saying I'm bad looking – that would be disingenuous. At five foot eight, I'm tallish. I've got boobs and hips but I'm not fat to look at (the squishy middle bits don't bother me). Most people assume I play sport (I resolutely do not). My features are regular; I don't hate my nose or crave collagen injections, but neither are my lips bee-stung, pillow-soft or any other Scarlett Johansson-esque adjective. Eyes (two) are hazel and look in the same direction. The one thing I'd change is my hair. Not the color (blonde) but the way it comes out of my head. Other people have waves. I have reverse cowlicks and sticky-outy bits that fuzz up like candy floss. It's out of control. Picture Helena Bonham Carter. Then rub her head against a balloon for twelve hours.

I knew Sam wasn't looking at me with his eyes, but with his heart. I wasn't seeing him in a wholly impartial light either. To me he was as adorable as an unshaven boy next door could be. His eyes are startling and green, his jaw square, and stubbly in keeping with rather long, unkempt curls. The only pinkie-sized bone I could possibly pick was his questionable fashion sense. 'Nice shirt,' I pointed at Che Guevara on his chest. Socialist-lite.

'Thanks. Power to the people.' He kicked his untrendy flip-flops (no Havaianas for him while George was designing for ASDA). As a man working for the government, his statement lacked a certain amount of revolutionary credibility. 'Here,' he said through the cheekiest grin this side of Matt Damon. 'Let me get your bag. No wait, let me kiss you again. Come here.'

He was so utterly sexy. Just thinking about him gave me that tickly stomach-churning feeling. He was the kind of kisser you definitely wouldn't want to be away from for almost two months. 'Thanks,' I panted when we surfaced for air.

Hoisting my hot pink tote over his shoulder made him list slightly to one side. He grabbed for my hand again, possibly to steady himself. 'What have you got in here?'

'Only necessities.' Wait till he saw my checked luggage. 'You never know what the weather's going to be like.' I didn't want to sound defensive, but jibes from fashion-backward boyfriends in the past had left their scars.

'The weather's hot. You don't need much.' He patted his rucksack, which was no bigger than a decent packed lunch. 'I have all I need in here.'

I squeezed his hand. Hard. No one liked a show-off. I'd love to have been one of those girls who dressed (or packed) appropriately for the occasion, but I wasn't. If it wasn't an evening dress at a business dinner then I was wearing stilettos at a picnic. Like the fruit machine that never quite paid out, my fashion choices were always off by one event. That was how I found myself wearing cashmere in Bangkok: a city where you could fry an egg on the sidewalk. While very stylish in powder blue, every so often I got a whiff of damp dog.

Outside, a pack of hopeful cab-drivers and assorted touts peered through the doors, plotting to pick off the young and the weak.

'Taxi? Taxi?' A boy materialized at my elbow as soon as we stepped into the chokingly humid morning air.

'No, thanks.'

'Where you goiiing?' He persisted. 'Bangkok? You take taxi from meee.'

'Ah, no thanks. Sam, where are we going?'

He was trying to deflect his own pre-teen peddler while putting his arm over my shoulder. I nestled into him. 'I heard about this great hotel. It's right out of the nineteen forties. I thought you'd like that.'

A grand old colonial hotel! I imagined four-poster beds and mosquito nets. Creaking old butlers with sweating cold drinks. Maybe there'd be a veranda. And palm trees and ceiling fans. 'I can't wait! I just need to get some money first.'

'Over there.'

He pointed to the cash machine. It wasn't even attached to a wall, just a free-standing plastic box. The kid who tried to sell us the taxi ride could have walked away with it under his arm. In fact, he might have put it there. 'Sam, darling, I don't think that's real.'

'I promise it is. I used it last night when I got in. Don't worry; I'll watch your bag. I mean your bags.' He sniggered at my luggage.

Twenty minutes and five hundred baht later, we were speeding along the motorway to the beat of cheery Thai pop at ear-bleeding decibels. Red and white flower garlands swayed from the taxi's mirror where Catholic drivers might have hung their crucifixes. In fact, there was a St Jude medal there too, and beside the dangling saint an entire shrine to Buddha perched atop the dashboard. The ceiling was papered in flock print to offset the tassels hanging from the door handles. It was more than a taxi. It was a speeding sitting room.

I tried not to be disappointed that we hadn't passed a single elephant. Still, it definitely wasn't London. Tangles of red and blue neon signs vied for space with colorful laundry hanging from the balconies of hundreds of rundown apartment buildings. Those buildings bristled with TV antennae and satellite dishes. Along the roadside, dozens of vendors with wooden pushcarts had constructed tarpaulin tents over scattered plastic garden chairs. They were serving up feasts from industrial woks, liberally flavored with exhaust fumes. Crowds of suited office workers shuffled along the highway's dusty edge, as oblivious to the Grand Prix running beside them as if they'd emerged from London's Underground. A family of four sped past on the kind of motorbike ridden by gap-toothed rednecks in the American South. A mom with babe in arms and two toddlers raced them on a mini-bike. And to think of all the money we wasted in the West driving our children around in vehicles with over-the-top safety features like seat belts, or locks. Or doors.

My observations were gleaned in the few moments when Sam and I weren't aligning our erogenous zones. Being denied smoochy access for so long made me desperate to catch up. It wasn't that we hadn't made an epic attempt at round-the-clock orgasms before he left. Eventually we had to curb our appetites or risk dehydration and permanent muscle damage. Besides, sex couldn't be stored up so, to be perfectly male about it, I really hoped the hotel was close.

The dashboard gods answered my smutty prayers when the driver put his indicator on for the first time since we'd left the airport. It wasn't the first time we'd turned, but indicators, like seat belts and the speed limit, seemed to be optional on Bangkok's roads. We drove past a beautiful, tall, modern hotel on the corner into a potholed street that threatened to shake loose my fillings. Keeping the uncertainty (accusation) out of my gaze, I peered at Sam.

Obviously my expression reassured him that I was confident in his hotel choice. 'Don't worry,' he said, beaming. 'I'm sure it'll be fine.' Two mangy (rabid?) dogs trotted alongside the car. I'd seen jackals on TV take down baby wildebeest this way. Several empty lots grew tall weeds and garbage heaps. It was dusty, dry and barren. There wasn't a tourist in sight. There weren't any locals either, and no cute shops, interesting bars, funky cafes or restaurants. Just dust. And dogs. My hopes for a miraculous detour into paradise were dashed when we reached the end of the street – a dead end. The building in front of us hadn't seen a coat of paint since Yul Brynner filmed *The King and I*. The windows were grimed over and the air conditioners hanging from them had peed great brown stains down the side of the once-white building.

'Is this it?' I didn't bring bedbug repellent.

'I guess so.' Now he looked uncertain, probably wondering why he hadn't just kept his room in the airport hotel.

'Three hundred fifty bahhht,' the driver informed us.

'Three fifty! Sam, I only took out five hundred. This guy's ripping us off.'

'Han, it's okay,' he said with a grin, holding my face to kiss my indignant lips. 'Three-fifty baht is about five pounds.' He took a wad of bills from his pocket, paid the man and wrestled my suitcase towards the curb. The odds on this match weren't in Sam's favor. That bag was costing me, and not just in reputation. The airline check-in clerk took a very inflexible view of my baggage allowance, even after I explained all about moving here, and meeting Sam, and most of the highlights of the last year. She warmed up a little towards the end, but the line was growing by that time, and she still made me hand over my credit card to pay for the extra weight.

Sam eventually got the case to the front door, after only a few astonished glances and one grimace like he'd strained something he might need when we got upstairs.

Despite its exterior looking like it had survived an assault by the Khmer Rouge, I shouldn't have doubted Sam about the hotel. Inside it was an oasis of forties glamour. The walls were paneled in red and the floors checkered in black and white. Funky red chairs and round tan leather footstools dotted the tall-ceilinged lobby. Nina Simone gently crooned from speakers in the rafters, giving the mood-lit, cool interior the feel of a sexy jazz club. Art deco signs dotted the walls and tables, wire fans stood in corners, and there was a groovy round sofa in the middle of the lobby. It was the perfect setting in which to lounge wearing an evening dress, with a cigarette holder in one hand and a martini in the other. Not that I'd brought an evening dress. Or smoked. Through an archway next to reception I spied a veritable jungle, and a pool. It was magical.

'Sawasdee kahhh,' sang the woman at the front desk, bowing with her hands in prayer formation at her breast. 'You pay first. Eight hundred bahhht.'

She reminded me of a cat, meowing in the tentative hope that I might feed her, but not in the mood to be demanding.

'Wow, that's cheap.'

'Get what you pay for room,' she said, smiling.

We kissed all the way up in the elevator, risking public indecency fines by the time we manhandled my suitcase into the room. Sam steered me to the bed where we fell together, still kissing. This was movie passion, only I wasn't acting. With Sam all sense of decorum disappeared, along with the embarrassment that usually made me back out of the room, geisha-style, when naked. That translated into some amazing sex. In fact, I'd had the best sex of my life with him. Being totally in love with him meant that every minute we spent on, in and under each other was perfect, because he was Sam.

… Even when there weren't that many minutes. 'Sorry, Han. I was excited to see you,' he whispered into my hair. I was snuggled into his chest, not even minding the sweat against my cheek. And I hated sweat. 'Oops,' he said, shifting away to grab his phone. 'It's just my boss, texting to see if I got here okay.'

'And you're texting her back now?'

'What? Oh, right. No, of course not. Sorry! I'll text later. It's not important.' He settled back down, opening his arms again for me.

'Good. Because that would be weird after, well, you know.' I sighed deeply, marveling that I was there with him in Bangkok. 'Thank you, Sam.'

He smiled, raising his eyebrows. Cheeky sod, misinterpreting my appreciation. Honestly, men sometimes. 'I *mean* for this holiday, not… that. Though that wasn't bad either. It's such a great way to start out together–' He smirked harder. 'Again, I mean the holiday, Sam, not that. Get your mind out of the gutter.'

'But I like being in the gutter. With you. Han, I'm so happy you're finally here. These last few months haven't been easy, have they? I didn't realize when I left how hard this would be. I'm glad you're here now. And we can do *this* again!' He made a playful grab for my thigh.

'Mmm, me too. I'm so happy, you can't even imagine. A huge thank you to your boss for letting you take time off so soon after starting.' Sam had just finished his PhD in political-economic something or other, and gone to work in Hong Kong advising the government about very important matters. That's why he had to leave London to take the new job. He was destined to be a top political-economic something or other one day.

'She knew it was important to me.'

Hmm, yes, I thought, so important that she texted you while you were with your girlfriend.

'Besides,' he went on. 'You can't see Bangkok and Laos in just a week.'

'Of course we could. We're American; we could see all of Europe in a week. We often do.'

'You're right,' he agreed, stroking my shoulder. 'Though not my friends. They can spend years travelling and call it research.'

'How nice to be perpetual students. Mmm, this is so nice. Sam, why don't we just stay here? Then we wouldn't have to take the extra flights.' I wasn't a great flyer under the best of conditions (and those conditions involved a GP's prescription). I couldn't point to any single traumatic flight, and it wasn't only small planes that made me chew away perfectly good manicures. Bigger planes meant bigger body counts. Over the years I'd developed a sharp sense of dread upon hearing the question, *Would you like a window or an aisle seat?* I descended into full-scale paranoia when the 'fasten seat belt' sign was lit.

'But then we'd miss Laos' he said. 'It's supposed to be such a magical, unspoiled place. You're gonna love Luang Prabang. There are hundreds of monks in the monasteries there. It's beautiful and peaceful, on two big rivers. The people are wonderfully friendly and kind…' He wore a beatific look. I was in love with a dreamer. I knew this when we first got together, when each date was like an adventure with the Pied Piper. This was the man whose recipe for English trifle ended in a chocolate custard fight that wiped out his security deposit. He positively glowed at the prospect of visiting Ikea's charming warehouse, or finding new season asparagus at Waitrose. He made it entertaining to wait in for the boiler man. Everything in Sam's life turned out positive and fun. Laos would be wonderful. I kissed him on the nose. ''Scuse me a minute.' As I got up I took my first real look at the room. 'Sam, what kind of hotel is this?'

'Hmm?'

'This. This— room.' The floors were puke-green linoleum. The walls were concrete blocks; the beds (singles) were metal. A desk squatted in the corner. We were in a dorm room. I expected a knock on the door any minute inviting me to a keg party. 'Who recommended this hotel?'

'My professor. He stays here whenever he's in Bangkok.'

Now I understood what the front desk clerk was telling me. 'You get what you pay for?' I said.

'Yeah, that's what these rooms are called. Isn't that great? Where would you find a place like this anywhere else in the world?'

I loved his enthusiasm. His capacity for joy at life's small wonders was astonishing. He'd texted me once in London, a few minutes before we were due to meet:

Sorry darlin', pretty sunset, 15 mins late.

Nature's light show had caught his attention and

he couldn't pass up the chance to watch it play out. For him it was pure bliss, and perfectly natural to stop his life briefly to marvel at it. I'd never encountered so much positivity, and it was infectious. Yes, this *was* great. I loved it. And I loved him for finding it.

Though we thought about staying in the room to perform all the prohibited activities we'd seen on the 'No sex tourists' sign in the lobby, Bangkok's treasures called to us. So after a quick shower we found ourselves back on the swanky hotel corner looking for a taxi. Every thirty seconds a young guy driving a three-wheeled motorcycle-cum-ice cream cart stopped and said 'tuk-tuk?'. The streets were full of these belching accidents waiting to happen, and they didn't seem to be just for tourists. Like the motorbikes, entire extended families thought them a nifty mode of transport.

'They want to know if we want a ride,' Sam explained as he shook his head at another hopeful driver.

'Don't we?' My shoes weren't what you'd call walk-friendly.

'In a tuk-tuk?' He looked like I'd just told him I knew how to tune an engine. 'I didn't think you'd want to ride in one. Don't take this wrong, Han, but you're more of a taxi girl.'

'I am not!' I really was, of course.

'Well, great! Okay then.' He whistled at the next cart to pass. 'Grand Palace please. How much?'

'Two hundred bahhht.' The teenager flashed a grin to melt the heart.

'No way, it's not that far. Fifty.'

'One-fiftyyy.'

'Sixty.'

'Three hundred and ping-pong show, okay?' He cocked his thumb in the universal sign for now-that-that's-settled-jump-aboard.

'No, just to the Grand Palace please.'

'No ping-pong show?'

'No ping-pong show. Just the palace. Sixty. Deal?'

His smile faded to a mere 300 watts. 'Okay.'

'What's a ping-pong show?' I bellowed as we zoomed along, the wind blowing exhaust into our faces. The whole noisy contraption was open except for a metal roof on four posts. Taxi, indeed. I wouldn't want to travel any other way. I could have used an industrial face mask though.

'Believe me, you don't want to know,' Sam shouted over the din of the mid-morning traffic. 'It's a kind of sex show,' he answered my expectant look.

'They have sex playing ping pong?' I realized that table tennis was an Olympic sport, but surely not.

'Nooo, but the woman uses ping pong balls.'

'For what? How?' The penny dropped. 'Oh. *Really*?' And they said girls had bad aim. 'Have you ever seen it?'

He looked embarrassed. 'Well, yeah, when I was here with Pete. You're going to love him when you meet him.'

Pete is Sam's apartment mate. They're best friends but he'd already moved to Hong Kong by the time Sam and I got together. 'Is it gross?' I ask, referring to the show, not Pete.

'Yes, but oddly fascinating.'

'Then maybe we should go.'

'You're not serious.'

'Sure, why not? Would they let me in?'

'Of course, but–' he shook his head.

'What?'

'You never cease to amaze me. I love an adventurous girl!'

Did you hear that? Sam loved an adventurous girl. In my mind I was the most adventuresome girl on the planet. In reality my cowardice was legendary, but Sam needn't know that. Not when he practically just said he loved me.

By the time we got to the Grand Palace I'd ingested enough fumes to shorten my lifespan by a couple of years. Like a carnival ride that spun at vomit-inducing speeds, tuk-tuks were only fun till the thrill wore off. The ride was worth it though. A fairytale village lay before us. Multi-layered, ornate, steep-roofed green and gold buildings with soaring spires housed the Thai people's national treasures. The whole enormous complex literally glittered with so much gold that I was nearly at a loss for words. My fingers intertwined with Sam's. I felt like we were kids standing on the threshold of a wondrous new world. I guess we were, in a way.

We spent the day sharing out our wonder, gawping at the grandeur, and each other, in turns. By dinnertime we'd settled back into our rhythm together. Time and distance were brushed away, leaving us a couple again. It was perfect, our reunion made all the more sweet against such a spectacular backdrop. We even had foot massages, which gave me hope that we were starting as we meant to go on. But that wasn't meant to be.

Forty-eight hours later we were riding in a truck through the Laotian jungle towards the start of our hike. Naturally I was there under duress. And to make matters worse, we were sharing the ride with Lara Croft. She wasn't Angelina Jolie as Lara Croft – that would imply that she was actually human, with possible flaws. She was the computer-generated model of perfection that was the Tomb Raider. Sam couldn't have been happier with the whole adventure.

I tried not to be jealous, but I hated her. I'd have been happy to share the excursion with a nice older couple who thought we were adorable kids, or a sexy man who liked to flirt. Lara's presence was unacceptable. Aside from the fact that I thought she was gorgeous, it was obvious that Sam thought so too. They didn't stop talking and he'd barely looked at me for at least an hour. Granted, I probably wasn't at my best, given that we were riding in the back of an open jeep, and it was raining: my hair isn't great in the rain. It isn't exactly magnificent in the sun.

I was cold, which raised goose bumps all over my body. Lara appeared immune to the weather, except for her nipples, which pointed straight at my boyfriend.

It hadn't seemed like a terrible idea when Sam suggested a little walk in the mountains. But as we left the truck and headed for the hilly, steamy, wet jungle that was no doubt full of bugs, I reconsidered.

'Hannah? What brings you to this part of the world?' Asked Lara in what I had to admit was a very sexy Eastern European accent. She was skipping along the path as if strolling downhill instead of climbing Mount Kilimanjaro.

'I'm moving to Hong Kong,' I wheezed. 'Next week.' Exercise and I weren't close companions. I went through a blessedly brief phase after college in which I joined a gym and had a personal trainer. A blinding crush on the trainer had been my sole motivation. It took three months of daily workouts to get him to kiss me. To my horror, he was a face licker. Since then, exertion beyond walking to the bus stop was, to me, wasted effort.

'Oh, Hong Kong is wonderful. Will you live with Sam?'

'Uh, well…'

'We're not living together,' Sam volunteered cheerfully.

'Oh,' she said.

It's funny how a single word could convey a sentiment.

It didn't matter that we were only at the beginning of our relationship, or that we were in complete agreement about not rushing things, or that I wanted to be independent. I didn't want a gorgeous woman misunderstanding Sam's status. If I were a dog marking my territory, at that point I'd probably have peed on him.

We walked in silence through the jungle. It was still uphill. It was still raining. Sam was no doubt mulling over Miss Perfect's CV. She worked for an NGO that built schools in war-torn countries. She was taking a little break from her post in Cambodia where she also volunteered for a landmine charity. She made Mother Theresa look like a selfish bitch. I couldn't bear to think what she made me look like. What had I ever done for charity except donate clothes after I was positive they'd never come back in style?

Our guide, wearing flip-flops, ambled along like a goat up the muddy hill. I'd had visions of me and Sam meandering hand in hand down a verdant jungle path, perhaps with monkeys swinging through vines overhead. Instead we were trudging single file to what felt like Everest base camp, and the monkeys were smart enough to stay out of the rain. As we rounded a corner I spied a river. It wasn't along the path – it was across the path. Undaunted, our guide flip-flopped through it, still smiling. 'Come this way,' he chirped.

I hadn't scoured London's streets in search of the perfect trainers to have them ruined in a Laotian river. Suddenly Sam's preoccupation with Tevas made sense. They were the amphibious assault vehicle of the shoe world – ugly and indestructible. My pretty shoes, on the other hand, were not, which was why they were going to travel raj-style on my head across the raging torrent. Unfortunately balancing on one shoe while unlacing the other wasn't easy. I wobbled, heaved sideways and stepped resolutely into the yellow squishy muck. 'Damn it.'

'Why don't you just wade across in them?' Sam called from the other side.

'Because they're suede!' Were. They were suede.

I swear I caught Lara roll her eyes. 'Want a hand?' She volunteered.

'No thanks.' Angrily I wrenched off my other shoe.

'Nice toenails,' she said.

'Thanks!' Gazing fondly at my Chanel Fire red toes through the rippling water, I couldn't resist accepting the compliment.

'I never seem to have the time to paint mine,' she addressed her own perfectly formed, perfectly varnish-free feet. Of course not, you were too busy teaching children and saving people from landmines. How much did I hate thee? Let me count the reasons.

Reason number one. In a fire Sam would rescue her first. How did I know this? Because within minutes we came upon another river, which looked suspiciously like the one we'd just crossed. Lara began hopping across the stones in her Tevas when she slipped. My boyfriend, who'd been holding me while I pried off my shoe again, dashed to Lara's side and helped her across the river. By the time he came back I could have drowned. Well, if I'd been in the water at that point, I could have drowned. When push came to shove we knew who'd get the fireman's carry.

Reason number two. Take reason number one and double it. I felt like I was watching my future crumble in the jungles of Laos. It made me sick to my stomach. I feared this might happen, and yet I let myself get carried away. Why didn't I learn from my mistakes? Even rats, after being electrocuted, eventually learned to avoid the shock. Wasn't I more intelligent than a rodent? Not judging by my dating history. As I stood in the rain, muddy and miserable, I flashed back to Jake, the truly dark smudge on my self-respect. What is it about the extra X chromosome that makes us resurrect disasters of boyfriends past when we're already down? As if the present humiliation wasn't filling enough without heaping on extra helpings from history. I'd stalked Jake into submission after meeting him briefly at a university party. He went home with another girl that night but I was smitten. Miraculously – or so he believed – we ran into each other at most parties/bars/coffee shops for the rest of that year. But despite my best efforts, to him I was nothing but the pack of biscuits at the back of the cabinet. Not a favorite but I'd do in a pinch. Eventually Jake ate the biscuits. Over time we settled into a pattern of sorts. I dragged Stacy around campus till we accidentally on purpose ran into him. If he didn't go home with someone else we'd spend the night together (I warned you this wasn't a flattering story). What was obvious to everyone but me was that I wasn't his Miss Right, just his Miss Right For Now. Eventually Stacy gave me a dose of reality. That's when I finally realized that no matter how fun, funny, sexy and smart I was around him, he was never going to see me as anything more than a runner-up.

And here I was in second place once again. It was sickening. So much so in fact… I actually felt like vomiting. My mouth started to sweat. Then the hot flush came.

I threw up on my clean shoe.

'Hannah!' Sam rushed over. 'What's wrong?' He rubbed my back, concern furrowing divots between his eyebrows.

I had no idea what was wrong. I didn't usually throw up in the face of emotional trauma. I overate. I started to shiver. 'I don't feel good.'

'Does it feel like the flu?' Lara asked. 'Or food poisoning?'

'I feel fine,' Sam said. 'And we've eaten all the same things. Han, how does your belly feel?'

I didn't have to answer him. My stomach was gurgling like a drain that'd just been unblocked. 'Uh…'

'We have to go back,' Sam told our guide, playing translator to my belly-rumbles. 'Phaivanh, my girlfriend doesn't feel well. We need to go back to town please.

Quickly.'

'This way is fastest,' he said, pointing up the hill. 'There's a shortcut over the hill. Will you be okay?' He gently stroked my arm, peering into my face, and I was touched by his concern. I was touched by everyone's concern, even Lara's. So touched that I threw up again.

Our journey took on a sense of urgency. I wasn't sure which end of my body planned to protest next. I couldn't stop shivering. The driving rain didn't help. We trudged up the hill on a path that got increasingly narrow. Soon it was no more than eight inches wide. Eight inches of treacherous slipperiness. My pretty, impractical shoes weren't helping.

'Here, Han, this'll keep you steady.' Sam handed me a big stick. 'Use it like a ski pole.'

I couldn't ski either. I bet Lara had giant slalom medals. 'Thanks.' At least we were cresting the hill. In fact, the path down was pretty steep. And still narrow. And carved into the side of the hill high above the valley floor.

'Watch out there,' Phaivanh called over his fit, retreating shoulder. 'There's a little slide.'

'Here, Hannah, wait.' Sam shimmied past me as I hugged the cliff face. Even in a life-threatening situation, the feel of his body as he slid past was hot. 'Let me go down first. Then I'll be able to help you.'

He meant catch me. Lara descended acrobatically, and stood with Phaivanh, waiting for the afternoon's entertainment to begin.

What little traction my shoes once had was lost along with my dignity at the first muddy puddle. Tentatively I placed a foot on the sledge-run that was the only route to a toilet. Cartoon-like, my feet began to spin.

'Oof!' I landed on my back in a bath of potter's clay. To add insult to injury I slid at least ten feet in this position.

'Hannah! Are you okay?' Sam struggled to get back up the hill to my prone body.

'Do I look okay?!' My underpants had just collected a quart of mud.

'Are you hurt?'

'Just my pride. Uh-oh. Bleurgh.'

He wore the same expression that children did when faced with a plate of Brussels sprouts. 'We have to get you to the doctor. I'm afraid this is serious.' He smoothed my matted hair away from my vomit-flecked face. 'I don't want anything to happen to you. I don't know what I'd do.' He stared at me with a funny expression. Suddenly he broke eye contact. 'I don't know what I'd do.'

'I'll be okay, Sam. I'm sure I will. Don't worry.'

'Well, I am worried. What if– Hannah, you're important to me. You're very important to me.'

He was telling me that he loved me. There, in the rain, when I'd just been sick on myself. Lara wasn't a threat at all. 'I understand. I feel the same way. And I can't wait to start our life together in Hong Kong.'

Suddenly he looked away.

'What? What is it?'

He helped me to my feet. 'Here, let me hold you. No, go on my other side.' He put himself between me and the abyss at the edge of the path. 'It's just that… I have to be away from Hong Kong for a few weeks.'

Something in the way he said it meant my chills were no longer just from food poisoning. 'When?'

'I have to be in Ho Chi Minh City on Friday.'

'But we fly together to Hong Kong on Friday.'

'I know we were meant to, and I really wanted to be there when you first arrived,' he said. I noted the past tense. 'I'm sorry, but it's the start of the assignment. I have to go straight there. They wanted me there this week, but I said I couldn't disappoint you. I hope you can understand.'

He looked so hopeful. Unsure, but so hopeful.

A few more weeks apart wouldn't matter in the scheme of things. We were crazy about each other. In that jungle, mud-smeared and vomiting, we both knew that. 'Right. Of course,' I said. 'Don't worry.' I wished I felt as cool as I sounded. 'It's only a couple of weeks, right?' At least we had a few days left together.

3

My, how trichinosis can take the shine off a romantic holiday. On the bright side, after spending four days sharing a room the size of an office cubicle, Sam and I took intimacy to a whole new level. Nothing more was said about the 'L' word, or if it was I didn't hear him through the bathroom door. Never mind, when the chips were down (and everything else coming up), Sam couldn't have been a better boyfriend. He was also the perfect nurse, though I made him leave the room to be the perfect tourist too. Given the unsavory nature of my condition, it was definitely better that way. Plus, now I've got loads of photos of our holiday, even if only Sam is in them.

He did leave for Ho Chi Minh City though, as threatened, and it'll be a few weeks until Stacy's visa comes through. So for now I'm on my own in Hong Kong.

Stacy has been my rock. As my lifelong friend, she's contractually obliged in this regard. She calls me daily, like she did when I first moved to London. Then, her calls were tinged with the guilt of having played a key role in my (rather accidental) move. I didn't relieve her conscience. She should have known that if you're going to get your suggestible friend drunk on the day she gets fired, you're partly to blame for what happens. If you challenge her to change her life when she complains that she's in a rut, then point her to a British Airways sale when she threatens to move to London to find a new job, then not try to take her credit card away before she books the flight, you've got a bit to answer for. I was as grateful for her calls then as I am now.

'How are you feeling? Did you try a spa yet?' She asks first thing, like always. A girl needs this kind of caring support, and reminder to pamper, when moving across time zones.

'I'm okay. Slowly finding my way around. No spa yet, but I've got a recommendation for a foot massage place.' Stacy takes American grooming habits to a new level. As a nation we're obsessive and Stacy makes the rest of us look like untweezed, unbuffed, frizzy, spotty amateurs.

'Email me as soon as you go and tell me what it's like,' she demands. Thank the ether for email. Being able to regurgitate an entire day's worth of minutiae in writing, without regard for time zones, makes these calls easier on the purse. Stacy gets my dramas daily by the paragraph. 'Are you ready for your interview, Han? What time is it?'

'Three o'clock tomorrow. I think so. I mean, there are only so many ways you can spin crappy jobs.' So far I've spent three months having my online applications nearly universally ignored, and two phone interviews that ended when I said, 'Work permit? Uh, no.' I'm not asking to be CEO. I'm happy to be the lowest rung on a very long ladder. I had no idea that being a buyer's assistant's assistant's assistant was such a coveted role.

'What are you going to wear?' she asks.

'Well. I found a dark grey sleeveless shift dress just before I left London—'

'Galaxy-esque?'

'Yep, but sleeveless, not cap sleeves, and a higher neckline. But it's got the same silhouette. It's got a faint check through it. I thought that would look good with my peep-toe black platforms.'

'Hmm… I'm not sure about the shoes. Have you got red? Or mustard?'

'I've got the red flat Mary Janes.'

'No, too clunky. I've never liked those shoes. They just don't try hard enough. I know! Your metallic grey ballet pumps.'

'Really? Not too, I don't know, meeting friends for shopping?'

'No way. Think Holly Golightly. Wear your Hermès scarf and it'll be perfect. It's got yellow in it, right?'

'You're right, perfect, thanks. Now all I need is the perfect interview.'

'Hang in there, Han, the right company will snap you up,' she says. 'And I'll be there soon to celebrate your new job. That's why I called. HR told me yesterday that they're just waiting to get the paperwork back. I've booked my leaving drinks for Friday. The power of positive thinking, eh? Also, if it's delayed I can have another party next week. It shouldn't take much longer.'

'Okay. Be sure you pack all your summer clothes. It's hot already.'

'But CNN says—'

'I know, but it's deceptively hot. It's the humidity.

And don't forget about the rainy season in summer.'

'Eww, but...'

'Tell me about it. My hair. I'll look like I've been electrocuted.' This kind of thing never happens to Stacy. For one thing, she's immune to the environmental factors that make the rest of us frizz up or break out. For another, good things happen to her. 'Maybe you can come anyway and then start when you get the paperwork through?'

'I think Immigration takes a dim view of that. Besides, I want to spend as much time with Tyler as I can before I go. He's turning out to be quite satisfying in bed. He takes foreplay to a new level. I don't know how he doesn't cramp up. We called in sick to work the other day. And it's not like I'll see him once I move.'

'I totally understand.' Tyler is Stacy's latest conquest. Like hurricanes, there's usually a string of them in season. That's how I know she doesn't expect us to talk about this one. She'd like to talk about Sam, but I won't let her.

Stacy's got a real grudge against him for "moving me" all the way to Hong Kong. Even though she knows I couldn't have stayed in London anyway, thanks to my poisonous boss. Of course it sounded crazy when Sam first suggested it. But my alternative was to move back home, or to another city where I didn't know anyone. At least Sam is here.

Or he will be here, as soon as he finishes his assignment in Vietnam.

Meanwhile, I proved that I could make a life for myself in London, and I can do it again in Hong Kong.

'So you think it'll just be a week or two then till you get here?' I ask, trying to veer towards a topic that doesn't call my judgment into question.

'Probably,' she says, playing along. 'Most of my shoes are packed, so I'm ready to go as soon as I get the okay. Any luck on an apartment?'

It's a bit of pressure being our designated housing scout, but I know Stacy's tastes as well as my own. Plus, I'd never pass up the chance to spend other people's money. Unlike me, Stacy gets to move here on an expat package. 'Not yet but I've got one to see before lunch. I have a good feeling about it. I'll call you tomorrow and let you know.'

Stacy shouldn't be so confident in my apartment-hunting skills. Jack and the Beanstalk drove a better bargain than I generally do.

The estate agent that I meet at the entrance to the tall concrete building senses this immediately. She's a perfectly coiffed, Chinese clone of the awright-mate-I'm-yer-friend hucksters filling these positions in the rest of the world. I distrust her intensely.

'Very nice apartment,' she gushes. 'Built in 2004. Big. Good value.' She's gesturing around the living room, carefully restraining her arm gestures to keep from touching two walls at once and undermining her claim.

The young woman she's brought with her is nodding through an enormous grin. She looks like an accessory to the con. How can she be so enthusiastic when these apartments all look the same? There may be slight variations in the decor of the lobbies and elevators, but they're all modern high-rises. How different from central London's accommodation, where we're grateful for a kitchen, and a housemate who doesn't steal. I miss London's architecture. Its charm lies in the hodgepodge of eras in the same road, from Edwardian to post-war. Not here. Hong Kongers don't like living in anything built before the Spice Girls broke up.

'Uh-huh, very nice,' I say. 'Just one thing. Shouldn't it have two bedrooms?'

'Yes, yes, two. Here. This way.' She opens a door in the kitchen that I assumed was the laundry room.

I was right. 'It's a laundry room.'

'Maid's quarters. Bed goes here.' She pats the countertop that Mom would use to fold clothes warm from the dryer.

'You put a bed on that?'

'Yes, very good price.'

I admit the price is good. For a two-bedroom apartment. Human rights violations aside, it's disingenuous to sell closets as maid's quarters. I didn't think accommodation could get smaller, or more expensive, than the submarine torpedo launch tubes masquerading as bedrooms in London. 'Thanks, can I let you know?'

She nods, shooing me away as her phone rings. Clearly she's got bigger fish to fry. I'll just let myself out.

'It's kind of small,' I say to the woman who's followed me to the elevator.

'It's not too bad, compared to some I've seen,' she says with a giggle. 'She was surprised when you objected to the maid's quarters.'

'Well come on, who would put a person in there?'

She grins knowingly. 'It's your first viewing, isn't it?'

I sigh. 'No, I've seen a string of them. That's the first one that tried selling a box room as a bedroom though. I'm already tired of this process and it's only been a week!'

'I know what you mean. Eventually you'll lose the will to live and just pick the next one you see. I'm at that point. I'll probably take that one. You sound American. Did you come from the US?'

'I am, but I came from London. Where are you from?'

'I'm Canadian. From Vancouver but my parents moved here when I started college. When do you need to move in?'

Now that I no longer think she's a professional plant, there's no reason not to be friendly. She looks around my age. And she hasn't stopped smiling. This fact, added to her huge blue eyes and big loopy chin-length blonde curls, makes her seem a very jolly gal indeed. 'In a couple of weeks,' I tell her. 'I'm in a corporate apartment now, but I'll move in with my friend when she gets here.'

'Ah–' giggle, giggle '–that makes sense now. That's why you need two bedrooms. I'll be on my own.' Her words pour forth from her megawatt grin. It's a bit like watching sound come from a ventriloquist's dummy.

'You said your parents live here? Then why don't you…' If I lived within sleeping distance of my parents' sofa I wouldn't be looking for an apartment.

'I'm living with them now.' Her expression tells me all I need to know.

'I understand.' We've reached the front entrance. Even though it's still relatively cool (that's relative to the sun), the atmosphere has a sponginess about it that I'm not sure I'll ever get used to.

'Do you feel like grabbing a coffee? Hee hee! If

you're not busy, I mean.'

Maybe she's got a nervous tick. Or maybe she sucks laughing gas from her handbag. I think she's just being friendly. I don't want to suggest that I'm a babe-magnet, but accepting invitations from strange women have resulted in a few misunderstandings. Short of a woman lap dancing on me, I haven't always read the signals very well. 'Sure, I've got some time before lunch.' Who am I kidding? The Man in the Iron Mask had a more active social life. 'I'm Hannah.'

'Rachel. Nice to meet you. We can head towards the escalator if that's not out of your way. There's a cafe there that does organic cakes.'

I'd trade a kidney for a proper piece of cake. The bakeries here are filled with a heartbreaking waste of calories. They may look delicious, but taste of nothing.

'Do you mean real cakes?' I ask hopefully.

'Sort of.' She shakes her head, clearly as distraught as I am. 'But they get a bit healthy. You know, apple juice for sugar, fat-free, that kind of thing. Mom makes proper ones for me.'

I wonder how to wangle an invitation to her mother's house without seeming forward.

After being completely alone for more than a week, it's a relief to talk to someone who answers me back. Grocery clerks across the city are getting tired of my conversational attempts. Rachel seems happy enough to indulge me though, which I soon realize isn't because she sees me as potential friend material. It's because she speaks in c-r-a-z-y and needs an audience.

She's just explained that she's moving out because her parents disapprove of her chosen career path. She talks to rocks. She claims they tell her when people have illnesses. Like medical Magic 8-Balls. 'Uh, that's interesting. And you make a living from this crystal stuff?'

'It's called crystal healing. It's not about the money.' She chuckles, seized by another gas attack. 'It's about helping people. I'm, like, a physician!'

Yes you are. Except for the training and the medical degree. 'Mmm. How long have you been… practicing?' Am I supposed to call her Doctor Rachel?

'Six weeks.'

'I see. Well it sounds like you've got a long career ahead of you then.'

'It's not a career, it's a calling,' she says, suddenly taking a turn for the serious. 'I've had jobs before, lots of them. After university I was a barista, although I don't like to define myself by my career, you know? I wasn't a barista. I worked as a barista. There's a difference. Then I worked in Lane Crawford… it's a department store,' she adds, seeing my confusion. 'I wanted to help people there, but you'd be surprised how few women want honest advice when clothes don't suit them.' Her already wide eyes are positively fish-like with the shock that a woman might not appreciate unsolicited advice about the size of her ass. Imagine. 'Then I worked for a bank. I'll never do that again. It was way too much pressure.'

'What did you do there?' I've burned off a layer of taste buds in my haste to finish this coffee and make my escape. And she was right; the cakes are much too wholesome, though the cafe's tables are full. It must be the place for ladies who lunch, this jumble of bars, restaurants and cafes running along the escalator.

My body may be hostage to this hippy but my mind

can come and go as it pleases. I watch the world's longest outdoor escalator running alongside the cafe. It may sound like an epic indulgence, until you see the hills here. What they spent on mechanics they more than saved in coronary unit hospital costs. And it's as functional as it is curious. It runs up the hills or down, depending on the time of day, between Central and the Mid-levels in a series of moving stairs and sidewalks. Every so often a narrow street bisects the system, where little red and white taxis hopefully cruise for fares.

Stairs run alongside the escalator for those who'd like a calf workout, or find themselves needing to go up, or down, when the escalator is running the other way. The moving sidewalk is on the less steep bottom bit, which makes even me feel lazy, and the whole thing is covered on top, but open to the elements on the sides. It's probably a real treat in cyclone season. It's wedged tightly between multiple-story buildings on either side, but these aren't the shiny glass high-rises like those in Central's business district, or the Mid-levels' swank and towering apartment blocks. They look like they were built in the fifties or sixties, concrete, painted at one time in pinks, creams and yellows, up to about ten stories high, and they've been adapted to their occupiers' uses in a staggering array of inventiveness. Air conditioners, antennae, washing lines and all manner of signs, neon and otherwise, grow from their sides. The many balconies are variously used for storage, drying laundry, and as gardens, smoker's areas, workshops and informal room extensions. On the escalator I get to watch an ever-changing tableau of Hong Kong life. It's light and airy to ride, but a bit dark and claustrophobic here in its shadow.

Rock-talking Rachel is still going on about the evils of bank employment. 'I worked in reception,' she says. 'It was grueling. I never had a minute to myself. The staff, the bankers, they were all rude. Like it was my fault when they forgot their passes. And the visitors were totally unappreciative. I was at rock bottom. And then I met Neil.'

'Who's Neil?' Why isn't she sipping her tea? It's like she wants this conversation to continue. Clearly we can't be friends. The giggles alone would force me to strangle her.

'He's my guru. He showed me the path to enlightenment. I'll be eternally grateful to him. Eternally. In all my lives. So now I can help people forever. It's so liberating to recognize your calling and know exactly what you're meant to do with your life. Like Mother Teresa,' she says earnestly, her fish-eyes popping again. 'You could use a session, you know. Your aura's very dirty.'

'My aura is fine, thanks.'

'No it's not. It's awfully dark blue.'

'Is that bad?'

'It's a bit muddy.'

'Thanks anyway. Listen, Rachel, I've got to run to lunch now. I've got a reservation. Nice to meet you, and good luck with the apartment. Who knows, maybe we'll see each other again. If the cosmos wants it... *M goi*, and *baaibaai*,' I say, carefully trying out my very first polite Cantonese phrases in public. I resist the urge to flash her the peace sign as I bolt for the exit.

'You're welcome and,' she says, waving *baaibaai*. 'Bye!'

Half an hour later in the restaurant I'm still contemplating that weird experience. I'm all for alternative medicine, but I don't see myself getting my aura vacuumed by the crystal whisperer. Especially when I've had eyebrow shaping that's lasted longer than she's been playing psychic geologist. And a guru called Neil? He's not even authentic enough to have a proper swami name. That's Marketing 101, Neil.

Goodness, listen to me, talking like I'm afraid they'll knock my chi off-kilter. Do I believe in all that? I guess I do, at least a bit. There's definitely good and bad energy. Haven't we all gravitated towards some people and been repelled by others? My muddy aura is definitely putting the waiters off in the restaurant. They're avoiding me like I'm that uncle at the family picnic who always wants a hug. Every time I catch someone's eye and smile to get his attention, he smiles back. Then he walks away. It's getting ridiculous. The other patrons are being served. I want dim sum, not a bone marrow donation.

'Excuse me. I'm ready to order.' The waiter, smiling, approaches. He looks confused, gently snatching what looks like a survey from the table's corner. 'No order?'

'Yes, order.'

He's scanning the paper. 'No order.'

I knew it. I've missed lunch. 'Can't I order?'

'Yes, order.' He sets the survey on the table.

'Thanks. Can I have a menu?'

'Menu.' He's pointing to the survey. It's not a survey. It's the menu, with some words in English, written on a wonkily photocopied sheet of paper. 'Hmm, do the pork buns have scallions in them?' He doesn't answer. 'Okay. I'll have those, and the... are these prawns big or small? Could the chef...? No, okay, then these please, and this one and, is this the chicken...?' I really want to know if they are the little steamed chicken and prawn dumplings like I get in New York, but given that the waiter isn't even pretending to smile any more, I won't continue my line of questioning. 'And this one, please.'

'You write.' He's gesturing at the paper again.

'I write what?'

'Write order.' He hands me a pen.

He has completely missed the point of being a waiter. 'Is that too much food?' I ask as I tick the boxes.

He smiles and walks away to ignore his other customers.

How can I get a job like that? I could learn to speak Chinese menu, couldn't I? No, of course I couldn't. I couldn't even speak English in London.

I have applied for loads of jobs online though. It's not nearly as much fun as shopping for a new dress or a handbag. And there's a big difference between browsing and buying in online recruitment. It's not like that Mulberry bag will say, 'Thank you for your interest. We've had many applicants and have found the shoulder we were looking for. Good luck in your search for the perfect spring accessory.'

In a way I envy Rachel. She might be clinically insane but she's found her dream job. I have a dream; I just don't have the job. Not to put too many eggs in one basket, but if I'm not hired tomorrow I'm out of options. Done, finito, kaput, doomed to live under the Star Ferry pier with the water rats. I just hope they don't get a whiff of desperation when I arrive. I'll be sure not to cling to the boss's leg or intimate that I'd be very grateful for the job, wink, wink. I simply need to gloss over the work permit issue. Just for a few weeks till I prove that I'm made to be a buyer's assistant's assistant's assistant. Maybe I'll take a page out of my waiter's service manual. I'll smile sincerely and walk away when the subject comes up.

The waiter sets my lunch before me, neatly stacked in covered steamers to maximize that whatever-could-be-under-this-lid quiver of excitement. They're pork buns! Just like the ones Stacy and I get in New York when we're really hung-over but eschew McDonald's because it's a fat day. This is quite a moment for me. It's the first time I've ordered a dish here that I'd meant to. And the second and third dishes are recognizable too!

The only problem is getting them into my mouth. Perhaps I rushed the decision to move to a country without forks. I'd feel less self-conscious if I weren't the only Westerner in here. The Chinese at the tables, and serving, and clearing aren't hiding the fact that they're staring at me. So no pressure.

Poking the dumpling sends it skidding across my plate, triggering a Rachel-worthy giggle attack at the thought of flipping it into the lap of the diner beside me. Now I see why everyone is eating straight from the bamboo steamers. Traction. Even experts take shortcuts. Good. While stabbing the morsel through the middle and levering it into my mouth may not win me any technical awards, at this point it's any fork in a storm.

'Bdllling!'

I loved that sound before I taught my mother to

send texts. Naively I thought giving her the means to send these supposedly unobtrusive messages would limit the number of middle-of-the-night phone calls. I was wrong. It's now 4 a.m. at home and I expect there'll be a message on my machine when I check it later. Mom simply views texting as an extra weapon in her arsenal.

Hannah, do you wantto come home for your bdat? We'll pay and you shouldn't be alonee.

Nice try, Mom, but I won't be alonee. I'll be with Sam. And Stacy. Besides, she must know I wouldn't willingly let her wear me down in person.

Mom isn't happy with my move. She doesn't mean to sound judgmental, and I do appreciate her genuine concern. After my rather out-of-the-blue move from Connecticut to London last year, this relocation probably has a whiff of déjà vu about it. But she should know me well enough to understand that it's no use trying to bully me into returning home. It's not just that I'm stubborn. She's fighting against an inviolable mother-daughter dynamic, a formula that has held true through the ages:

$$N(T+12) = -L + S2$$

where a mother's nagging across time zones is responsible for her daughter's unwillingness to listen, plus her exponential capacity for spiteful digging in of heels. It doesn't take Pythagoras to work that one out.

Thanks, so thoughtful! I text. *But Sam will celebrate with me. Having lunch now so can't text longer. x*

Turning to my lunch, I find a gelatinous mass of meat beneath the last steamer. I've seen more appetizing biology experiments. I definitely wouldn't have pointed it out to the waiter and said, 'Mmm, mmm, I'll have some of that, please.' Nevertheless, it must be the chicken. I take a bite.

It's vile. I can't spit it out. After that durian fruit incident in Bangkok, when I heaved it up on the street in front of Sam and the woman who'd offered it to me, I don't exactly have a reputation in Asia as a cultural ambassador. Luckily, as it's covered in such a thick layer of fat, it slides down rather easily in one piece. Check, please.

The waiter is much quicker with the bill than he was with my order. But there's no fortune cookie. How is that possible when we're in China? I look forward to these petrified portents of the future. Not that I believe in them. Completely. It's just that I got one in Chinatown right after I told Sam I'd move here. It said: *Following your heart will pay off in the near future.* I love that it endorsed my decision. It's safely folded in my wallet, and I'd like another choice-confirming cookie.

What I really want, of course, is Sam. I miss him so much that it actually, physically hurts. I find myself feeling short of breath, panicky when I think about him. When I think about his absence. I know he's coming back soon, but still I miss him with a visceral gut-wrenching sense of loss. This can't healthy, being so in love. It's madness, just like the poets have always claimed. It does feel like madness. How is that possible? Surely we haven't known each other long enough. How can I know he's the one so certainly? I don't know. I just do. I'm feeling it, not thinking it. I've certainly never felt this way before. He's The One. I know it as surely as I know I'd never eat that chicken dish again.

He picks up on the third ring. 'Hannah, hi! How are you, darlin'?'

My belly flips upon hearing his voice. To the wider world I'm sure he's no Barry White, but Sam could read fungicide application instructions to me and I'd melt. 'I'm great, so glad to talk to you! I just finished eating dim sum, and now I'm walking back to the apartment. I viewed an apartment earlier. You're not going to believe this. They're trying to sell the laundry room as a second bedroom! What are you doing now?'

'Hah, you've seen the maid's quarters then. They're shocking, aren't they? Pete and I saw a few of those when we were searching. It's appalling. Definitely not suitable for you and Stacy! ... I'm glad you called, Han. It's always a nice surprise at work.'

'Oh, do you have to go?'

'No, that's okay sweetheart. I can use the break.' I can picture him as he blows out his cheeks, wiping sweat from his brow after a grueling day being an economist. 'I planned to call you later, but tell me about your day now. Li Ming just went to get us some early dinner – it's gonna be another late night here.'

'... Oh, well I don't want to keep you from... anything,' says I, suddenly struck by an insidious jealousy-inspired martyrdom. 'I'm sure Li Ming will want you, so I should let you go.' I don't know why, when I'm a perfectly intelligent woman, I feel so insecure when it comes to this man. Surely when you're in love with someone you're supposed to feel more secure, not less.

'No, Han! I can talk. Tell me more about your day. There's nothing interesting to report from here. Where are you now?'

'I'm not sure. I got a little turned around when I left the restaurant. I think I'm heading towards Sheung Wan.'

'Ah, I love it there. It feels like old Hong Kong. Where was the apartment you saw?'

'In the Mid-levels. There was someone else looking at it, and you can't even imagine this girl. She didn't stop giggling the whole time we were together. She invited me for a coffee, which was nice of her, but she's so flaky, Sam. She claims that crystals heal people, and has a guru called Neil. Seriously, what guru is called Neil? Apparently my aura needs cleaning.'

'Oh, that's great. I'm sorry darlin', but can I call you back? Mr. Nguyen just came in. Okay Mr. Nguyen, I'm happy to go through it again. Sorry, Han, I'll talk to you later, okay?' He hangs up. Convo interruptus.

I suppose it was a little unfair to expect him to kick his feet up on the desk for a chinwag at work. I should be more understanding. When I worked for my horror boss in London, I wouldn't have been able to take a personal phone call, let alone enjoy it. Still, now I feel unfulfilled and frustrated. I wanted our conversation to ease the panicky loss I'm feeling. Instead, it just sharpened it. Given that he's done nothing to make me feel insecure, I have to admit the possibility that it's me.

This is not a comfortable thought as I pick my way through Sheung Wan's higgledy-piggledy streets, careful to avoid the shallow woven baskets that are strewn across the pavements. Most are full of urchins and scallops that have been drying in the heat of the day.

One basket holds what look like reptilian lollipops.

They're actual lizards, splayed out flat on sticks. Do diners gnaw on them like jerky, or soak them in water till they reconstitute into their fleshy former selves? Their heads are still attached. I'm not crazy about eating something that could, theoretically, watch me fork it in. This feels a million miles away from the sleek skyscrapers in Central. In street after narrow street shops sell things that I've never even contemplated putting in my mouth. Most look a bit like garages, with wide roll-up doors on the front, some with shelves along one wall and a counter, some with hundreds of bags of mysterious dried things. This is what I expected when I moved – the sheer foreignness is overwhelming, and exciting! Wonderful pungent smells waft through the street, herbs and grassy, hay-like aromas, fish and a spicy, smoky smell. It's strong but not off-putting.

It's one of the true joys of this city. You never know what's around the corner. The next street is lined with Chinese medicine shops. Although they're probably just called medicine shops here, like Swedish massages are simply called massages in Stockholm. Window labels tell me they're selling deer antlers. They're rich brown and fuzzy, chopped into sausage-sized pieces. And there are dinosaur teeth. Surely those are supposed to be in a museum. And… what on earth is that? Through the window I glimpse a man, a customer, standing in front of a tray of dark, rounded, fleshy-looking objects. He's picking each one up and weighing it in his hand. I notice one on a tray in the window. It has definitely come from an animal. I wonder which part? Uncertainly I enter the shop, catching the clerk's attention as the customer leaves. 'Do you speak

English?' I ask politely. He comes over to the counter as if ready to answer my question, so I point to the object. 'What is this?' He smiles, but doesn't answer. It feels rude to walk out now, so instead we begin a game of charades.

I point to it, then to my tongue. It could be a tongue. A burst of laughter erupts from the corner. I hadn't noticed that another clerk, a lady, is sitting at a little table shaving pieces off an antler. The man shakes his head, looking unsure now. He splays his fingers out from his ears. I get it, it's from a deer. Not antlers though. He takes his hand and moves it to his midsection. Oh. Oh no. I'm about to make this nice man mime deer penis. I wince in anticipation. Then he puts it on his bottom and flicks it up and down.

'A tail?' I say hopefully, praying he hasn't got his anatomy wrong.

He nods. 'Tail, yes.'

Before I can stop myself I ask him, 'What is it used for?'

Now why can't I just leave well enough alone? I'd hate to make him mime impotence, or constipation, or—

'For kidneys. Good for kidneys.'

'Oh, I see.' Good to know, should a case of honeymoon cystitis ever strike. And since Sam arrives in two weeks, I just might find myself here again.

4

I haven't come down with cystitis yet. Instead, I'm suffering from a backwards case of dater's remorse. I don't mean that I'm filled with regret having just woken up next to a halitosis-filled mouth-breathing troll. I mean that I'm filled with regret because I shouldn't be on a date with Sam on Stacy's first night in Hong Kong. She's sitting alone in my diminutive apartment, surrounded by her worldly belongings, while I sit atop The Peak with my boyfriend quaffing Chardonnay. I am a Bad friend. Capital B, small f (very small f).

It was a real *Sophie's Choice* moment in the terminal this morning when they both arrived. My breath caught in my throat when I saw him. And then I saw her. But it was Sam. And Stacy. Both coming towards me. Who to kiss first? Was I the kind of woman who'd choose a man over my best friend? Or to side with the sisterhood when my boyfriend was puckered and waiting? Stacy had just flown 9,000 miles. I hadn't seen Sam in nearly three weeks, and I was in love with him. I hadn't expected that kind of soul-searching in Terminal A.

The decision was made for me when Stacy beat Sam by a nose. 'Oh my God,' she'd said, hugging me as I caught Sam's eye over her shoulder. 'That flight was like a million years long, I can't believe I'm finally here!'

'Welcome to Hong Kong, Stace! And this is Sam.' He stood a little shyly beside me, reaching for my hand. Then he kissed her cheek, and she blushed. Actually blushed.

'Hi, you,' he said to me, enveloping me in his arms. His lips were magic. Just seeing them, imagining, remembering their remarkable abilities, made it hard to keep from panting. He kissed me with his whole mouth, soft and slow, so sensual, his hand holding, then caressing the back of my neck and pulling me closer, keeping me firmly with him. His other hand explored my jawline, our bodies pushing against each other. Kissing him was like being in a sensory deprivation chamber; I was aware of only my body, and its reaction to him. Somewhere in the back of my mind my mother reminded me that there were hundreds of people who may not care to see us humping each other in Arrivals. I respectfully asked her to shut up.

'Ehem.'

Right. Stacy. 'Sorry,' I said after our last (well, third to last) kiss. 'Are you ready for Hong Kong? Though you must be exhausted. You should probably take it easy tonight.' Even as I said the words I was plotting to ditch her in my apartment. Bad friend, capital B, small f.

The fact that I feel so guilty isn't nearly enough penance. When I shuffle off this mortal coil, Saint Peter will scoff at me and slam shut the Pearly Gates. And I'll deserve it, because I should not be having the time of my life, holding Sam's hand, gazing at what might be the most gorgeous view on the planet.

Think Fiji, Hawaii or one of the Caribbean jewels like St Lucia. Put the Manhattan skyline on the shore, and wire up all the buildings with jaw-dropping illumination so that the whole scene lights up like a pinball machine. Finally, build a restaurant with panoramic views atop one of the green-carpeted mountains. That's The Peak. It's supposed to be one of the most romantic places on earth, but surely that depends on your date. The troll with the bad breath still wouldn't stand a chance here, whereas Sam could have his way with me in a Tesco. It's all a matter of perspective.

At the moment my perspective is trained on Sam. I've just told him my news.

'What? How? When? Congratulations! When do you start?'

'In a week. I know, it's fast, and I can't believe it. I found out yesterday when Josh called but I wanted to tell you in person. Can you believe it? I'm going to be a fashion buyer's assistant!'

Sam pushes back his chair and strides around the table to kiss me. That's why I didn't tell him on the phone. A momentous occasion like this should be shared personally. Preferably with skin-to-skin contact.

I'm still in shock that I got the job, though I was pretty awesome in the interview, if I do say so myself. I told Josh all about my PR assistant background, embellishing just enough without tipping into 'Bless me Father for I have sinned' territory. When I told him about my party-planning stint he started grinning, and I knew I was in. Who'd have thought that a CV consisting solely of menial jobs would be a career-enhancer?

'Hannah, I'm so happy for you, really, this is great. It must be such a relief now that you've got a job, to know that the move was a good idea. And Stacy's arrival too… I'm relieved it's all working out so well for you. So tell me about this Josh. He's your boss?'

'Uh-huh.' I can't stop grinning. Sam is right. It is such a relief to have a job. It means I'm now a fully functioning grown-up living in Hong Kong. And it seems like I've found a great company to work for. Josh's granddad started it in the fifties, selling blouses and dresses to high-end boutiques in London and Paris, who went crazy for Chinese silk. Then, when designers started outsourcing manufacturing to Asia, he craftily changed gears to stock knock-offs. He made a fortune, and Josh's dad shifted the business again when the knock-offs market got too crowded. Now the company supplies fashion apparel to shops across Europe. It's got just a dozen or so employees, but it's very successful, and Josh seems great. When his dad died he took over the business. He was born in Hong Kong, though, oddly, he speaks the Queen's English, and referred to England as 'home' in the interview.

'Josh seems super, very friendly,' I say. 'And really happy that I'm going to work for him.'

'Well, I hope he's not like Mark,' Sam murmurs.

'You mean a weasely slimeball?' Mark owns the events company I worked for in London, where Sam and I met. He was quite the fisherman, in that he loved reeling them in from the company pier. I willingly took the bait, that is, until I found out he had a stocked aquarium at home. Men like that deserve to be kicked in the tackle box.

'I mean hiring you just to get in your pants,' my boyfriend says.

'... Why wouldn't he hire me because he thinks I can do the job?'

'I know about men like that, Han, remember? I worked for Mark too. Just be careful, that's all I'm saying.'

'You know what? You said the same thing about Mark when we first met. You assumed I was only there as a bit of eye candy.'

'I was right.'

'What?!'

'What I mean is, Mark was an ass and he was only interested in your, you know, your other assets. That doesn't mean you didn't do a great job, or that you're not going to be amazing at this job. It just means you should go into it with your eyes open.'

'What about you? I could say the same thing about your boss.'

'Li Ming? Why would you say the same thing about her?'

I realize I'm grasping at ridiculous straws, but I don't like the sound of this Li Ming character. She seems to always be there when Sam calls. I know they're sharing an apartment with the two other colleagues. I still don't like it. 'I think she likes you.'

'What? Hannah, she's my boss. We're on an assignment together, along with the *rest of the team*. Trust me, she doesn't like me. You're not jealous, are you?'

'No.' Yes. Why am I jealous? I shouldn't be jealous, should I?

He takes my hand. 'Good, because I think you'd

really like each other. She's very nice. You have nothing to worry about.'

'I know.' What is wrong with me? This dinner has the potential to go seriously downhill if I don't stop this silliness. 'Why are we fighting?' I force a smile. 'All I did was tell you about my new job.'

'Aw, Han, you're right. I have no idea why we're arguing. I'm sorry. Here,' he says, raising a glass. 'To you, and your new job, and your boss who hired you because you're wonderful and because you're going to be the best buyer's assistant that Hong Kong's ever seen. You'll be great, and I'm so proud of you. Cheers.'

We clink glasses but the night seems a tiny bit dimmer now. It's not just that this bickering came from nowhere. A question has been niggling.

How long does Sam plan to stay? I want to ask, but I'm afraid to hear the answer. I'm going to be seriously unhappy if the milk in my fridge lasts longer than his visit. It's not that I haven't asked before. And by 'before' I mean every day that we've spoken for the last two weeks. Sam simply hasn't been able to say for sure. I guess when you're working for a government you're expected to work around their schedule. I also suspect that he (rightly) thinks I'll seize on any information like a bull terrier. He doesn't want to disappoint me. Of course he could best avoid disappointment by staying permanently, but it's probably a little selfish to expect him to quit his job to be available for my dating needs. So I have to ask. But I don't want to. But I have to. I'll just finish my wine first. And make a quick call. ''Scuse me a sec, I should check on Stacy.'

'That's a good idea,' he says with a smile. 'Han?

You know you're a good friend, right? You do, don't you?'

He has such a gift for saying the right thing. 'I know, thanks. See you in a minute. I'll just call her from out front.'

The wind buffets me as I round the corner of the building. It's unseasonably cool tonight (which means that the temperature has dipped below five-minutes-to-soak-through-a-blouse). To look at the locals you'd think we're dining on the Arctic ice cap.

As usual I'm inappropriately dressed, but goose bumps are worth the sacrifice to wear my new shoes – hot pink satin, diamante encrusted, in the fashion-forward sense rather than the aging-Hollywood-has-been sense. They're impossibly delicate, sky high and pretty enough to bring a tear to the eye. They're also uncomfortable enough to raise a quiet sob.

Stacy picks up on the first ring. 'Stace? It's me. I just wanted to see how you're settling in.'

'Oh. Hi.' It's her angry voice.

'Did you find everything okay?' It's a rhetorical question. We're sharing a room the size of a walk-in freezer

'Yes, thanks.'

'How about towels? I bought you a scrubby glove – it's in the shower.' As if a loofah can slough away the feeling of desertion. 'And there's tea, and milk and sugar, in the kitchen. Have you eaten?'

'Where would I eat? I've never been here before.'

Oh yes, definitely her angry voice. 'If you take a left out of the building and walk a couple of minutes, there's a whole row of restaurants. Tomorrow I'll take you to lunch at a dumpling place that you'll love.' As best friends, we sometimes know each other better than we do ourselves. So we know that if either of us cracks and admits to being mad (her) or guilty (me), the argumentative floodgates will open and we'll end up on the phone till morning. Like the proverbial elephant in the room – I will not mention it, I will not. And I hope she's too tired for a fight. 'I'll be home by midnight so if you're still up, I'll see you then, okay?'

'Sure, okay, see you later.'

'... Bye.'

'... Bye.'

I don't know why I thought that'd make me feel better.

'How's she doing?' Sam wants to know when I navigate back to the table, slightly weaving in my shoes.

'She's angry.' I could sugar-coat it, but it wouldn't do any good to lie to him. He has an eerie sixth sense that sees through me.

'Well, she did just land today,' he points out.

'So did you!'

'Darlin', I'm not judging you. Really I'm not. I love being here with you. It's selfish of me, but I'm glad you're with me instead of Stacy tonight.'

Okay then. Because, for the record, he asked me here. I was ready to sacrifice my happiness to stay with Stacy. I wouldn't have been good company, but I was ready to do it. 'Stacy isn't sharing your point of view at the moment.'

'Let me ask you something. How would you describe the relationship between you two?'

He's always asking me questions like this, and often much more random (like, if you could have any superhero power, what would it be?). He's a real ponderer. 'We're best friends.'

'I know that. But what's your relationship? I mean, who has the upper hand?'

The thought pops instantly into my head. 'She does,' I say. She always has. I'm her canary in the coalmine, ready to play the warm-up to her headline show…

Or am I? Certainly that was my role when we were growing up, and such an instinctive role for me that I never questioned it. I happily followed her natural lead, generally without touching the brakes of common sense. Once, when she decided that brunettes have no fun, she stole her mother's Nice 'n Easy permanent color and turned me into a blonde. Fortunately, or unfortunately, her mom caught us mid-rinse, and put an end to Stacy's dreams of fair-haired partiality. We were nine. I spent the fourth grade growing out my roots.

But if I'm honest, our relationship did change when I moved to London. Certainly at first we talked every day. I needed her advice, her support, and that connection to home. But as I settled in and made a few friends, the power shifted. I think Stacy even started getting a little insecure. So I revise my answer. 'Maybe I have the upper hand now.'

'Yes, I think so. After all, she followed you here, right?'

'Are you trying to make me feel bad?' I frown at him.

'No, no. Come here.' He holds my face as he kisses me over the table. 'I just mean that you're not the same people you were before you left the US. It's going to take time to establish your boundaries again. She's probably a little unsure about where she fits in your life now, and that's hard for her. I'm sure that's the only reason she's acting mad now. It's not really because we're here and she's in your apartment. So don't be so hard on yourself. Think about it. You know her best. Besides, I'm really glad you're here with me.'

'Me too.' Ah, the way he's looking at me! Like I'm his one true love and we're the only two people in the world. Like he wants to tell me something. Oh. Is this it? Is he going to say it?

'Han.'

'Yes?' He's going to say it. I wish I hadn't eaten the spinach.

'I need to tell you something.'

Despite the typhoon blowing across the balcony, this is the perfect setting to declare our love. I've dreamed about this moment since we first kissed. 'What is it?' That garlic mayonnaise was probably a mistake too.

'I have to go back to Ho Chi Minh on Sunday.'

'What?!'

What about 'I love you'? Or at least 'I'm staying longer than the sell-by dates in your fridge'? Who wastes a setting like this delivering bad news? Unless this is the dating equivalent of dumping a girl in a quiet restaurant, counting on the setting to keep her from sobbing into her tarte Tatin. Oops. Too late.

'Oh sweetheart, please don't cry,' he says, wiping my tears, and probably not a little mascara, with his fingers. 'I hate that my job keeps me out of Hong Kong, and away from you. I didn't expect there to be this much travel, not at the start. Hey, please stop crying. I can't stand to see you upset because of me.

Really, Han. I miss you so much when I'm away. I'd much rather stay here, but I've taken this job and this is the assignment. I don't have a choice unless I quit. I've thought about that, believe me, because this isn't what I want. Living out of a suitcase isn't exactly my ideal. But I can't quit. At least not till I've given it a chance, and put in my time. You understand that, don't you?'

'Yes.' No, not really.

'Darlin', I'll be back again soon, in just a couple weeks. And we've got a few days before I go. We'll make the most of it. How 'bout we take Stacy sightseeing tomorrow, maybe to see the Ten Thousand Buddhas in Sha Tin? It's a monastery, she'll love it, and I'll spring for lunch.'

A monastery is no substitute for a boyfriend. 'Okay, that'll be nice–' sniffle '–But Sam, I'm already thinking about Sunday. I'm going to miss you so much!' I hate it when I blubber. I don't cry daintily; I effuse copious amounts of bodily fluids.

'Oh, please don't worry about that now. It's not Sunday yet. And of course I'll miss you too. But we can talk every day. We do now, don't we?'

'I suppose.'

'Besides, you've got Stacy here, and you're going to need to find an apartment, and start your job. You'll be so busy that you won't even notice I'm gone.'

Why do men say stupid things like this? I had a boyfriend once tell me that I shouldn't worry about him meeting his foxy ex (his words, admittedly in a different conversation) because even though she was still in love with him, he'd made a commitment to me. How is that supposed to make a girl feel better?

'Should we get the bill?' I suggest. If I'm going to

make the most of our few days together, we need to skip the coffees.

'Sure,' he says, making the universal check-please hand signal to a passing waiter. 'It's a nice night. What do you say we walk back to your place from the tram?'

'I, erm…' I say that's a terrible idea. Stacy is sleeping a meter from my bed. And he can't have failed to notice my footwear. 'Why don't we take a taxi to your apartment?'

'I didn't think you'd want to stay on Stacy's first night.'

This is going to get very awkward if I have to spell it out. 'I don't plan to stay…'

'A quickie?' He's grinning. 'But I'd feel so used.'

'Are you upset to know you're wanted for your body?'

'I've never been so proud in my life. Come on.' He grabs my hand and hurries me, as fast as my shoes will allow, towards the tram. I don't care that we're making a spectacle of ourselves as we navigate the stairs in a pre-coital embrace. And Stacy will have to forgive me if I'm a little late.

I'm very late.

'Have fun?' Her words cut through me as I gently close the front door. I guess there's a small chance that they've been sharpened by my guilt rather than her anger.

'It was a magical night, Stace. I've missed him so much! It seems like forever since we've seen each other, even though I know it's only been a few weeks. And it was amazing to catch up, and finally get to spend time together here. It was like we'd never been apart, I guess that's a sign isn't it, to be so connected? And this was our first time together in Hong Kong, our christening I guess you'd call it, and it was fun, we went to The Peak for dinner, I'll take you there, it's got an incredible view, though different from Kowloon, sort of the opposite view if you know what I mean, and the food's good, but we can just go to see it too, and go somewhere else to eat…' Maybe hyper-babbling will stave off the inevitable conversation.

'Good.' She's still mad.

'Are you tired?'

'No. I feel rough though.'

Stacy is one of life's beautiful women, with sleek blonde hair and flawless skin that always looks tanned despite her bat-like aversion to sunshine. For her, feeling rough translates into slight shadows beneath her eyes that only she can see. When I arrived I looked like I'd just been sprung from solitary confinement. 'Aw, Stace, it's the jet lag. It takes a few days to adjust. Want to watch TV? They dub Friends into Cantonese.'

'No thanks.'

'Well, I'm exhausted.' I mime a stretch. 'Mind if I head to bed?'

'Hannah.'

Damn. 'Yes?'

'I wanted to talk…'

'Oh, sure.' Remember the comfortable ease with which Sam and I passed the evening? This is nothing like that.

'I'm worried about you.'

When people say this, they usually mean they're about to criticize me in some hurtful way. 'Really? Because I'm doing great.'

'I've been thinking a lot about this. It's… you're… I think you're getting too wrapped up in Sam.'

'Well, I love him.'

'And that's great. But you should be a little careful.'

'Why?' I definitely don't like the course this conversation seems to be tracking. 'Be careful of what?'

'Well, it's such a new relationship, and it's moving really fast. Don't you think so?'

'Yes, and I'm thrilled. That's not always a bad thing, Stace.'

'No, I know. But what's the rush? You could still see other people here. After all, you've just moved to a new country. And Sam will be away a lot. Don't you want to have some fun?'

'No, Stace, I want to be with Sam. I love him. Why would I want to be with someone else?'

'It's just that you're making it too easy for him. If you wait around for him to show up, and then drop everything at his beck and call, you're not doing yourself any favors. You should play hardball a little more, don't be so available.'

What's the point of pretending not to like him when I really like him?

'That's how the game is played,' she continues. 'Believe me. He'll want to see you all the time then.'

'But he's only in town for a few days. He wants to see me all the time now. And I don't want to play a game!'

'Come on, we all play games.'

'Stace, you know how crap I am at that. You remember school, right?' My game-playing ability is on par with my checkbook-balancing ability. I haven't got the stomach for either one. 'Why can't I just be myself and do what comes naturally?'

'Well… don't take this the wrong way,' she says, guaranteeing that I'm going to take what's coming the wrong way. 'But you become a little, pathetic, when you're hung up on a guy. And you know I say that with the utmost love for you.'

Well, at least that didn't hurt. 'Thanks very much.'

'I just mean that you change when you have a boyfriend.' She tips her head. 'That's not always a bad thing, sometimes you change for the good.'

Again, thanks very much. 'I don't think I change.'

'Oh, come on! You take on the personality of the guy you're seeing. You always have… I see you've bought Tevas.' She stares pointedly at my footwear collection.

'You know what, Stacy? Why don't you give me some credit for having my own personality? That's really insulting. And I bought them because they're practical.'

'I'm sorry,' she says. 'I don't mean to insult you. I just wanted to point out that the reason Sam likes you is because you're you. And you're wonderful the way you are. If you then become him, you'll lose what made him like you in the first place. Sorry, I really didn't mean to offend you. Although,' she pauses before delivering her coup de grace. 'You've never been practical when it comes to shoes.'

'I'm not going to play games with Sam.'

'Well, you know him best, so that's up to you to decide.'

'Stace, it sounds like you don't think this was a good idea.'

'Well…' She sighs. 'I'm just glad that I'm here.

Don't worry, Han, whatever happens we'll have a great time together.'

So it's official. Everybody I love, except Sam, has judged this move to be a Very Bad Idea.

5

'Wakey-wakey!'

'Mwhuh?' Stacy is standing over my bed with, it looks like, toast. I'll know for sure when my eyes can focus beyond my pillow. 'What's this?'

'Move over.' She shoves me to the edge of the mattress. 'Breakfast is the most important meal of the day. Especially for our first day of work.'

Of course. It's Monday already, and Sam's gone back to Vietnam. Both these thoughts hit me in the gut, and neither makes that toast look appetizing. After such an amazing weekend together, finely balanced between cultural exploration (the monastery) and sexual exploration (everything else), I feel his absence more than ever. Stacy, good friend that she is, did her best last night to distract me from his departure. It worked, briefly, but oh, my head.

In her attempt to find the hotel where the eponymous hooker from *The World of Suzie Wong* plied her trade, instead we found a Mexican restaurant. That would have been fine if dinner hadn't been mostly margaritas with a side order of food. Ay caramba!

'What time is it?' I ask.

'Relax, it's only six-thirty. We've got plenty of time.'

'Yeah, like another hour before my alarm goes off. This is brutal, Stace, it was after midnight when we went to bed.'

'Glad you appreciate the gesture, Han. You're welcome very much. I couldn't sleep. It must still be the jet lag. But you want to start early on your first day, don't you? Impress the boss?'

How can she look so alert while I've got a hangover doing the salsa on my synapses? 'Yeah, I guess so. Yes, definitely, what am I saying? I've waited all my adult life for this kind of chance. Thanks, Stace. Here, get in,' I offer, patting the mattress. 'You know something? I'm actually going to miss this little apartment when we find our new one. I've grown used to having everything in arm's reach.'

'Not me.' She shakes her head, snuggling under the duvet. 'I hate having to unpack my whole suitcase just to find something to wear.'

I scan the room, which is a cross between a jumble sale and a natural disaster site. 'I see what you mean. Are you excited for your first day?'

She grins. 'I can't remember the last time I was so nervous. Honestly, I'm not even hungry.'

This could be serious. She is never not hungry. Her ravenous appetite, and willingness to indulge mine, is what keeps me from resenting her physical perfection.

'You shouldn't be nervous,' I tell her. 'You'll be great. Your boss already thinks you're a superstar. He made space for you to come, didn't he? I wouldn't worry about it.'

'Oh I know,' she says breezily. 'That's not what I'm–' She sighs. 'The job is the job. I can be an analyst anywhere. It's the people I'm worried about. I loved everyone at home. We weren't just colleagues, we were friends. Some were really good friends. What if nobody socializes after work? Or what if they do, but I hate them all? What if they're geeks,' she whispers.

'You might love them,' I point out.

'I guess. It's a stupid thing to worry about. Right?'

She sounds uncertain. Why, she is uncertain. Of course she is. I've been so focused on her arrival, so that I was comfortable, that I didn't think about what she must be feeling. She's probably going through exactly what I did when I moved to London. First time away from home, away from everyone she knows, not knowing what's ahead, or whether she's going to succeed or fail. It's exciting, yes, but it's also terrifyingly disorientating. 'Stacy, trust me. You're going to love them and they'll love you, just like at home, and you're going to be great at your job, just like at home. And you've got me. Just like at home.'

'This is a huge adventure, huh?' She crams most of a piece of toast in her mouth, ending what might be the briefest fast in history.

'It is. That's the best way to see it. Otherwise we'll just scare ourselves. I'm so grateful that we're doing it together. Thank you for coming here. It's the best thing I can imagine.' I'm trying to resist the urge to wrestle her into a bear hug and weepily shout, 'I love you, man!'

'Aw, Han, I thank you. If you hadn't moved in the first place I'd never have done it. You have no idea how much I admire you. You've got balls, girl, serious cantaloupe-sized cojones. You realized what you wanted and you went for it and you made your life in London. That's incredible. And now you're doing it again. No matter what your family says, or me, you've made this move. That takes guts, to take that kind of risk despite… despite what everyone thinks.'

Uh-oh, here comes that bear hug.

'Thanks. It definitely hasn't been easy. I can deal with my parents because, well, they disapprove of most things. But your approval means a lot to me, Stace.' I'm trying my best not to sound scoldy. 'I made the right decision you know, to be here. I know I did, even though no one else thinks so. I'm so excited for the chance to make my life here, just like I did in London. Having you here, and Sam, is the icing on the cake. Although I wish he was here now.'

I don't want to ask the next question, but I have to know the answer. 'What did you think of him?'

She pauses, mopping up crumbs with a wet finger. 'Han, I'd love to tell you that I'm one hundred per cent sure about him, and that he's definitely the right one for you. I'm glad I got to know him a little better over the weekend, and I do see what you see in him. He is really nice. He does truly seem to be crazy about you, and he says and does all the right things. But I can't be completely sure about him yet. It still bothers me that you're not living together. Hold on,' she says to the objection forming on my lips. 'I know that was never the plan, and it's a new relationship. I know all that. I also know I'm not the best person to judge when it comes to love. So please don't take my reservations as a judgment against your relationship. I'm just wary. I don't want you to get hurt. So until I'm completely sure that Sam's going to come good, I'm gonna watch your back.'

'Thanks, Stace. That's what friends are for, right?'

'Exactly. You'd do the same for me… Who knows? Maybe I'll fall in love with someone you hate one day and you can repay the favor.' Her face says she's realized what a clanger that was. 'I don't mean that I hate Sam. Not at all, he was quite sweet. You know what I mean.'

She's not telling me she doesn't trust Sam, just that she doesn't trust him yet. I feel better. Sam was right. Our trip to the Ten Thousand Buddhas was an excellent idea. He was his usual friendly self and he definitely charmed her. Quite literally. He sneaked off to buy us little bracelets at the monk gift shop. 'This is for you, Stacy,' he'd said, handing her an intricately woven gold string with charms dangling from it.

She was flabbergasted. 'For me?'

'Yeah, to welcome you to Hong Kong. This little stone is for luck, and this one here, this is for prosperity, and this is for wisdom. And the little jade butterfly, that's for love. I hope you'll love it here.' Shyly he kissed her cheek.

'I don't know what… thank you! Thank you so much, Sam. It's so nice of you.'

'Aw, it's nothing really.' In a fifties sitcom he'd have kicked the dirt and mumbled 'shucks ma'am' before going off for the morning milking. That's not to say his trinket bought her undying devotion though. I did have to run interference when I came back from the loo a little later. Judging by Sam's rather hunted look when I interrupted, I got there just in time. Stacy is always going to look out for me. That's the kind of relationship we've got.

'I know what you mean, Stace, don't worry.' It's comforting to know I'm not the only one who puts her size sixes squarely in her mouth. 'Do you want to get in the shower first or should I?'

'You can go first. I'm going to have some more toast. Aren't you going to eat that? I'll have it.' Happily she slides another piece on to her plate, pads to the kitchenette (technically she could simply stretch out an arm) to pop two more slices into the toaster. Sumo wrestlers have daintier appetites. 'We can walk down to Central together,' she murmurs through her buttery breakfast.

'Are you nervous?' she asks an hour later as we shuffle to the escalator with the rest of Hong Kong to begin our morning commute.

'About the job?' I say. 'You know, I thought I would be but I'm just excited. I'm nervous about getting there though. I hope I don't get lost.'

'You got there for the interview,' she points out.

'Stace, that was a fluke. You know what my sense of direction is like.' Columbus aimed for India and found the Bahamas. I wouldn't have made it out of port.

'True,' she admits. 'Do you want me to walk you to the station and make sure you get on the right train?'

I'm touched that she'd do this for me, if a little embarrassed that she feels she needs to. 'No, that's okay. I'll have to learn to do it on my own at some– Wow, look at that!'

The escalator is heaving, exactly like London's Underground at rush hour, except we're hovering above street level. 'Do we just get on?' People are streaming onto the stairs at the platform. Some have their noses buried in books or newspapers, their feet carrying them on auto-pilot to the office. I've always marveled at commuters able to walk while reading. I'd concuss myself on a lamppost.

'Dunno, I don't see any turnstiles, do you? Is it free?'

'I think so. The underground isn't, but the escalator should be, don't you think?' It's not like the escalator has drivers to pay. On the other hand, the people who built it might want their investment back. I did notice last week that there's something called an MTR Fare Saver machine on the platforms. Unfortunately the instructions are all in Chinese. For all I know it's dispensing daily astrological forecasts. If I get caught by the transport police, that's exactly the argument I'll use. 'I don't know, Stace. I guess we just get on. Ready? … Uh…' The commuters are reluctant to let us join them. 'Maybe we're supposed to barge in. 'Scuse me, pardon me.' I grab Stacy's hand and we make a jump for it. We will not fall at the first hurdle less than ten minutes into our morning commute. Especially not when, for me, this is a long-distance race. Stacy's office is just five minutes from the escalator in Central. Mine is deep in the New Territories, across the harbor and far away from Hong Kong side. Working for a family-run exporter will mean regular top-ups to my travel card, and probably my patience. It can't be more frustrating than London though, where a power walker can beat your bus to work.

Hong Kong's traffic looks little better but after

only forty minutes and two wrong turns I've found my way back to the office that has hired me. Call me Magellan.

'Hello?' I shout above the traffic into the call box outside. 'This is Hannah, I'm here to see Josh. I'm starting work today.' The door buzzes briefly. Too briefly. 'Oh, sorry, I didn't quite… Can you buzz again? Please?' My competence must really be shining through.

'Nee how,' I greet Mrs. Reese, the receptionist, when I finally get up the stairs to the top floor.

'Hello,' she says back, refusing to humor my scant Cantonese. She seems quite sour and bears an uncanny resemblance to Margaret Thatcher. That lacquered hair could survive a jet engine at full throttle, and her aqua blue skirt suit, complete with brooch, buttoned-up blouse and black pumps tell me she's not one to blow with the winds of fashion. Her broad-shouldered frame is tensely still, as if anticipating attack, and she's openly assessing me through rather beady, watery eyes. 'Please take a seat. Josh will be out in a moment,' she says, her voice imperious and clipped. I don't get the feeling she's going to head up my fan club.

Josh. My new boss. Already I love him, just for hiring me. I've never been what you'd class as a strong candidate. I don't generally 'ace' interviews; I'm more likely to be thanked while shown to the door halfway through the allotted time. And I don't show up very well on paper either – my CV is more pixelated than high-def. So far, my career has included:

1) A once-a-week job making pizza in college. I can actually spin a paper-thin pizza crust, but have found little use for this skill in the wider world.

2) A brief stint working at a turkey farm. For the record I had nothing to do with the care, feeding or eventual dispatching of the fowl. I worked at the store that sold the farm's output. I was fired for my lackadaisical approach to pricing. I don't think minimum wage should require my encyclopedic knowledge of every vegetable's price per pound. The turkey people disagreed.

3) A summer waitressing in a pizza restaurant. After coming home for the umpteenth time with less than ten dollars in tips, stinking of cheese, I quit. The manager was grateful for this.

4) Weekly babysitting during high school, for which there is not enough money in the world.

5) My first 'proper' job, with my first proper title that wasn't 'Excuse Me, Miss, Where's My Pizza?' As a PR junior account executive, I had the noble task of proofing my boss's releases, and eventually even writing my own, as long as the topic was sufficiently boring to risk tears or tantrums if assigned to the higher-ups. I was fired when they outsourced my job to Hyderabad.

6) My second proper job, in London. Assistant party planner to initially uptight, ultimately poisonous Felicity. Things weren't going so badly until I was forced to blackmail her to keep her from firing me. After our showdown, the cleaning staff had more sparkling career prospects than me.

So my career was the twenty-first-century equivalent of Henry VIII's marital record, from the wives' point of view: graduated, fired, quit, graduated, fired, survived.

'Welcome, Hannah.' Josh grins as he shakes my hand. 'Come through this way please.' He's a natural salesman, but not the kind who'll peddle his grandmother. He's the sort of person who puts you at ease right away. I knew in our interview last week that this was someone I could work for. Though after foul Felicity back in London, I'm still a bit punch-drunk. I'd now find working for the Marquis de Sade only mildly uncomfortable. My former boss started off dismissive and belittling, only to turn the dial to abusive and vengeful when I'd settled in. Who'd have thought that earning my stripes slaving for such a bitch would work in my favor?

'Your desk is here.' He points to the cubicle near the door. 'Mrs. Reese will get you anything you need. Once you're settled in, come into my office and I'll give you the lay of the land.'

Mrs. Reese stands beside my desk, ready for orientation. 'This way please,' she orders. 'I presume you've worked in an office before, and therefore you know how they function. You will know that without clear rules, an office cannot operate efficiently. I run an efficient office. This way.' She gestures to a doorway off the main corridor. 'This is the kitchen. Coffee, tea and sugar are here. Filters are here, cutlery here. Milk is, obviously, in the fridge. That is where it must stay. In the fridge. Is that clear? It cannot be left out or it will go off,' she explains. 'This is the tropics. You may have been lax about hygiene back in London, but here it cannot be.'

She points to a sticky pad. 'When things run low, please write them here so that we can replace them. Don't wait until they are gone. Now, in here–' She stops, waiting for me to catch up with her at the other doorway leading off the kitchen. 'You'll find the printer. It is also a photocopier, but it's to be used for business purposes only. If you need personal photocopies, please use one of the many print shops. The same goes for printing documents. This is the fax machine. You don't need to worry about that. It's used by the sales staff. Here is the stationery cupboard. Please feel free to take what you need but don't hoard stationery in your desk. I ask that people take only what they need, otherwise we appear to run out when in fact employees are simply hoarding. It's customary to take lunch between one and two but it's not a hard and fast rule, so you may go at any time. It's best, though, to keep a consistent lunch schedule so whatever time you choose, please take lunch at that time only. Food must under no circumstances be brought into the office. That includes cereal and other breakfast items. It encourages roaches. I will not have roaches.'

They wouldn't dare come here, I think as I follow her back to my desk, clutching two pens and wondering if I'm being decadent. 'Josh will see you now,' she announces, depositing me at his door.

'Did you find everything all right?' he asks, as if I've just completed a tour of the Pentagon. Believe me, it's not the Pentagon. The office was a surprise when I came for the interview. I expected a modern glass skyscraper, the kind with efficient elevators whooshing between deep-pile carpeted floors. I expected stick insects in couture living out a Chinese version of *The Devil Wears Prada*. I expected someone obsessing over Miranda Priest-Li's green tea. Instead, it's grimy outside with narrow cracked linoleum stairs leading to the industrial steel entrance door. Inside is chaotic. Despite Mrs. Reese's obvious love of organization, prisons after riot have been more orderly. Wires hang from the walls and computer cables crisscross the floors. The offices are overcrowded with ancient, steel, olive green desks, swing-arm lamps clamped to each in an attempt to offset the flickering overhead strip lighting. Half-crushed cardboard boxes are piled beside the desks. It looks like a fashionista has detonated on the site. I wonder whether the employees get to use all the wallets, bags, scarves and shoes that have rained down into piles on the desks and floor. 'Mrs. Reese showed me around, thanks,' I tell Josh. 'And thanks again so much for this chance. You won't be sorry.'

'Why would I think I'd be sorry?' His quizzical look tells me that most employees don't start their careers by promising not to screw up. My party-planning scars are clearly not quite healed.

'You shouldn't. I'm sorry. It's just that after my last boss, I'm… Never mind. You shouldn't.' What a stellar impression I'm making. Maybe I'll round off the morning by telling him I don't steal too often.

'I understand. Hannah, you strike me as very capable, and your ability to deal with the difficulties of your last job… your last two jobs, actually, are part of the reason I hired you. Things don't always run smoothly here. We're a small operation–'

'Bdllling!'

'Would you like to get that?' Josh asks patiently. 'No, no, feel free.'

'I'm really sorry! It's just a text.'

God luck on your first dat. If it doesnt work out you can always come home.xx

What a heartfelt vote of confidence, Mom, thanks. 'I'm so sorry, it's on silent now. You were saying?'

'So, we're small. Profitable but small. Everyone has to pitch in to get the work done. We're very much a team, and a bit like a family. I mentioned that my grandfather started the company. Well, Mrs. Reese was with us when my father first took over. She's seen me in nappies... as a child, of course.'

My sycophantic guffaw takes us both by surprise. 'Sorry, go on, Josh.'

'A few of the others have been here for decades.' He sighs. 'In a way I'd like some new blood. It's easy to get stuck in our own ways when we're surrounded by the same people year after year. But the industry is changing quickly. That's why I created this position a few years ago. So I'm looking to you to be my right-hand woman.'

'Sure thing. I'm yer woman... You said you created the job a couple years ago. Who had the job before me?' I don't like to tempt fate by discussing the recently departed, but hopefully she's gone on to a better place. Maybe to the big luxury house in the sky (top floor of Louis Vuitton).

His smile flickers. 'Oh, that was Sandra. She was with us for just a few months actually. Very nice woman. We had to let her go because there were some irregularities. But never mind, you're here now, and I know you'll be great.'

'Thanks, Josh. One question.' Now that I'm officially hired I'm justified in asking. 'What'll I be doing exactly?' We were having such a nice chat during my interview that it seemed churlish to talk nitty-gritty job details. 'I know I'm your assistant, but what does that actually mean?'

'Ha, good question. In fact, I've got a project for you to start off with. Given your obvious flair for fashion, I dare say you'll enjoy it. That's very nice by the way.' He brandishes his hand like a game show host. 'Nice nod to the designers.'

'Thanks. It's mostly Cos and H&M, but Miu Miu inspired.' My ensemble is possibly over the top given the rather down-market surroundings, but I wanted to make an impact. Nothing says capable like a royal blue silk tank dress and camel platform shoe boots. Stacy was right. The ballerina flats were perfect for the interview but I don't want anyone wrongly assuming I won't appreciate any sky-high samples they'd care to throw my way. The office is a long walk from the MTR station and my feet may bleed by lunchtime, but I'll look good as I mince on my shredded stumps.

'You've got an eye, as I thought. Excellent. So this will be easy for you. We have around forty shops that we buy for. They vary from very low end to high street. And we've got a couple hundred suppliers in China that we buy from. Our job is to identify the clothes our shops will want to stock each season, from the suppliers that provide the best options in terms of quality and price. Easy. Here.' He pushes a foot-high pile of magazines across his desk. 'These are some of the product line catalogues we're buying from for the autumn/winter collection. There are several online as well. Come, I'll set you up with access to our database. You can see what orders each shop has placed in the past, and how many pieces they normally take in an order. I want you to choose pieces for the shops. How does that sound?'

'It sounds like I've died and gone to heaven! When can I start?'

He chuckles. 'I like your enthusiasm. I'll be doing the same thing of course, but I want you to start getting used to the process.'

A young Chinese woman knocks tentatively on the doorframe.

'Ah Winnie, come in. Hannah, this is Winnie, our head of sales. Winnie, Hannah, my new assistant.'

We're all smiles as we shake hands. She's a Chinese poppet in Prada, mid-twenties I'd guess, so she must be a sales prodigy to be the head already.

'Winnie's going to show you around the sales side. It won't take long. As you saw on your way through, we're a cozy group.'

Sure enough it takes only a few minutes to see the entire sales operation. Unsurprising for a women's fashion exporter, the staff is mostly female. 'Have you worked here long, Winnie?'

'Fourteen years,' she says, smiling.

'Fourteen! Did you start as a child?'

'I'm thirty-seven. You white people! You can never tell how old we are.' She chuckles.

'… Can you tell how old we are?'

'No, you all look the same to me. Want to have lunch later?'

'I'd love to, thanks.' I can tell from her lopsided grin that she's got a wicked sense of humor. Either that or she's incredibly comfortable about being a racist. And it doesn't matter that most of the clothes in the catalogues are flammable imitations of next season's designer catwalks, or that I don't have any real power until Josh relinquishes the controls and lets me fly solo.

I can't believe they're going to pay me to buy stuff from fashion catalogues with other people's money!

After work, Stacy and I clink glasses in the bar we've chosen to celebrate our first day. 'It's truly a dream come true,' I tell her. 'I'm so excited!' My squealing is drowned out by the hundred other after-work revelers spilling on to the street.

Stacy, scanning the crowd, says, 'It's a little different from home, huh?'

'Yeah.' Our hometown has just a handful of bars. There's little room for maneuver should one occasionally suffer from wine-induced indiscretions. Hong Kong's bars are plentiful across the city, high atop office buildings, malls and trendy hotels and low, here in Lan Kwai Fong. It reminds me of Soho in London's West End, except that here, a wet T-shirt contest could break out any minute. Picture American Spring Break circa 1995 (judging by the music) where the students dress as office workers, get blind drunk, sing in the streets and try to shag everyone in sight. Mating rituals are unfolding all around us with varying degrees of success. The women are preened, laughing in groups of two and three and throwing come-hither looks at the men. Stacy's going to be just fine here. 'Tell me about your office, Stace. Were they as bad as you feared?'

'Definitely some eggheads, but I guess that's normal considering how much time we spend building models.' I know she means computer models but when she says this I always imagine her gluing wings to balsa wood airplanes. 'There were a couple cool people. I guess it was silly to be worried that I wouldn't like them. An English guy called Stuart showed me around at lunchtime today. He's fun, and really nice. I can already tell we'll be friends… No,' she says, seeing my face. 'I'm definitely not interested in that way. There is one hottie though,' she says lasciviously. 'I haven't officially met him yet, but there's much to admire from afar.'

'Stacy, no, you can't. Remember what happened with William.' When I mentioned that Stacy's love interests have been rather fleeting, I wasn't including William in that definition. He was her kryptonite. She was miserable working with him, every day hoping for a glimmer of interest, each day disappointed. He lives on in best friend lore now as a cautionary tale, The Hopeless Crush.

'I know, I won't through that again. You won't either, right? Promise me you won't fall for your boss this time.'

She makes it sound like I've slept with all my former managers. It was just the one, really. 'No way—' My phone is chirping. 'Excuse me just a sec. I— I should take this… Hi Chloe! It was great, thanks. Yep. I'm going to love it. He's the best boss! Guess what I get to do? Only choose next season's fashions. I know. I know. I—'

Stacy is trying to bore a hole through my forehead with her stare. 'Uh, I'm with Stacy celebrating. Can I give you a call when I get home? I can call your landline, will you be in? Oh. Well where are they? No, if they're lost then I guess you wouldn't. Do you have to change the locks then? Okay, I'll call your mobile. Oh. Well then charge it. Where's your charger? Maybe in one of your bags? Then I'll call you tomorrow at work, okay? Thanks, see you, bye, bye.' I swear that girl is so forgetful she could literally misplace her virginity. 'Sorry, Stace, what was I saying?'

'You were promising not to sleep with your boss, before Chloe interrupted us,' she says pointedly. She's never liked Chloe, and at this point probably never will. I assumed that because I love Stacy, and I love Chloe, that Stacy would love Chloe. But affection can't be transferred between friends like inky hand stamps. If only it had been as easy as licking them both and rubbing them together. I wish Stacy would get over this jealous little snit she's nurturing. We're twenty-seven, not seven. Chloe is all the way back in London and Stacy lives here with me. She should be a graceful winner (yes, I'm calling myself a prize). But she won't even admit she has a problem with Chloe, let alone acknowledge that she shouldn't.

'Right,' I say. 'I'm definitely not going to sleep with Josh. First of all, he has absolutely no interest in me. Second, he's kind of funny looking. Definitely not attractive.'

'How funny looking?'

'Well, he's skinny, and tall, and pale. His face is sort of drawn, and all weather-beaten, and oddly wrinkly. He must have spent too much time in the sun. He looks like he's in his late thirties.'

'Does he have good teeth?' Graced with a blinding grin, Stacy's got a dental obsession.

'Uh, yes, his smile is nice. Very open. Dimples too, between the wrinkles.'

'He sounds sexy.'

'Actually, I was being kind. He's really nice, but definitely rather ugly.'

'Ooh, he's sexy-ugly then. You know what I mean, like Billy Bob Thornton or Steve Buscemi. Not conventionally handsome but with that je ne sais quoi.'

'Billy Bob Thornton is je ne sais gross.'

'I'd sleep with him,' she says through a wicked grin.

'You have odd tastes. No, Josh isn't sexy. Just funny looking. And his hair. Well. It's mad. It's too long and it sticks up in all directions, straight off the top of his head. He must use gel. You know how I feel about gel on a man. And he dresses like a nineteenth-century dandy. He actually wore a cravat today. Anyway, it's a moot point. He could be the best-looking man in the world but I'm in love with Sam. I can't even imagine looking at someone else.'

'Really? Not even him?' She gestures to a group of young men eyeing her up like she's the last pudding on the fat farm buffet.

'They're interested in you, Stace, not me. Oh look, one's breaking away from the pack. He's coming over. Bold move.' He has the swagger of the smug, which reminds me of something Laughing Gas Rachel told me. She said the women here aren't backwards about being forward. She made it sound like they're not above hog-tying a man and dragging him back to their place. I object to this, not because it's unladylike, but because it artificially inflates a man's ego. A guy with a dinky winky is king among the eunuchs. Meanwhile we fight each other for the pleasure of mediocrity. It's unfair.

'Hello ladies. Having a good evening?' he says, staring at Stacy.

'Great, thanks,' she says. 'I'm catching up with my

friend. It's been a long day. Enjoy your night!' Somehow she manages to sound dismissive and friendly at the same time. She's a master. I always overshoot the mark when I try the same thing. Either the guy latches on like a tick or runs away to tell his friends about the bitch he just met. Candy-coated rejection is a real balancing act.

'Stace,' I say when he's left. 'He was cute. Didn't you want to talk to him?'

'Nah, there's plenty of time for that. I'm here with you. We're celebrating. That's more important.'

This is a True Friend. Capital T capital F. She'd never leave me alone on my first night to go to The Peak with her boyfriend. I wonder if I'll feel guilty about that for the rest of our lives. Knowing me, it's possible. After all, I did just treat us to a guilt-induced foot massage. 'How do your feet feel?' I ask her. It wasn't the pampering experience I was expecting. It's a bit hard to relax with a four-and-a-half-foot harridan of Hulk-like strength working her knuckles into the tender parts of your feet in an effort to draw blood. Every time I grimaced, she chuckled, gripped harder and stabbed again with her steely digits.

'Like I've run a marathon,' she admits, wincing.

'Maybe it gets better once you get used to it.' I did notice the man next to me sleeping while the masseuse did her best to break his toes.

'They say that about a lot of things. Like anal sex, or a bikini wax,' she muses.

'Did you get a bikini wax?!' As best friends of course we've shared our views about anything going up the back stairs, but we've been daring each other to get bikini waxes for years. We've been put off at the thought of having our pubic hair torn out by a stranger earning minimum wage.

'Only for the last two months!' She snorts, looking like she's just confessed to a secret, torrid and very satisfying affair.

'Get outta here! Did it–' I lower my voice. Stacy won't thank me for discussing her lady parts in front of Hong Kong's eligibles. 'Did it hurt?'

'Not as much as you'd think, actually. And it was incredibly fast.'

'Ninja waxer.'

'Exactly. Another drink?'

I love this. We're back to normal. This is what I hoped for when Stacy said she'd move. I just have to figure out how to add Sam into the mix without spoiling the batch.

6

The phone line sounds like I've accidentally dialed 1956. 'You mean you're finished in two weeks?' My heart's doing the samba. In fourteen days Sam will come home to start our life together properly.

He says, 'I can come back in two weeks.'

'For good?' I clarify.

'For the weekend,' he offers hopefully.

'Then why did you say you had good news and that you were coming back in two weeks?!'

'Because it is good news, Han. I'll see you in two weeks. It's not that long.'

'I'll say it's not. It's only two days.'

'I mean till I come back. To. Visit.' He's speaking like I'm a child.

'It's fourteen long days,' says I, the child. Our conversations lately have been fraught with confusion. We never used to misunderstand each other. It's the distance. And it's Li Ming's fault. I'm not sure how, but it is. 'How's Li Ming?' Funny how when I speak, green-eyed monsters come out.

'She's fine. But I think the project's getting to her. It's the long hours. They're getting to all of us. It's worse for her though, because she's leading the project. She's been very stressed. She actually even yelled at me yesterday. That's not like her at all. She's usually very sweet. You'll see. She's coming back the same weekend I am, so you'll get to meet her.'

'Why would I want to meet her?'

'Because she's my boss? And you've been obsessed with her since I started the assignment?'

'I wouldn't say I'm obsessed…' I have a healthy interest in the woman my boyfriend is spending every waking hour with. That's not obsessive. It's prudent.

He chuckles. 'Come on, Han. You asked me to take her picture the other day. Isn't that obsessive?'

'Well, I just… I… I'm simply curious about your colleagues. That's perfectly natural.'

Yeah, perfectly natural for a freaky weirdo. I am obsessive, but only because I'm so in love with him. Of course I'm terrified of losing something this incredible. Who wouldn't be?

'You haven't asked for stats on the rest of the team,' he points out.

'I'm starting at the top?' I know I sound ridiculous. Sam knows it too, which is why he's turned my admittedly odd request into a joke. Otherwise he'd have to face the fact that he's dating a psychopath. 'Oh Sam, I know I sound crazy. It's just hard being apart. It's making me insecure.'

'You've got nothing to worry about, Han. I keep telling you that. Li Ming is only interested in me as far as my job is concerned. She's not a threat. She's really sweet and nice, that's all. And this isn't forever, you know. The assignment should be finished in a couple of months. Then I'll be back with you. Trust me, the time will go quickly. It probably already has, with your job, and searching for the new apartment. How was your day today?'

I know he's just trying to sound as normal as possible, as if we were able to see each other without the use of aerodynamics. 'I don't think Mrs. Reese and I are going to become best friends,' I tell him. 'And thank you so much again for the flowers. They were the perfect way to end my first day. I'm looking at them now.' In reality they're about twenty-four hours away from self-composting but I can't bring myself to throw them away. Every time I've seen them this last week they've reminded me that Sam is thinking of me.

'Well, hang in there, Han. Josh likes you, and he's your boss, not the old bat. I've been thinking about your job, you know, and how diligent you've been to find it. I know it wasn't easy… you're really a strong woman, Han, you know that? I admire you. I guess I have since your party in London. Even if you did have a death theme for someone with terminal cancer.' He snorts at the memory. 'You really worked hard to make a success of that job, in spite of Felicity. You're gonna be great at the job, I know you will. And I'll be back in just a couple months for good. Think how nice that will be, living in the same city. We'll go on dates as much as you want. We'll make spectacles of ourselves. And it'll just be a few more months.'

'Promise?' Too late to take the word back. I hate sounding so needy. 'I mean, that'll be great. Goodnight, sweetheart, I'll talk to you tomorrow.'

Just as I hang up, Stacy crashes through the door, laden with grocery bags. 'Here.' She hands me a card. 'It looks like it's from your parents. How's Sam?' She's ever alert for his transgressions to justify his suspected rat-hood.

'He's good. He'll be back the weekend after next.'

'For good?! That's great news. Finally.'

'No, just for the weekend.'

'Oh. Well, I guess that's something. Nice of him to visit at least.' She frowns. 'Are you okay?'

'Oh yeah, I'm fine.' I grin. 'Great! It'll just be for a few more months. Then he'll be back for good. And he's doing really well in his job, so this assignment is excellent.' I sound like an eighth-grade cheerleader but I just can't bring myself to tell her how I'm really feeling. I don't want to risk another I'm-worried-about-you talk like we had her first night here. I want my confidence in Sam to be unshakeable, not to have evil little whispers in my ear making me doubt him. Sometimes friends don't realize the power of their words.

'Oh, good lord.' I've just opened Mom's card. It reads: 'Enjoy your freedom. You deserve it.' I show Stacy. 'She's subtle.' I tuck the card back in the envelope.

'Well, Han, you should enjoy your freedom. I've told you that.'

'Or, even better, I could enjoy the fact that my boyfriend is coming in two weeks. Anyway, thanks for going to the store without me. What's the milk situation?'

She sighs under the weight of Hong Kong's dairy peculiarities. 'Okay. Remember the blue one that tasted funny? I think it was soy milk. I just checked and it was in a different section from this one.' She brandishes a carton with a cow on it. 'Plus, as you can see, it has a cow, so it has to be regular milk, right? Want to taste?'

'After the last one? Let's do it together.' Milk doesn't taste like milk here. And the surprise to the taste buds isn't a pleasant I-was-expecting-milk-but-got-cupcakes sensation either. Bread doesn't taste like bread, either, but at least it only tastes of Styrofoam.

Hong Kong's food stores are truly an adventure in foreign palates. Pushing my miniscule cart through narrow aisles, I didn't even recognize everyday foodstuffs. Anyone who's had a self-catering holiday abroad knows the disorientating feeling of staring blankly at rows of boxes or bags without having the faintest idea what they are. Sometimes there are helpful drawings, but they're mostly a mystery. Might be sugar, might be flour. It's not a mistake you want to make as you stir your morning coffee.

Our supermarket has more varieties of rice than I'd ever imagined possible, yet there's virtually no cheese. And the milk, well, I spent a long time staring at cartons labelled 'milk beverage' or 'milk drink' with lots of Chinese lettering. So far we've failed to find milk that tastes like it came from a cow.

'Those flowers reek, Hannah. You've got to get rid of them. Seriously, I'll buy you new ones. Oh, by the way, Chloe called yesterday. Sorry, I forgot to tell you. It's on the machine.'

'Thanks.' It's not the first time Stacy *forgot* to tell me about Chloe's calls, but I don't want to fight over it. I guess there are some things we both gloss over. 'Have I got time to call her now?'

'Not really. The guys said it'll take a while to get to the Buddha. We can take the MTR to Lantau, but then there's a bus. We're meeting them in half an hour in

Central.'

By 'the guys' she means her colleague Stuart and his identical twin brother Brent. In just the few weeks since they met, Stuart has already become Stacy's favorite work playmate. I met them a couple days ago and they are just as nice and fun as Stacy said. Being ginger, neither sibling holds any romantic potential whatsoever, so they're in the running to become our safe best friends. That means there's no risk that they'll suddenly come down with a case of the wish-I-could-kiss-yous.

Within two hours we're on a hilly Lantau road with our fates in the hands of a bus driver who thinks he's driving for Team Ferrari. To be fair, he'd have more time for the road if his pesky mobile didn't demand all his attention. We had a little fright when its ring sent him diving into the bag wedged under the brake pedal, but the damage from sideswiping that lorry wasn't too bad. This is one of those bigger-vehicle-bigger-headline situations. There are at least fifty victims on the bus. It catches air as we crest another hill. Stacy has even stopped talking. 'Isn't he going to slow down?' she finally entreats.

'He must know what he's doing,' Brent reasons, in a rather bouncy Somerset accent that sounds as if his words are on elastic bands. 'He drives this route all day.' He's seated nonchalantly while I dig the stuffing out of the seat back with my fingernails.

'That's not an established fact,' I say. 'How do you know this isn't his first day?'

'Is he driving like it's his first day?' Stuart thinks he's joking but since he's brought it up...

'He's driving like it's his first day behind the wheel. Any wheel. Plus, there's construction. Look, it's only one lane.' Concrete barriers divide the already narrow road, protecting the digging equipment from maniacal bus drivers. A well-used guardrail runs alongside the edge of the road and a temporary stop light signals the entrance to this slalom course. The light is red. The bus carries on. Clouds float level with the guardrail.

'Did he just run the light?' Even Brent looks a little nervous now.

'I think he did.'

'Maybe the light doesn't work.'

'Or maybe it does, and there's a bus coming the other way.'

We all squint into the hazy distance, but the hairpin turns make it impossible to see more than a couple of hundred yards.

Kapunk! Something bounces off the side of the bus. Or, more accurately, the bus bounces off the side of something, ricocheting from the barrier towards the guardrail, and the abyss beyond, while the less continent passengers soil themselves. 'Yeeaahh!'

We come to rest a little way up the road. I swear I see the driver take a swig out of a bottle in his bag. It looks a hundred proof.

'All right me lover?' Brent grins, like he's waiting for our exclamations of praise for planning this adventure just for us.

'I think so.' Aside from my fingertips, which are knuckle-deep in the seat back, there doesn't appear to be any damage.

Stuart twists around to address Stacy, who's wedged between me and the window. 'You all right?'

She's hyperventilating.

'Hoo. Hoo, yeah. I'm okay, hoo.' Women in labor sound less distressed. 'Isn't there another way to get to the monastery?'

'Brent?'

'Sure, we could have taken the gondola.'

There's a gondola? As in a nice, slow, safe, not-driven-by-maniac mode of transport? 'Is there a stop close by?'

'Nah, it's back where we got the bus.'

'Stace,' I say. 'Do you want to lie down for a minute?'

'Okay.' Docile as a lamb, she lays her head in my lap. Now I know she's not all right. Stacy's not the type to show weakness.

'Here, buckle up.' I don't want my best friend bouncing around like popcorn in the pan when we start moving again.

'How can you not be scared?' I ask Brent, who looks like he's about to have a quick nap. I'm really warming to him. He's remarkably easy-going, and reminds me a little of my housemate, Adam, from London. Adam is the kind of big, cuddly man who women want to be friends with, the type who suffers under the curse of the nice-guy syndrome. Always a best friend, never a lover. Brent has the advantage of a runner's build (which would be yum if it wasn't covered in ginger fur), but his happy, open face tells you that he is nice-guy afflicted. He wouldn't be bad-looking if he didn't have quite so much forehead, but Mother Nature can be cruel. His eyes are a pretty light blue but his face is a little too delicate for a man. It's his pointy nose and very archy eyebrows. Plus, his accent makes him sound simple. As endearing as this is in a friend, few women want to hear it when being smutty-talked in bed. His brother, sharer of chromosomes, is identically challenged. They're only differentiated by their bellies; Stuart has one and Brent doesn't.

'Nah, I'm not frightened. I have faith that I'm not going to die on a back road in Hong Kong. So I don't worry about things like that.' He shrugs.

'You're a fatalist then? You believe there's a time and place, and you're not going to go before your number is called?' I'd love to have that kind of faith. Being a lapsed Protestant and a devout worrier, there's no chance.

'And that's the truth,' he states with a nod.

Their accents will take getting used to. And they keep calling us lover, which I assume is just a figure of speech in the West Country, not a declaration of intent. 'What makes you think your ticket's not going to be punched on the ride back?' I ask.

His smile briefly falters. 'Well, I just don't. It doesn't do any good to worry, does it? Might as well live your life as you'd like to. Otherwise you're just biding time.'

'Like reading magazines in the waiting room,' I propose.

'That's right. I'd rather just turn up when my appointment is called.'

The driver's unusual application of brakes makes Stacy bolt upright. 'Are we there?' She's much more chipper with the risk of suicidal plunge behind us.

'It seems so.' Seven thousand stairs meander to the top of the hill. They have painful journey written all over them.

'Do we have to climb all the way up?' I ask. 'I can

see it fine from here. Big Buddha, very nice. I'll get a photo.' In the dim distance, practically ringed with clouds, Buddha sits smugly watching tourists hyperventilate towards him.

'Come on, Hannah, don't be lazy,' Stuart cajoles as we leave the bus. 'Think how lovely it'll be when we get up there.'

Lazy? I'm not lazy. It's hot. Stairs and I are not firm friends. We've almost died once already. I don't want to add stroke risk to my day. 'Sure, okay, let's go.' I'm hardly going to let our new best friends think I'm lazy, am I? Besides, I can tell these are men who believe that rubbish about the journey being part of the adventure. Stuart is clearly the leader among the twins, although he's more a benevolent dictator than a Chairman Mao. He was probably born first and his two-minutes-younger brother lives happily under his regime. I know exactly how Brent feels. After all, I've gladly followed Stacy's lead most of my life. It's comforting to have someone you trust take control. She's already staked her friendship claim on Stuart, having planted that flag firmly between his eyes on the day they met in the office. It is fun having them to play with. And they've worked here since graduation, Stuart in business and Brent in architecture. So we've got real, live, know-their-suey-from-their-wonton tour guides.

Twenty minutes of breathlessness later, I've proven to myself that a giant Buddha close up is just a more in-focus giant Buddha.

'Isn't that a nice view?' Brent enquires. After a climb that would give Edmund Hillary a nosebleed, he isn't even winded. I guess the fact that Hong Kong is the world's most humid StairMaster keeps one in shape. It really is remarkable how tenacious those first colonizers were. I'd have taken one look at the steep mountainsides and set sail for Bali.

'Yep,' I manage between breaths. The twelve-foot high bronze attendants surrounding the big man are very pretty too, each kneeling, serenely offering up a gift of some kind. I admit they're almost worth the deodorant lapse. Quietly I count the statues, savoring the few local words I've learned. '*Yut, yee, sam, say,* erm…'

'*Mmm*,' Brent says. 'That's the word for five, not erm. And *luckh*! Have you been learning Cantonese?'

'Oh, just a few phrases. I figured it's the polite thing to do.'

'Go on then, can you keep counting?'

'*Yut, yee, sam, say, mmm, look, chut, bot.* oh damn, I know it... *Sep, gau*!' I announce triumphantly as a few people turn to acknowledge my efforts.

'Oh no, Hannah, that's not what you mean! Oh me lover. Oh dear.' He laughs. 'Nine, is *gow*, not,' he lowers his voice. '*Gau*. Ten is *sup*, not *sep*. Maybe it's best not trying to say nine anymore. If you have to, just say it in English.'

'What did I say?'

'Wet cock.'

'Oh Jesus.'

'It's not your fault. It's a very tonal language. You have made my day though!'

No wonder those girls are giggling behind their hands. Apologetically I smile, sending them into another fit. 'Moving swiftly on, please,' I say as seriously as possible. 'Do you do a lot of these excursions?'

'Nah, just when new people come to town. We tend to stay in Central and drink instead.'

'Good, then we can be friends.'

'Not a fan of nature? I'd never have guessed.'

Given that we'll never have first-hand exposure to one another's reproductive systems, there's no reason to lie. 'You'd never think it to look at me.' I gesture to my inappropriate dress. 'But I'm not really a nature girl. I'm not crazy about hills either.'

'You've moved to the wrong city! Though everyone takes the escalator so we don't much notice. Your new flat will be on Robinson Road, right? Then it won't be too bad for you. Speaking of your flat, Stacy says you're moving at the weekend. Stuart and I could help you move if you like. We're just up the road.'

After Stacy's co-workers warned her that it was impossible to find a decent apartment, I didn't have high hopes. So possibly our standards are lower than the norm – we weren't competing for a family apartment, or one with a pool, concierge or underground garage, and we didn't mind living in a building older than last season's shoes. We chose our new place in an afternoon. It's close to the corporate apartment so we could relocate using a wheelbarrow. 'Thanks, that's really nice, though it's not far, and it's furnished so we're just moving our clothes.'

'But we'd love the company, thanks!' Stacy interjects as she approaches, glowing with fitness. 'And we'll cook you dinner. It'll be fun! Han, you two should have a look inside the Buddha – it's very cool.' She's been milling around for a while already, having virtually jogged up. I don't know how she does it. Actually, I do.

Stacy is a gym bunny. She's signed up with the meat

market gym near her office, and she's sure that my life won't be complete until I'm spinning with her in a room full of Lycra-clad hard-bodies. I'd like to think I'll hold out, wearing my squishy belly with pride, but I know I'll join. At the moment I risk being mistaken for a walrus and rolled into the harbor.

'Can we please take the gondola back?' I plead as we start our descent. 'Not that the bus ride wasn't exciting and all.'

'I second Hannah's suggestion,' Stuart says. 'All those in favor?'

'Aye!' It's unanimous. We'll live to play another day.

7

I was right, the move was easy. It wasn't quite wheelbarrow-easy, but nobody strained any muscles and we did try to cook for Stuart and Brent as promised. Our efforts ended with pizza delivery, but the thought was appreciated. And thanks to an unexpected flash of negotiating brilliance I've staked my claim on all of the closets outside Stacy's bedroom. So I'm justified in expanding my wardrobe.

That's why I'm now being felt up by an old Chinese man. In fairness he's groping me in a professional capacity. Mr. Chan is a tailor. I'm hoping he's the tailor that I'll fondly refer to as the genius who makes all my clothes, the man who perks me up, reigns me in and fills me out all with a wave of his magic needle.

He's certainly not shy about wielding his tape measure. Technically he's measuring my inseam. I've had less intimate dates.

'You stand.'

I am standing. Am I meant to stand somewhere else? Or stand still? Or simply to keep standing?

'You stand!' He says again before disappearing

through a tatty curtain into the back. I don't want to cast aspersions here, but a torn curtain in a tailor's shop is like a closet organizer with mismatched hangers at home. You have to wonder how seriously to take the advice you're paying for.

I've harbored this dream of handmade clothes since my first grown-up job, in PR. Landing it was pure luck, and a fair amount of pure Jose Cuervo. My friend had introduced me to her boss in a bar and around last call he offered to let me work for him. Despite these questionable circumstances, he had no ulterior motives. He was far too enamored with himself to bother admiring anyone else. As a result, his favorite conversations revolved around him, and he loved telling anyone who commented on his suits that he'd had them made in Hong Kong. Being twenty-one and not the worldliest of girls, I didn't recognize the pretension in that oft-repeated statement. I recognized the possibility. It became my dream. And now Mr. Chan is about to make it my reality.

'You pay,' barks the sprightly sewing angel.

'Okay… How much?' We haven't discussed these details. Once I finally found the shop and asked if Mr. Chan makes ladies' clothes ('Yes, very nice clothes. You want?'), before you can say Balenciaga his assistant had unfurled dozens of bolts of sumptuous cloth. I was mesmerized by the colors, the impossible delicacy of the fabric. He had me at the first shantung silk. The whole shop is lined with shelves, each filled with vertical bolts of cloth arranged by material and color. The stalwart summer wools look serious and masculine, while patterned cottons and silks are a visual feast. It's quite beautiful in its chaos.

'Very good price for you.' He punches some numbers on his calculator and formally slides it towards me. There's a nine in his proposed price. I will not say *gau*, I will not say *gau*. He'll think I have Tourette's. Am I supposed to accept his offer? Or punch a number back? It does look like a very good price. That's probably because we're sweating in a condemned rabbit warren of rooms up a million flights of stairs on a rundown street off Nathan Road in Kowloon. There'd be another zero if we were in the air-conditioned splendor of the malls on Hong Kong side.

'That's fine,' I say. His lightning quick smile tells me he expected some haggling. Hello beanstalk? This is Jack again.

'When do I come for the fitting?'

'Two weeks. Very busy.'

'Great, I'll come at lunchtime again, okay?'

'No, too busy at lunchtime. Important clients. You come at three.'

'Sure thing, Mr. Chan. I work on Kowloon side. Not too far.' By not too far I mean quite far. I'm not sure how I'll get here and back to the office without raising an eyebrow. But he has important clients. That must mean he's good, right? I'd hate for my dream of a lifetime supply of Chanel-lite couture to be crushed.

It's not like I can wear anything from the Aladdin's cave of samples at work. Clothing, clothing, everywhere, and not a frock to steal. It's because my size eight frame is too big. All the women in the office except Mrs. Reese are Chinese. On a good day I feel like Gulliver. On bad days I am Shrek. And it's not just the office freebies making me feel ungainly. The shops too only stock little-lady sizes. I nearly danced with excitement the first (only) time I went into Prada, but aside from the key rings, nothing fit.

I've just broken a sweat hurrying back to the office in the vain hope that Mrs. Reese won't have noticed my absence. No such luck. She continues to be the grit in my oyster. 'Miss Cumming.' She sighs. 'Please keep your absences from the office to lunchtime.'

'Sorry, Mrs. Reese.' Her outfit is particularly arresting today. On Jessica Rabbit an orangey-red skirt suit might stand a very slight chance of being stylish. Mrs. Reese looks like a Royal Mail post box.

'And please do remember to close the cover on the photocopier when you have finished.'

'Sorry, Mrs. Reese,' I sing again in my most false of voices. 'I'll try to remember.' I should be more tolerant, because she's worked here since the last ice age. But tidying the copy room is a bit like sweeping the floor in a coalmine. The sales personnel simply ignore her repeated requests, and emails, and memos, to follow the clean desk policy. Still, she maintains her one-woman crusade against disorder.

'And Hannah, you need to go back out. Josh wanted some rubbers.'

I do a double-take. 'I'm sorry?'

'Rubbers, Hannah, for Josh. I've been meaning to go but haven't had the chance. Here.' She hands me a few notes. 'There's a shop just over the road. Go now, please.'

'But I've got my meeting with him in twenty minutes.'

'Then you'd better hurry.'

As if I didn't already have Jurassic butterflies

threatening to oust my breakfast. After two weeks spent poring over China's knock-off factory catalogues, I'm about to present my choices to Josh. Buying his sex aids wasn't meant to be part of the pitch.

Oh God. What if, like the cystitis medicine, I have to explain what I need? I'll be miming a thrusting gau to the pharmacist.

Mrs. Reese is acting like buying rubbers for your boss is all part of a normal day. She won't take no for an answer, so across the street to the pharmacy I go. Hurrying up one aisle and down the other, I'm hoping against hope. Of course they're not on display, because that would take a tiny bit of the humiliation out of this experience. 'Hello,' I say to the young man behind the counter. Sigh. 'I need condoms, please.'

'What kind?' He asks.

Kind? I've never bought them before. Because that's a man's job... and definitely not an assistant's job. 'Uh, regular?'

'Size?' He can see from my face that I'm about twenty thousand leagues out of my depth. Patiently he lines up a dizzying array of boxes across the counter top. Boxes with hearts, boxes with horses (for 'Big Boys'), ribbed, dotted, three-packs, six, twelve, and the ironically named twenty-four family packs.

'These, please,' I say, pointing to the least weird-looking three-pack. If he wants more, let him buy them himself. 'May I have a receipt, please?' Mrs. Reese is a stickler for petty cash procedure. 'And yes, a bag, thanks.'

I'm careful crossing the street back to the office. I do not want to be struck down by a speeding taxi knowing that the personal effects shipped to my parents will include a box of rubbers.

'What am I meant to do with them?' Mrs. Reese scowls when I try to hand her the brown paper bag. 'They're for Josh. Take them in with you. You may as well take these as well.' She hands me a mechanical pencil, lead refills and a notepad.

I'm not going to argue with her just before the most important moment in my work life so far. Ready. Set. Go.

'Hi Josh,' I say, trying to settle myself unsuggestively in the chair opposite his desk… 'These are for you.'

'Thanks,' he says, distractedly opening the bag. '… Hannah? What is this?'

'Did I get the wrong kind? Do you, uh, prefer something else?'

'Nooo. These are, ehem, fine. I'm just wondering why you'd give them to me.'

'I'm sorry, Josh! Mrs. Reese insisted I bring them to you. I feared it might embarrass you. It's sure embarrassing me!'

'Mrs. Reese knows you bought these? For me? What, exactly, did she say?'

'… That you wanted some… rubbers.'

'Oh, Hannah.' He shakes his head. 'I'm afraid there's been a translation error. Rubbers are pencil erasers.'

'Oh no, they can't be.' My face is as red as that condom box. 'I can't believe I just did that. I'm so sorry!'

'Well, it's certainly the most interesting opening to a presentation I've ever had. No harm done though, don't worry. I needed a laugh today actually, so thank you. Now, if there are no more surprises–' He waits for my denial. 'Good, then let's hear what you've come up with.'

'Sure. Okay. Phew. Thanks, Josh, for understanding. That could have been really bad. I mean even worse.' I take a deep breath. 'Ehem. So, I've given this a lot of thought. The clothes I mean, not the– Never mind. The less said the better, right? Anyway, I think that the trend for next season will be… peasant.'

He looks perplexed. 'Peasant?'

'Well, peasant-ish. Stylish, of course, with a nod to peasanthood. I don't mean dressing like milkmaids, but a little embroidered embellishment, hand-woven wools, that sort of thing.' I can feel the worry lines forming as I wait for his judgment.

'Help me understand your thinking on this.'

'Sure, okay…' Where to start? Oh yes. 'My friend Chloe, she's back in London, she was telling me how she's turned over a whole new leaf, and pampering is now her middle name. She's gorgeous but I always thought she needed some polishing. Nothing major, she doesn't have a moustache or anything, but her cuticles are a mess, and her heels are an embarrassment. She's finally come around to my point of view, thanks, she said, to lastminute.com. They're running £10 beauty treatment deals. At really good spas too, in London, not just the rundown ones outside the M25 that can't drum up any business without dropping their pan– … prices. She booked a couple of treatments a day for like, the next month. Massages every day, plus weekly facials, mani/pedis. I'm quite jealous actually, although the foot massages here are great, now that I'm used to them, and the pedicures aren't bad. Is there a lastminute.com here? No? Shame. Anyway, I said, isn't that tying up your evenings? She's going out with Barry, he's my old boyfriend, sort of, and they're getting along great so I figured she'd want to meet him after work, not spend every night in a treatment room. But she said she was doing them during the day. That's one of the downsides of the deal, probably why they're so cheap, because the appointments are just during weekdays. So I said: how can you take all that time off? Because it's at least two hours for each appointment by the time you get there and back. And she said she's got no work so nobody cares whether she's there or not. She's a recruiter. She says the companies aren't hiring. Just like a few years ago. So that got me thinking. My parents freaked out when some of the banks went bust, or got bailed out or something. I wasn't living with them at the time though, I had my own place, with Stacy. That's my friend who's here now, living with me. But we went to my parents' each week for dinner. It was sweet really, that they worried about us even though we both had jobs. Some people might not want to see family every week but I liked it, and they really appreciated it too. Dad, especially, loved it when we were there – we gave him a fresh audience. Actually, Mom was probably pretty happy about that too. Every week Dad had more bad news. He was constantly talking to Stacy about the economy. I admit it was pretty boring, but it must have sunk in because one time, after dinner, we stopped by the mall on the way home, and I noticed that the Gap had gone all tweedy and chunky sweaters. And it hit me. People were feeling tweedy. Home-baked bread and nights on the sofa. Once I'd noticed it, I saw it in all the shops. So when you asked me to pick next season's orders, I talked to Stacy and asked her what'll happen in Europe in the next year. She says recession for a couple of years. So I figure that, since the last couple years haven't been great, women are probably economizing. And if everyone is worried about her job, it's not the time for flashy fashion statements. And women probably want comfort. Not in a that's-so-comfy way, but they want to be comforted. So they'll be harking back to simpler times. Uh, so that's why the peasant influence will be strong.'

His brow is still furrowed, but there's a hint of a smile playing over his face. 'Hannah, that's the longest, most round-the-houses explanation of a fashion trend I've ever heard.' He nods his head. 'But you may have something here. Well done. Let me see what you've chosen.'

Winnie is sitting on my desk when I leave Josh's office. 'How'd it go?'

'God, can we please go to lunch?' I say.

'It's eleven-thirty. What will Mrs. Reese say?'

'She'll complain that we've gone to brunch. Come on.' It's thanks to Winnie that I don't have to make my own Styrofoam sandwiches or try to mime noodle soup any more. Aside from fast food and chopped salad bars, Western restaurant options are thin on the ground out here in the New Territories. She happily navigates me through the baffling local options. In fact, we spend most lunch times together. She's teaching me some useful Cantonese words, hopefully with the correct pronunciation, and we chat about our lives now and back in London, where she studied.

At thirty-seven I'm surprised she's single, because I think she's fantastic. But she doesn't date much. She's got a group of lifelong girlfriends and she always seems to be doing things with, and for, her family. It sounds like the Chinese spend a lot of time with ancestors, visiting cemeteries and sweeping graves and, as the eldest daughter, she's usually busy with living relatives as well.

Winnie sees only humor in Mrs. Reese's request. Over our chopped salads she says, 'But rubbers are what we call them. You said Josh really did ask for them, right?' I admit that's true. 'You know I don't like the old witch, but looking at it objectively, she knows you've come from London, where they're called rubbers? And we call them rubbers here. So she wouldn't call them anything else.'

'But I never used an *eraser* in London, so I've never heard them called rubbers!'

'She doesn't know that though, does she? And even if she was being malicious, what could she think would happen? That they'd make you jump Josh in his office and he'd fire you for sexual harassment? I don't know, Hannah, I think it was innocent. And very funny.' She grins.

I guess she's right. Mrs. Reese didn't act like anything was amiss. And she did have me give him the pencils that he'd asked for too. No, I can't blame her for my mistake. Besides, she's got nothing to gain from making me look foolish.

After a healthy lunch with Winnie, walking through the wide gym doors makes me feel healthier-than-thou. True to her word, Stacy didn't give up on her campaign to see me in Lycra. But I am proof positive that you can lead a girl to the gym but you can't make her sweat. Stacy's in spin class. I'm in the juice bar, and the smoothie is delicious. Incidentally, so is the buff Chinese man who just made it for me. We have an understanding, he and I. He pretends that I don't spend all my time hiding here and I try not to drool on his biceps.

Ten more minutes and Stacy will finish. She thinks I've been on the treadmill. It's nearly time to get into position for when she comes to find me. I just need to drop my bag, which is full of magazines for my smoothie-reading pleasure, back in the locker room. She might ask questions if she sees me toting so much reading material during my hard-core workout.

There are escalators between each of the many floors, up to the locker rooms at the top. Surely if people enjoyed exercise they'd have installed stairs instead. 'Bdllling!' I hear the new text. I bet it's my mother, wondering how today went. I dig around in my bag, looking for the phone while balancing on the escalator. I wish I didn't always overstuff my bags. I dig a little deeper. I'm at the cardio floor, still fidgeting. Got it.

Hannah, I saw Mrs. Friedman she says Jake is back home. Shoild I give him your email?

She isn't seriously trying to tempt me away from Sam with my high school crush.

Thanks Mom, good to know. Has his bald spot gotten bigger?

Send.

Uh-oh.

Suddenly my bag starts to wobble. Things start

spilling out. I can't catch them or risk dropping my iPhone on the floor. I meant to get that insurance. More things rain out of my bag. A tampon drops out. Of my bag. At the feet of a fellow member. A man. A courteous man. Whose first instinct is to pick it up. And hand it back to me. I've been handed a tampon in my gym by a man in front of the cardio floor. I'm cancelling my membership.

Stacy is still glowing from her workout when we get back to the apartment. I'm still red from humiliation. I can't even tell her what happened; it would mean confessing my non-cardio ways. I told her I'd put the incline up on the treadmill when she asked why I was purple.

'Ah bubbly, we've earned it today,' she proclaims, unperturbed that the champagne cork came within an inch of blinding her.

'Thanks, Stace. And thanks for leaving work early.'

'Don't mention it. I didn't have time for the gym at lunch anyway, so it was fine going later.'

'You have been working a lot lately,' I point out. She's always worked harder and longer than I have, but now she works twelve-, fourteen- and fifteen-hour days. Sometimes I feel like the stay-at-home wife, waiting for the apologetic phone call.

'I know, but that's what's expected here. Nobody leaves before eight, and even that's considered slacking off. I guess it's the price to pay for being in such a booming place.'

'I just don't want you to miss out on living here. Couldn't you go in earlier or something and then leave at a reasonable time? You're a morning person anyway.'

'I thought of that, but we've got to put in our face time. It doesn't matter how early I'm in. If I left before everyone else they'd think I was a slacker. As it was, there were comments tonight when I left early. Oh, they were jokes: Working a half day today, are we? But beneath the joke is a message. I don't think there's any way around it.'

'Maybe you could get everyone to shift a bit. If you're all coming in early and leaving on time then it's not unusual.' I don't like that she keeps saying 'early', when seven p.m. isn't early. She's being brainwashed into thinking that it's normal to spend your whole life in the office. I'm afraid for her. And selfishly, I'm afraid for me.

'Hah, call me Norma Rae. The union organizer?' She tries in answer to my blank look. 'Sally Field played her in the film? Oh never mind, it's not funny if you've got to explain it. Anyway, let's toast your success. Congratulations, sweetie, I knew you'd be great at this job. Josh is really letting you put forward all your suggestions!? That's incredible you know. He must be so happy he hired you. You've found your true calling and that's wonderful.'

'I know. I send the proposals to the companies on Monday!' It is wonderful, so I don't mind her changing the subject. I'm finally in a job where I don't feel like I'm a step away from meeting with HR to discuss my future. Is this really what it feels like to be good at what you do? 'It seems like everything is falling so perfectly into place, Stace. And it's all the more sweet because it wasn't an easy start.'

'That's an understatement. You didn't really apply for all those jobs, did you? You must have been exaggerating to Stuart and Brent.'

If only. They weren't laughing at me, they assured me. They were laughing with me. If only I'd been laughing. 'Stace, you overestimate my ability to get a job, and I love you for it. Thirty-eight applications exactly, for every job even remotely related to fashion. I counted when I realized I wasn't hearing back from any of the companies. Only a handful even bothered to email me. But it was worth it to find the perfect job. I'll ask Josh to get me a work permit soon.'

'I can't believe you're working without one,' Stacy says. 'Do you realize how risky that is?'

I nod. 'I also know that Josh has to be totally happy with me to go through the time and expense of getting me the permit. I'll ask him soon, don't worry. The important thing is that I'm here, standing my own two feet, and the apartment worked out, and you're here…'

She nods sympathetically, knowing what I'm saying with my silence. 'He'll be back soon, Han. And you'll see him in less than forty-eight hours. That's good I suppose.'

'I know. It is good. It's just so hard. It'd be different if we were… if we knew when the assignment was ending.' I nearly slipped up and said 'living together'. I can't give her that kind of statement to latch on to. It'd only (wrongly) convince her that I'm not happy with Sam, with the situation. 'I guess we'll stay at his place this weekend, okay? Even though Pete's there, we can't exactly stay in my room.'

Sam and Pete live in Wan Chai. It's not a bad area, if you like cruising brothels. His apartment is wedged between two such establishments. Technically they're hostess bars. I can guess what kind of hospitality is on the menu.

The fact that my boyfriend lives in the red light district was at first a little perplexing, but he really seems to like the area, and I admit it's lively. So I'm trying not to be all Connecticut on the subject, though needless to say I glossed over these details when describing Sam's apartment to my mother.

'We could look at making bunk beds in your room.' Stacy smirks. 'After all, they stack washers and dryers in there.'

When I said that our apartment standards might be lower than usual, I meant my apartment standards. We (I) had to be realistic to find an apartment in our (her) price range. So we've (I've) compromised. The apartment is definitely nice. Its living room and dining room are faced by sliding glass doors leading to a miniscule balcony, looking up the hillside instead of down over Hong Kong. Ironically my room has the only view of the harbor, through a little window set high in the wall. I can see water when I stand on my bed.

And it's easy to stand on my bed, since it covers the entire floor. That's why I get all the closets. As long as I pretend I'm a sailor when I'm in my room, it's not too bad.

'What are you doing this weekend?' I ask. 'Are you seeing Brent and Stuart?' They're now attached at the diary.

'I'm meeting them on Friday night. I think we'll try one of the rooftop bars. It's a shame you can't come– I know, I know,' she says holding up her hand to my objection. 'Sam's coming, and I understand. Maybe we can all meet on Saturday night instead. I have to work but I'll be done by dinnertime.'

'I'd rather not plan anything if that's okay, since he's only here for the weekend.' I feel guilty saying this to my best friend, but surely she understands. It's not like she's dying to see him anyway. 'We're lucky we met Brent and Stuart, aren't we?' I say instead to change the topic. 'As long as you're sure Stuart doesn't like you.' This does tend to happen with Stacy. She's every man's dream, though she's not a tease. She'd never purposely hurt a guy, but some men can interpret a smile as an invitation to test your mattress.

'He definitely doesn't like me,' she confirms, smiling. 'He worships one of our colleagues though. He talks about her non-stop. He's working up the courage to ask her out.'

'Oh, good for him! He deserves someone nice. Do you like her?'

'I don't know her, really. She's on a different desk. But she seems kind of stuck up and cold.'

'She doesn't sound like much of a catch. And Stuart's so friendly. Why would he like her?'

'He's got yellow fever.'

'Oh no! Poor Stuart.' I got vaccinated before I moved – the nurse said people can die from it.

She laughs. 'Not that kind of yellow fever. It's when white men only want to date Asian women. You've noticed all the men here pawing at the Chinese girls, haven't you? Or the creepy fat bald men with the Filipinas?'

'Yeah, I guess so. I just didn't realize it was a medical condition… Do you think she'll go out with him?'

'It's hard to say. She's pretty much got her pick of the office. Even the married guys, and the ones with girlfriends, are all trying their luck. It's disgusting really, but it sounds like cheating is a national pastime when you're an expat. You wouldn't believe some of the stuff that goes on. I wouldn't move out here if I were attached–not that all men cheat. I didn't mean that at all. Stop making that face, Han, I didn't mean Sam.'

'Oh, I know you didn't. Sam's completely devoted.' He just happens to be living with his Chinese boss. Suddenly I feel less like celebrating.

8

'Hannah.' Winnie appears suddenly behind my office chair. Instinctively my finger finds the close button on-screen. Goodbye eBay. 'Josh wants to see you right now,' she says.

'Ah, it's only you. Mrs. Reese likes to sneak up on me like that. We need to fit her with a bell or something.' Last week she caught me on facebook and accused me of stealing the company's internet. And just yesterday she warned me that my one little call to Stacy from the office phone could cost me my job. I just know she keeps a log of my transgressions in her drawer, ready to cite as evidence at the first opportunity.

'Really, Hannah. He wants to see you.'

This sounds serious. 'Did he say why? Did he sound mad?' It's not like Josh to be demanding.

'I don't know, but I'd hurry if I were you.'

In London whenever my boss demanded my presence it was because she wanted to lecture or humiliate me, or send me for her lunch and dry cleaning. Josh gets his own lunch. That can only mean I've screwed up somehow.

'Sam!' I say when I see my boyfriend standing beside Josh's desk. 'What are you doing here?!'

'Surprising you. Surprise.' He sweeps me up in his arms, sticking a big bouquet of flowers into my side.

'Ouch.' I'm glad they're not roses.

'Sorry, here – these are for you. I know it's probably not very practical, but I saw them on the way here and thought you'd like them.'

'Thank you, but what are you doing *here*? I expected you tonight. How did you know where I work?' Josh and Winnie are standing like proud parents at Sam's side. Josh's grin says he probably gets misty watching romcoms. Winnie may start humming 'Unchained Melody'.

'Han, we talk every day remember? You told me where you work. It wasn't rocket science to look it up and call Josh. I wanted to be here when you finished so we'd have the whole night together. I got an earlier flight.'

This is wonderful. However, I'm far from boyfriend-ready. I didn't sleep well last night, thinking about the weekend, and was late getting up. My hair is unwashed and I've got no make-up on. Sam's not supposed to see me like this. I meant to rush home, shower (I haven't shaved!) and wait, primped and gorgeous, with a glass of wine in my hand for him to from his flight. Three hours from now. Obviously I can't tell him that. I need to avoid direct light until I can get to a pharmacy for emergency supplies. Hopefully he's so blinded by love that he doesn't notice I look like a refugee. 'Josh, Winnie, were you in on this?'

'Of course,' says Winnie. 'You never stop talking

about Sam. We had to meet him.'

So much for being cool. 'Thanks. I'll go now if that's okay.' They only just refrain from making kissy-face noises to our retreating backs.

'Sam, this is great! Where are we going?'

'Let's start with drinks, then I thought dinner and we'll see what we want to do from there. How's that sound?'

'Super! I just have to stop at a pharmacy on the way, okay?' I need some eyeliner, and mascara, some blush, a lipstick... dry shampoo, a bit of mousse. And a razor.

Wait a minute, why am I worrying about these little details? My boyfriend is standing in front of me! 'I'm so glad you're here!'

'Me too, Han, I've missed you these past few weeks. We've got a lot of catching up to do!' His lascivious grin says he's not talking about films.

'I missed you too.' I smile and kiss him again. 'But you're here now and we're going to have an amazing weekend. We don't even need to get out of bed if we don't want to.' I'll definitely need that razor. I'm at risk of making cricket noises if my legs rub together.

'Well, not until tomorrow night anyway. I've arranged a little dinner with my colleagues so you'll get to meet everyone. I didn't want to presume what you'd want to do, but I thought that'd be fun. They're getting a table at a really nice restaurant that's famous for its duck. It'll be great.'

I don't mean to sound ungrateful but he spends every damn day with his colleagues. Okay, I do mean to sound ungrateful. 'Couldn't we just spend the weekend together? I told Stacy that I'll be staying with you. I didn't plan to see her. I see her every day,' I add pointedly.

'We will be together the whole time, Han. I just thought you'd like to meet them. You've been very curious about them.' I wish he'd stop bringing that up. Geez, cross the boundary once and you're labelled for life. It's not like I asked him for Li Ming's urine sample. It was just a photo.

'You're right, it'll be fun. I'm sorry. I'm just being selfish because I've missed you so much.'

'Aw, come here.' He kisses me sweetly. 'We've got tonight, and tomorrow, and all of Sunday alone together. Pete won't be around that much, which is a shame because I really want you to get to know him. But he'll be at dinner. You're going to love him.'

'Based on the way you talk about him, I'm sure I will.'

'Yeah, I know.' He cringes. 'I do sound like I worship the guy. In actual fact, he drives me nuts sometimes. I'm kind of pissed at him now, actually, but it'll blow over.' When he sees my expectant face he continues. 'It's not even worth talking about. He– he's in a disapproving phase, that's all. He'll get over it.'

'Is it because you're seeing me?' Guys can be weird about their friend's girlfriends.

'No, not exactly. Never mind, it's no big deal. The point is that we've been best friends our whole lives, like you and Stacy. Even when he's being a dick. Which isn't often! I'm making him sound awful now when he's really pretty great. He's like a younger version of my friend Charles. Did I ever tell you about Charles?'

'Mm, no, I don't think so,' I say, still fretting about Pete's disapproval as we wander hand in hand along the crowded street. Commuters stream past, making their way to the MTR for their journey home. That, at least, hasn't been a culture shock. The public transport is as crowded here as it is in London, with the same jerk forcing his way on the packed train instead of waiting three minutes for the next one. There's only one real difference, which literally hit me on the head the first time I wedged my way into the center of the carriage. The handles dangling from the ceiling assume a certain lack of stature. I guess that makes sense. It wouldn't do to ask commuters to boost each other up to suspend from the ceiling like trapeze artists.

'I interned for him in high school,' Sam reminisces as we walk. 'He had a company, a consultancy. They're economists, advising local governments and clients like that.'

'Did you always know you wanted to be an economist?'

'God, no! I wanted to be a rock star.' He looks embarrassed at this confession.

'You play an instrument?' My boyfriend, a musician! I couldn't carry a tune in a basket, with both hands.

'No, and I can't sing either. It wasn't a very realistic dream.'

'That's why they're called dreams.'

'They were pure fantasy, in my case. No, my father got me the internship the summer of my senior year. One of his friends put me in touch with Charles. He was great. I had no real idea what an economist did when I met him. I figured he'd be a geek with a clipboard and tape on his glasses, writing papers nobody ever read. But he was so cool. He could explain why anything in the world was happening, in an accessible way, and make it sound interesting. I loved that guy. He was like a better version of my father.'

'I thought you got along with your father?'

'Yeah, we get along okay. He's just not very engaged with my brother and me. He's a brilliant man, but he's an academic. He doesn't connect very well with people.'

'You're not people though, you're his family.'

'Ironic, isn't it? But Charles and I weren't like that. He was a sort of a mentor for me, not just in school and career stuff, but in life…'

'What happened?' Because something must have happened or we'd be discussing Charles in the present tense.

'He had a hacking cough even when we first met. Heavy smoker. By the time he was diagnosed, he had just a couple months left. He died almost three years ago.'

'I'm sorry, that must have been really hard.' I hate being confronted with news like this. My responses always sound so trivial. And occasionally stupidly flippant. I still kick myself for responding to a colleague who said she'd just lost her granddad with the question, 'Did he fall through a hole in your pocket?' Nervous idiocy.

'Yeah… but,' he says, smiling again. 'If reincarnation is real then he's out there somewhere, right? So he's not gone. Maybe we'll meet again.'

How I'd love to have his belief that every cloud has a silver lining. By my calculation, his mentor would just now be out of diapers if he were reincarnated. But Sam loves the idea so much that he doesn't care that little Charlie would be drooling strained carrots.

The streets we wander are jammed with people,

noisy with traffic and a feast for the eyes. The whole city is saturated with color. Unlike London's majestic, restrained buildings, or Connecticut's shopping strips and malls, detail crowds every square inch of Hong Kong. Neon glows everywhere, giving the city a carnival atmosphere. Every shop is stacked to the ceiling with merchandise, on floors, walls, countertops. Posters and hand-lettered adverts paper many of the display windows. Magically, like sweet shops, they draw my foreign eyes.

In fact, it is a sweet shop! 'Will you look at that?' I say, dragging Sam inside the busy shop. Most of the labels are unintelligible but one section is in English. It's stocked with dried prune products – chamomile prunes, basil prunes, green tea prunes, yogurt prunes, rose prunes. Europeans must get awfully constipated here. Just next to nature's laxatives is the Asian hillbilly section, full of codfish jerky. Mostly, though, the shop is filled with baskets of beautifully, individually wrapped morsels. The customers are milling around filling plastic bags. They don't look like pick "n" mix candies though. I think they're actually dried fruit jellies. We watch, uncertainly, until a lady snatches a sample from a dish in the middle of one of the colorful sections. 'Here.' I hand Sam one and free mine from its shimmery colored wrapper. 'Ready? Down the hatch on three. One, two, three.'

Bleurgh. It tastes of soap.

'That's horrible!' Sam laughs, putting his hand over his mouth.

'Squeaky clean breath though.' I kiss him, savoring the moment. This is exactly how I imagined my life in Hong Kong. With Sam. We'd meet after work, hold hands and chat about our days, our pasts, our future. We'd discover new places together, occasionally share too many bottles of wine in a random bar, not caring where it was or who was there, not even noticing, because we'd be so wrapped up in each other. We'd start shopping for things 'we' needed, each settling into the other's apartment, establishing little routines together. Sometimes we'd get together with friends and sometimes we'd spend entire weekends doing nothing but watching DVDs in each other's arms. We'd try different spots for dinner, and share food that we'd never eaten before, and find our favorite haunts. We'd be a normal couple. I want that so much.

'So, here it is,' Sam says when we've walked all the way to Tsim Sha Tsui at the tip of Kowloon. 'It's kind of a weird entrance for a restaurant but trust me, it's cool.'

We're standing on a narrow, very upscale shopping street. 'Chanel does dinner?'

He laughs. 'I told you it was a weird entrance. Here.' He guides me through a sleek office lobby to an elevator guarded by a bouncer, and we ascend at the speed of light. 'Ow, my ears are popping.'

'Mine too.' He winces. 'We're going to the top. I'm tempted to cover your eyes when we go in, but I don't want you to trip. Ready?' He holds the elevator door open for me. 'I wanted tonight to be extra special.'

There's no need to cover my eyes. We feel our way in the murky light through the elevator lobby to the restaurant.

The whole front of the restaurant is glass. A shimmering panorama stretches to the edges of my field of vision. Across the harbor, lights from every skyscraper reflect off the water, but nature's light show is giving this perfect example of modern beauty a run for its money. Twilight intensifies from pale pink on the horizon to deep blue in the sky. Despite the light pollution (as if you could call such a beautiful sight pollution!), I bet there'll be stars tonight. 'Wow, it's so beautiful. Thank you, Sam.' I kiss him while the host waits patiently to show us to our table.

The table would be perfect if only Sam wasn't sitting on the other side of it. He has gallantly given me the seat facing the windows. 'Sit here next to me,' I propose.

'I don't think there's room.' He frowns, eyeing the small bench.

'Come on. Look at this view. Here, I'll squish over. There's room. It's silly to sit there when you can sit next to me.' As he snuggles in beside me with his arm over my shoulder, I know this is the best date I've ever had.

'This is perfect,' he says. 'It's my idea of the perfect life. I never thought I'd be so happy, so content. Not that I'm not usually content. I am. As you know. I loved grad school, and London. But this is better than I dreamed. Don't you think so?'

'Absolutely.' I couldn't be happier than I am at this moment. To hear my boyfriend say that confirms everything I'm thinking.

'I can imagine living here for the rest of my life,' he continues as the champagne arrives. 'I'm comfortable here, and it's the ideal place for my kind of work. The job is going really well, Han, and I love it, despite the long hours. I was really lucky to get it, don't you think?'

Work? Isn't he talking about us, and our wonderful

life? The paranoid terriers are snapping at my heels again. Why do I feel harrumphy because he's talking about loving his job? Considering how few people do, I should be happy for him. And I am. I'd be even happier if he included our relationship in his idea of perfection. After all, I do.

'Yes, although it is taking you away from Hong Kong.' Just a small fact I'd like to point out.

'That's the only downside,' he says. 'Think how perfect it'd be if you were in Ho Chi Minh!' He laughs at the look on my face. 'Han, I'm only joking. I'll be back here soon.'

'How do you know about this place?' I ask between bubbly sips. Most of the tables are full, with a mix of Chinese and Westerners. There are little round tables along the windows for couples to enjoy ringside seats to Hong Kong's show, and some bigger tables in the middle of the floor for groups of friends. Our table perches on a raised platform at the back, giving us an uninterrupted view over the heads of the other diners. A few of the men are in suits but it's clearly more a social restaurant than a business one. Although looking at the prices, an expense account would come in handy.

'It's one of Pete's favorites. When I told him I wanted to take you somewhere special tonight, he suggested it. It looked amazing from the photos online. It's even better in person. He takes dates here when he wants to cement the deal. It's sort of pricey.' His look tells me he regrets divulging Pete's seduction tactics.

'Don't worry. Pete's secret is safe with me. And, by the way, you didn't need to take me here to get lucky. You're going to get lucky tonight.'

'I'm already lucky.'

He's staring into my eyes. I feel lost in them. I'm so much at ease with this man. He makes me feel excited for our future. There are possibilities there.

I'm sure we could kiss our way through the night, subsisting on champagne alone, but the menu is too tempting. Everything looks delicious. I just wonder if the chef can make a few tiny adjustments.

'May I have the bresaola, please?' I smile at the waiter, who has finally overcome his reluctance to interrupt our kissathon. He looks pleased with his own trendiness. 'But instead of the salad, can I have figs? And instead of goat's cheese can the chef use mozzarella?'

'You want…?' His composure slips as he struggles to understand why a patron would come to a restaurant only to treat the menu like the pick 'n' mix at the cinema.

'Well, you have mozzarella, here in this dish,' I point out. 'And figs here in this one. I'd like a combination of the bresaola, figs and mozzarella. Can your chef do that for me?'

I guess they may as well know what they're dealing with from the outset. I guess the same is true for Sam. Smirking, he says, 'And can we please have some olive oil and balsamic, for the bread?'

'Yes, sir. And for your main course?'

'Let's decide that later,' I say. What I mean is that I'll give them a break before altering more dishes. The waiter already wishes he hadn't seated us.

Even though I'm savoring each moment, disclosure, joke shared, every look, and the seemingly infinite details of his face and body, time is flying by. I desperately want to slow it, but I'm too caught up in its momentum. We've been making out like teenagers for most of the meal and I'd love to muster the social conscience to be embarrassed. It's the very least my mother would ask. But I don't care. I love this too much.

'This is the best table in the house,' he says as our main courses are cleared. 'Look. Everyone in here is looking at us, wishing they'd done the same thing.' Sitting together he means, within kissing distance.

Why have I never sat next to my dates before? Probably because I've never felt like this before. I want to be in contact with this man all the time. It physically hurts when I have to leave him. My stomach clenches and I feel like sobbing. It's silly really, as this happens even when we part for just a few hours. Sometimes I wonder if it's healthy to be so in love. The emotion should carry a warning label. Caution: may cause panic attacks, sensitivity to harmless comments, and sinky-stomach upset. Can encourage long bouts of analytical discussion in some sufferers. Do not attempt to operate heavy machinery, and always follow your friend's advice.

By the time the waiter clears our main course plates I'm ready to alter his menu again. Something tells me he won't like it any more than he liked my starter and main course suggestions. 'I wonder if they have any dark chocolate, to go with the wine, for dessert?'

Sam looks bemused, dreading my next chat with our server. 'I can ask,' he continues gamely.

It's not fair to make my perfectly nice boyfriend make the waiter's life any more difficult than it already is. He has, after all, proven himself capable of ordering one of the chef's suggestions straight off the menu.

'Excuse me,' I say. 'Is it possible to just bring us some chocolate for dessert?'

The waiter definitely wishes he'd called in sick tonight. 'Chocolate? Here.' He's pointing to the chocolate mousse.

'No, that's chocolate already in the dessert. Is it possible for the chef to just give us some chocolate, pieces of chocolate that he uses for desserts? Just the chocolate.'

'I'll check.' He slinks off to hand in his resignation.

Another man appears a few minutes later. He could be the bouncer from downstairs, who's trained to deal with difficult customers. He claims it's not possible to give us chocolate because all the desserts are prepared ahead of time, so the chocolate is already in situ. Fair enough. 'Then can I please have a scoop of vanilla ice cream with a shot of espresso to pour over it?'

He nods, baffled as to why I'd ask the bouncer for dessert.

'Where's that?' Sam asks, perusing the menu.

'It's not on there. But they have ice cream, here with the apple tart, and espresso as a coffee option.'

I don't blame him if he never takes me out to dinner again. That's okay. I'm happy to stay in his apartment all the time. We can always ask the hookers next door to bring us some food.

The next morning I feel remarkably awake considering that we were the last diners in the restaurant last night, or rather, this morning. It might be the excitement of today's adventure. Or maybe it's because I've drunk enough coffee to give me palpitations.

There's a tree in Hong Kong that grants wishes.

Sam's as excited as me as we exit the MTR station, looking for a sign. It's not exactly the ancient setting you'd expect to find a mythical tree. I envisioned mist wafting through temple complexes, with perhaps a few Shaolin warrior monks. But the station is modern, squat, concrete and functional. The streets surrounding it buzz with cars and buses. Perhaps we're in the wrong place. There's no sign for the tree anywhere. Surely magic trees can't be so common here that they don't merit any acknowledgement.

'Can I see the map?' I ask Sam, as he digs his ringing phone out of his pocket. I only do this to show that I'm willing to help out. I'm not about to challenge a man's fundamental belief in his ability to navigate. Besides, my map-reading skills are on par with my driving skills. That is to say, best left to someone else.

'Sure, though we were off the map about a dozen stations ago.' He shrugs as if this is all part of a normal day. Everyone travels to the Chinese border looking for a mythical tree. ''Scuse me just a sec, it's Li Ming.'

What does she want now? They saw each other just yesterday at work. It's a little inappropriate for a boss to call her employee on his day off. I'm sure HR would be interested to know that she's cutting into his personal time like this.

He's telling her the name of the restaurant for tonight. He doesn't sign off with kissy noises or murmur endearments into his handset, but I still don't like it.

'Sorry about that. She's really looking forward to meeting you tonight.'

My stupid imagination is making me insane. 'Great, I can't wait! I'm sure I'll love her.' I force a smile.

'Should we ask inside about the tree?' The moment passes when he reaches for my hand.

The ticket agent says we're in the right place. Helpfully he writes down a bunch of characters. 'Number sixty-four bus. This stop.' He points to the slip of paper, smiling his bon voyage wishes.

As we wander to the bus stop opposite the station, I hand Sam the paper. 'You'd better hold this.' He's a man after all. He'll enjoy being keeper of the directions.

The bus carries us through densely packed streets lined with shops, the ubiquitous neon signs, and people. Down narrow side roads I spy little clothing and food markets. It takes almost half an hour of crawling in traffic but eventually we reach the outskirts and the shops recede, leaving long stretches of barren road. It's starting to look more like a place that wishing trees would live. 'Is that it?' I say, pointing to the bus's electronic sign, which has been flashing each stop as we approach. 'Hat, squiggle, four, squiggle, squiggle?'

'No, it's a house looking thing, seven, tepee, o with a line through it, chair.'

At the next stop I say, 'Is that it? Upside down V, squiggle, chair?'

'No,' he says patiently. 'It's…'

This goes on for most of the next twenty minutes until, disappointingly 'Lam Tsuen Wishing Tree' appears on the screen. Still, we could have read it in Chinese if we'd needed to.

The bus deposits us alone at the side of the dusty road. There's no indication of a magic wish-granting tree, just a hand-painted sign down an embankment. A red arrow points into the scrubland. 'Do you think it's down there?' I didn't imagine trekking through the underbrush.

'I don't think so.' He shakes his head. 'It doesn't look like anybody goes down there. Besides, there are probably snakes in there.'

'You're not afraid of snakes, are you?' This is the man who took me trekking through the jungles of Laos.

'Yes, I'm afraid of snakes,' he says, as if I've just asked him the most obvious question.

'Really? I used to catch them to keep as pets. Not poisonous ones obviously,' I hasten to add. 'Just grass snakes. And garter snakes, though those were stinky. They peed on you when you caught them.'

He's looking at me like something he's just dug out of the drain, but chooses to overlook my creepy confession. 'I think the tree would be signposted,' he offers. 'After all, it has its own bus stop.'

'Okay. Maybe we could ask that man?' A lone workman has been standing beside his truck, following our lack of progress. 'Where's that little piece of paper the agent gave us?'

Sam pats his pockets, looks sheepish, pats again, sinks deeper into sheepishness, pulls out his wallet, rifles, and flourishes the now well-folded if slightly tattered slip of paper. 'Excuse me,' he says loudly, to aid comprehension. 'Do you know?'

The man points across the street, away from the embankment.

'This way.' Sam takes my hand and hardly makes an 'I told you so' face at all.

Back across the road is an open gate, and to the right is a large tree. 'Are you sure this is it?' I ask.

'It's where the guy pointed.'

'It looks kind of…'

'Sick.'

The tree's sparse branches are supported by tall wooden braces, those few branches rather barren of leaves. 'How do you throw oranges into that?' I wonder aloud. Sam's guidebook definitely said that chucking our wishes, tethered to oranges, into the branches would make them come true. This is very disappointing, like finding out that Santa Claus doesn't come down the chimney at all, but simply walks through the front door. A big part of the magic is in the delivery.

A middle-aged woman wearing a conical straw hat sidles up beside us. Finally, some authenticity. 'You get wishes. Two,' she says, handing us each a sheet of yellow paper and pencil and leading us through a gap in the fence. My wishes pop straight into my head. I want to be happy. And I want to stay with Sam forever. Sappy, I know. I don't care. I scribble them down and follow Sam's lead, hanging the rolled-up sheet on one of the hooks drilled into a tattered board beside the tree. I'm smirking. He's smirking too. We're in this together, and I love it. The setting doesn't matter. We could be gazing at each other on my sofa and I'd be just as happy.

Maybe my caffeine buzz is wearing off, but now that we've found the tree, I feel a little deflated. That wasn't the magical adventure in my imagination. But I suppose the important thing is to be with Sam, right? Still, I feel like we we've been short-changed.

As if reading my mind, he says, 'I thought there'd be more. Maybe we should go to the fortune teller's temple on the way back for some actual mysticism?'

'Let's do it!' I've never had my fortune read. All I have is my fortune cookie fortune, tucked up in my wallet. It's been right so far, hasn't it? *Following your heart will pay off in the near future.* It certainly has. No one can accuse me of following my head. My heart has led me to Hong Kong with Sam, to this weekend, this day, this moment. So do I believe in fortunes? I think so. Unless the fortune teller says something bad. Then it's a load of rubbish.

Sam seems to know his way to the temple, which is a good thing because it's not easy to find. 'Have you been here before?' I ask.

'Uh, no. Well, once, but it was closing so we didn't go in.'

I have to keep reminding myself that Sam lived here without me. He started a whole life here with Pete, and his new job, and his colleagues, when I was still in London. He talked a lot about Pete (was he in a 'disapproving phase' then?), but he must have gone out with other people too. This is an uncomfortable thought. I can't help it, I have to ask. 'Who'd you go out with when you first moved here?'

'Mostly Pete. You know that. We talked every day, remember? Han, why do you ask?'

'I was just thinking that you've probably been to lots of these places that I haven't. Because you're away now, I guess I forgot that.' I mean, of course, that he's had an entire social life that I wasn't part of.

'I didn't go out that much. You know that though. I told you what I was doing every day. I spent most of those first months just settling in, sometimes going out with Pete for drinks or dinner.' He's peering at me. 'Does it matter?'

'No. I didn't expect you to sit in your apartment waiting for me to arrive. It just hit me that I wasn't part of that time. I *was* part of your life in London. I guess I felt a little excluded all of a sudden, which is ridiculous because I wasn't even here. Don't listen to me, I'm babbling.'

'I do listen to you, Han. If something's bothering you then we should talk about it. Hmm?' His thumb gently strokes my hand.

'No, it's nothing.'

I'm sabotaging this perfect day with inane conjecture. What do I expect him to do, invite me into his time machine so we can spend those first two months in each other's pockets? These imagined wounds are self-inflicted. Snap out of it, Hannah.

'I'm glad you're here now,' I finally say. We're walking alongside a tall stone wall leading to an imposing red and gold gate. As far as temples go, it's impressive. I had a look at the Man Mo Temple back in Central when I first arrived, but it's rather puny in comparison. Plus the lit incense hanging from the ceiling is a downright hazard. Health and safety would disapprove of dropping incendiaries on tourists.

A lone fortune teller is sitting beside the gate. 'Should we go to him?' I ask, a little nervous that he'll shut up shop for an early dinner and take my fortune with him.

'Nah.' He shrugs. 'There must be others. What if there are better ones?'

This strikes me as a typically male approach to choice. As women we're prepared to make a decision without exploring every last option. Which is why we're able to choose a mate without wondering if there might not be a better one out there. 'Okay,' I say, by which I mean, 'If we miss the fortune telling I will hold a grudge for the rest of my life.' Just so we're clear.

The stone wall hides a golden-roofed temple, ornately carved and painted red, green and gold, merry with hanging paper lanterns. It's thick with swirling incense smoke and mingling worshippers, walking, standing, kneeling, bowing or prostrate in the stone courtyard. It's much noisier than one would expect for a place of worship. I'm used to churches, where a whisper can send you straight to hell. We wander through the complex, careful not to step on the faithful.

Off to one side, nestled amidst the skyscrapers and grumbling traffic, is a garden. A very peaceful garden with koi ponds and bridges. 'Let's look,' Sam says. He really does seize the moment. I know it's a small thing, but so important to me. He's my ideal partner in crime. On a little arched bridge we stand shoulder to shoulder, watching the fish execute their hypnotic water dance. 'It's so peaceful.'

I mean this whole thing. The feeling is almost overwhelming, waves of the gentlest calming I've ever known, of complete peace, like being stroked until you're just about to fall asleep, floating in that limbo between slumber and consciousness.

'Bdllling!'

'Is that your phone?' He asks.

'Yes.'

'Do you want to get it?'

'It's just a text.' I sigh. 'From my mother.'

Hannah, are you with Sam? plese invite him home for 4th July.. Your father wants to bbq

As if Dad needs an excuse to char meat in the back yard. She's getting desperate now.

Thx Mom, that's v patriotic but I don't think we can make it. Maybe for Secretary's Day.

'My mom says to say hello,' I fib, pressing the send button. 'So what do you think, shall we find our fortunes?'

It takes less than five minutes to circumnavigate the grounds and see that there aren't any fortune tellers here. Maybe they've gone on strike. That man by the gate may have been the only scab to cross the picket line. I don't want to encourage strike-breaking, but I want my fortune told. Just as I'm about to suggest finding him, Sam spots a narrow lane alongside the temple building. That has to be it. Fortune tellers' alley. Little pink papers, fluttering in the breeze, are stapled to boards lining the walls. They're covered in red Chinese characters. This is definitely the right place. 'We'd like our fortunes read, please,' I tell the lithe young woman tending the boards.

'Number?' She asks.

'Sam, what number do you want?' I've always been partial to eleven. It was my soccer number, though I only played for a week before realizing that a) I have virtually no foot-to-eye coordination and b) sweating in a field wasn't as much fun as, say, anything else I could think of. They let me keep the shirt though.

The woman looks confused when I tell her this. 'Get number, in temple,' she says, clearly thrilled at having tourists riding roughshod over her ancient customs.

But there wasn't any place in the temple to get a number. The vendors are all out here. The temple was filled with people waving incense, and praying, and… Wait a minute… 'I know, Sam.'

There's a small open area neatly laid with straw mats where people are making an awful racket, shaking cans full of tongue depressors. I'm not sure how, but that must be where we get our numbers. We follow the small crowd up the broad stone steps, shedding our shoes as the others do. Ladies behind the can-laden tables offer them in exchange for a few Hong Kong dollars. Tentatively we join the devotees. What are we getting ourselves into? I feel like a fraud, kneeling at this shrine, shaking my sticks and trying to keep nervous giggles from erupting into full-scale mania.

Sam's wrestling with his own it's-inappropriate-therefore-I-must-do-it giggle fit. At least if we're destined for Taoist hell we'll be together. A young man notices our inexperience (read: agnostic disrespect for their age-old religion) and suggests, 'Think about your questions, and shake until one falls out.'

Oh, I see. I did wonder what kind of sign we were waiting for. The sticks are numbered. It takes a bit of technique but eventually they start creeping forward. Within minutes we've got our numbers. Suddenly I'm nervous. What if the fortune teller says something terrible? Will I really not believe him?

As we return to the alley, a young man is watching our progress. The minute we pay the woman, who hands us our fortunes, he appears at our side. 'I'll take you to my master now,' he says, greedily eyeing the pink papers.

I imagine a wizened old man with a long beard and Chairman Mao pajamas. I had a Chinese friend in school called Amy whose mother consulted her fortune teller before making any decision. Amy was embarrassed by her family's traditions, but maybe there's peace of mind in trusting your decisions to someone else. I'll judge after I hear what he says.

The young man leads us into a low corridor lined with stalls, brightly lit with ugly yellow fluorescent overhead strips. Wooden stools line our path, waiting to receive the faithful's bottoms. In one of the stalls sits a forty-something-year-old man behind a metal desk. His face is bathed in the glow of his computer screen. He looks like an IT programmer.

'You sit,' the man says, holding out his hand as his minion melts away. Eventually, from his pointed look rather than any polite request, I gather he wants my paper. 'What's your question?' he demands, scrutinizing the pink slip.

Well, I want to snap, you're the soothsayer. You tell me what my question is. Of course I don't. I sit silently, having not prepared for this exam, until he prompts, 'Work, family, relationship?'

'Relationship.'

He stares at the paper, making some notes on it, then says, 'Relationship okay. Marriage no. Marriage not happy. You make unhappy. Yes.' He sits back, like Yoda in a polyester suit, pleased with his proclamation.

Thank you. So, just to be clear, I'm not the marrying kind and will someday make a man very unhappy indeed. Forgive me if I'm not prepared to believe a man who may have been surfing porn when we interrupted.

It's Sam's turn. 'Relationship,' he says in a show of solidarity.

The fortune teller sighs, considering the paper. 'You

don't pay attention,' he says. 'You need to pay more attention in relationship. And you work too much. Too much time working. This is bad. Yes.'

'Great, thanks very much,' Sam says. 'Er, is that all?'

Having dispensed his cosmic insight, the master gruffly waves us away.

That was about as satisfying as a fat-free muffin. I suppose it is the end of the day. We probably got the last stale fortunes. That makes us 0 for 2 on the soothsaying front. At least the company is excellent. Otherwise this whole day would have been a washout. 'What do you want to do now?' I ask as we emerge from the building.

'Well, we've got a few hours before we have to meet everyone for dinner. I know what I'd like to do.' He grins. 'Shall we go back to my apartment? We could have a nap or, whatever we want…'

He's reading my mind. His bed is calling, and not for its restive powers. I'd love to skip the team bonding dinner and stay under the duvet till Sunday with my boyfriend, but he's really excited for me to meet everyone. I'm sure it'll be fun. Maybe not as much fun as the next few hours, but fun all the same.

9

I couldn't be having less fun in a dentist's chair getting a root canal. At least then I'd be numb with Novocain. Yet here I am, unmedicated, except for the better part of a bottle of wine, sitting beside Sam at a table of strangers, fielding condescending questions from his supposedly fabulous friend Pete. I'm sure Sam would jump to my defense but he hasn't got eyes in the back of his head. Which he would need to see me, since I've been staring at his shoulder blades for nearly an hour. His front is solidly engaged with Li Ming, whose conversation must be the most scintillating in the room.

It's not unlike a frequent nightmare I have, where I'm desperately trying to get someone's attention. It's always for a really good reason too, like their hair is on fire or they're about to walk off a cliff. No matter what I do I remain invisible, and the horror unfolds despite my best efforts.

I've gone twice to the loo for pep talks with myself. I haven't been as persuasive as I'd hoped. I should just leave. Drop by the table, breezily tell Sam I'm going, and walk out. Every minute I stay just deepens the snub.

I've pored over every minute of this farce, trying to see if I'm somehow overreacting. Unfortunately, Stacy has already left, and isn't answering her phone, which makes my analysis a bit lopsided. Wait till she hears what she's missed.

Sam and I arrived at the big, busy restaurant just as Stacy did. He suggested I include her tonight, which struck me as typically thoughtful if a little naïve. She's been dying to get another crack at him since I foiled her attack at the monastery. Now I wonder if he didn't risk her presence just so I'd have a friend close by when he ignored me. She was only able to stay for drinks and starters before going to meet Stuart. Now I wish I'd left with her, but things hadn't yet skidded downhill. In fact, we had a promising start, and much as I hate to admit this, Li Ming is friendly, and seems nice and fun. She's also plain, not the Lucy Liu of my nightmares. Her face is rather round and she doesn't wear much make-up. Still, she's a pixie. Not a beauty, no, but fragile and innocent. There's no reason to think she's a threat now that I've seen her. And yet her lack of obvious beauty makes her all the more worrying somehow. For she certainly has Sam's attention.

As for Pete, I don't understand what Sam sees in him. Though I do see what women see in him, at least at first glance. He's gorgeous – tall, broad and smoldering. It's a shame that his personality is so unattractive.

In all the months that I've heard about him, it never occurred to me that he'd act like this. Clearly he suffers from schizophrenia, since he was charm personified to Stacy before being a dick to me. His looks must let him get away with a lot. Highlights of his delightfulness so far include his implication that I've latched on to Sam like some bloated tick ('Your devotion is commendable but then, who wouldn't do everything they could to keep hold of Sam?') and a lecture on the exploitation of fashion ('It's unconscionable to warp consumers' minds with the bullshit that they should pay more for a pair of shoes than the child who made them gets in a year').

Sam's other colleagues aren't awful. They're just economists who like to backpack, wear hemp shoes and lament the 'bigger issues' in life. My concern about cashmere versus merino for winter doesn't qualify as one of these.

'Hannah, are you planning any travel?' Li Ming asks me over Sam's shoulder.

'… Yes, in fact, I'm… going to Phuket in a couple of weeks.'

'You are?' Sam asks.

'Yep. Stacy and I are going for my birthday weekend. Didn't I tell you that?' Of course I didn't tell him. I've just made it up. The surprise on his face says it's not a bad thing to push him off balance a bit.

'Maybe you did,' he says. 'That'll be fun.'

'It'll be great. Stuart and Brent might go too.' Why am I doing this? 'Actually, it was their idea. They want to take us away. To introduce us to Asia. And celebrate my birthday.' There. Now Sam is paying attention. 'I may have to take a few days off, but it'll be worth it. It's not every day a girl gets whisked off for such a fabulous holiday, is it?' I smile sweetly at Sam, who now looks much more sober than he did a minute ago.

'No, I suppose not,' he says, sounding a bit

deflated.

'Well, that sounds very nice, Hannah.' Li Ming grins. 'I'm sure you'll have a wonderful time. We've only managed to get to the beach once so far. Your trip will be much nicer.'

My stomach heaves at this news. 'The beach? Which beach did you go to?' My voice doesn't crack at the question, unlike my confidence. Please let him say he didn't go. Or that he went but Li Ming didn't. Or that the beach is actually a library in central Ho Chi Minh City.

'Uh, what was it called again?' my boyfriend asks his boss for confirmation of their love nest rendezvous destination.

'Ha, your memory really is terrible Sam. You booked it for us! Mui Ne Bay. You should take Hannah there. She'd love it. Hannah, maybe you'll visit us soon?'

Us? Yes, that's a great idea. Take me to your secret little lover's beach. I feel sick, and it's not just because I ate too many thousand-year eggs at dinner.

'Yeah, Hannah, that's a point. Why haven't you visited Sam yet?' Pete lobs his grenade into this already uncomfortable foxhole.

'Well, *Pete*, I haven't been invited.' Surely if he's Sam's best friend, he'd know that.

'What?' Sam interjects. 'Yes you have, Han!'

'You haven't invited me.'

'I have. I always tell you that you're welcome to come.'

'That's not the same thing as being invited.'

'Isn't it?'

'No, it isn't! An invitation involves extending a

specific request for your presence, not just a vague, "It'll be cool if you wanted to"'

'I'm sorry, Han. Would you like to come to Ho Chi Minh in two weeks for the weekend?' He's grinning in that way that usually melts me.

'Yes, that'd be nice, thank you,' I say petulantly.

'Wait, you can't, can you?' objects Pete. 'You're going to Thailand in two weeks. I'm sure you could visit Sam any other weekend though. Any weekend that Sam's free.'

Sam shoots his friend a menacing look. Finally, he's noticed the animosity. 'Oh right. I guess not then. Sorry Sam, maybe another weekend. I'm pretty tired. If you don't mind, I'm going to go.' I get up on shaky legs. It may be a late exit, but better late than never. 'Goodnight everybody, and thanks.'

Sam follows me out. 'Hannah, what's wrong? Are you okay?'

Does he really have to ask? God, men can be thick sometimes. 'I'm fine. I just thought I'd leave you to your friends. Since you obviously want to spend time with them.'

'Well, yes I do. But I want to spend time with you too. That's why I thought we'd all have dinner. Han, have I done something wrong? I feel like you're mad at me, but I don't know why. You're saying you're fine but clearly you're not.'

'Well, how would you feel if my friends were rude to you? Pete was awful and you didn't even notice.'

'I'm sorry about Pete. He's not usually like that. He shouldn't have been rude. His issue is with me, not you. He should apologize.'

'That's not the point. The point is that you ignored

me all night, and left me alone with a bunch of strangers.'

'I didn't leave you alone! I've been right beside you the whole night. Honestly, Han, I think you're overreacting.'

There's no surer way to make me see red than to tell me I'm overreacting. Of course I'm overreacting! Unlike most men, who are emotionally constipated, I have feelings. I'm not going to swallow my hurt. I'm going to make sure there's collateral damage.

'Overreacting? Let's see. You're home for forty-eight hours and decide to spend an entire evening with the same people you see every day. You invite me along, then spend the whole time ignoring me to talk to your boss. And you accuse me of overreacting because I'm upset about that.' I'm shaking. I think it's anger, but there may be some fear that this conversation isn't going to end well. That's possibly because instead of looking abjectly contrite, Sam's face is set in a rather less accommodating manner.

'Hannah. I arranged this dinner for you so that you could meet the people you're so curious about. You said last night that it'd be fun, and when I suggested you invite Stacy you sounded like you were really looking forward to it. If you didn't want to go then you should have just said so, instead of pretending you did. It's not fair to be mad when you didn't tell me what you were really thinking.'

So shoot me for not wanting him to think his idea sucked. Doesn't everybody do this, glossing over little aggravations so as not to make the other person feel bad? Maybe this was bigger than a niggle, but surely my fib is justified given that Sam's only here for two days.

Besides I didn't know my boyfriend was going to spend the evening with his back to me, did I? 'Sam, that's not fair. I didn't know I didn't want to be there until you started ignoring me.'

He shakes his head. 'I never ignored you.'

'You did too! You spent hours talking to Li Ming.'

'We've been talking together, all three of us! You and she went on about where to get handmade shoes, remember? And about your tailor. You told her all about your fitting. True or not?'

Sure, we chatted, briefly, about fashion. And a bit about my job, and new apartment, and my time in London because she studied there too, though not with Sam. But he had his back to me. I know I'm not making that up. 'I felt like you ignored me.'

'Jesus, Hannah, I'm sorry if I didn't spend every minute talking to you. I thought that since we were at a table full of people, it'd be okay to talk to the others too. Is that what you want? My complete, undivided attention?'

Yes. That's exactly what I want from the man I'm in love with. It would be different if we lived here together. Then we'd have the luxury of all the tomorrows. But we've got less than twenty-four hours left. He shouldn't want to share that time with others. 'Yes,' I tell him.

'Well, I'm sorry. I thought that flying early to meet you yesterday, and the fact that we spent every minute, waking and sleeping, together from then till now, alone except for this evening, would be enough for you. I don't know what you want from me. I can't give you any more than I am already. If it's not enough, I don't really know what to do.' Now he looks sad.

'You were flirting with Li Ming.' The words slip out before I can stop them.

'What?! I was not. Han, I wasn't.'

'You've got yellow fever.'

'What are you talking about?' He tries to grab my hand but I yank it away.

'Stacy says expat men all want to date Asian women. Why wouldn't you? Li Ming's tiny and exotic. You're in the same field and get along so well. Maybe she wouldn't mind being ignored. Not that you were ignoring her.'

He stares at me. 'Are you saying you want me to date Li Ming?'

'I'm saying I don't want to stand in your way. Listen, this has been hard, being in different countries, hasn't it? Not just for you, you know. I've moved 6,000 miles and I'm ready to start my life here, my social life and my love life. I can't do that while my boyfriend is living somewhere else, visiting every few weeks.'

That's shocking him back to his senses. See how you like the idea of losing me, Sam. He's nodding slowly, as realization dawns.

'… You're right.' He sighs, his eyes bright. 'This isn't fun. And it isn't fair.'

'Thank you.' Finally he understands. I take his hand and he squeezes it back.

'I don't know when I'll be back in Hong Kong,' he says. 'Honestly, the project seems to be dragging on. I'm sorry, I've been completely selfish. I've convinced you to move here and now I'm not even here. That's not fair to you. So you're right.'

'I am?' Is he saying what I think he's saying? He's moving back. We'll no longer be in limbo, and can start to live our life together as we, I, he planned. I can finally start answering Mom's calls. And Stacy will stop making I-told-you-so faces every time I mention my boyfriend.

'Absolutely,' he says thickly. 'I hate this but… it isn't fair. We should be free to see other people. I'm sorry I've been so selfish. You're right, it's not fair to either of us right now. Come here.' He pulls me into his arms, burying his face in my hair.

What just happened? Did I just suggest we break up? I don't want to break up. These tears should be evidence enough of that. We're not breaking up are we? Sam said we could 'see other people', he didn't say 'not see each other'. Right? Right?! I need clarity.

'Did we just break up?'

'God, no! At least I hope not! We didn't, did we?' He looks terrified. He probably looks like I do.

'No, definitely not. Phew, you scared me. I don't want to stop seeing you.'

'Me either, Han. That's the last thing I want. I want to see you so much. Even though I don't like the idea, you're right, this is the best thing for now.'

I wish he'd stop saying I'm right. I don't feel right.

'There won't be any misunderstanding or resentment this way,' he continues. 'I shouldn't have been so selfish up till now. I'm so sorry about that.'

'So we're not breaking up.'

'Han. We are definitely not breaking up. I promise you that. In fact, will you think about coming out for your birthday weekend? I know you're supposed to go with Stacy and those men, but I'd love to celebrate with you instead.'

Well, that was the shortest pretend holiday in

history. 'Okay, yes, thanks, Sam, I'd like that.'

He smiles shyly. 'Kiss me?'

As I fold myself into his body I feel the tension of these last hours draining away. I don't want to let go. I don't want the absent feeling that comes after the last contact. Neither does he. He keeps kissing, again and again, as if each last kiss reminds him that he wants one more. He doesn't want to break up. This was a stupid fight, and a stupid misunderstanding. The panic is subsiding now, but oh, how close we came to losing each other. That was terrifyingly close.

10

'But petal, if you were exclusive before, and now you're seeing other people, how is that not breaking up?' Chloe gently asks later in the week when we've finally managed to overcome the time difference, and her uncharged mobile, and lost handset at the apartment. Luckily her office doesn't mind its employees making international calls. Or I'm sure they wouldn't mind if they knew about them.

'We're not broken up because we're still seeing each other. After our talk everything went back to normal. I guess we just needed to clear the air. I've been kind of crazy about his boss, but now that I've met her I feel better. She's not what I imagined. She's really sweet and nice and friendly.'

'Is she ugly?'

'No, she's not beautiful but she's not ugly. She's regular.'

'Just your run-of-the-mill smart, sweet, nice, friendly Asian woman who spends every day with your boyfriend, and lives with him and their colleagues? Han, are you sure you're okay with that?'

'Well, you're making it sound bad. I didn't get a

threatening vibe from her at all.' Although I did feel sick when she mentioned the beach, didn't I? 'She's much less threatening than I imagined. I've got nothing to worry about. And Sam and I had a wonderful, relaxed day together before he had to fly back. Chloe, really, we're not even on a break. In fact, I'm visiting him in two weeks for my birthday. Broken up people don't do that. They stop seeing each other and cry a lot. This isn't anything like that. I'm not crying at all, I promise. And it's just until his assignment ends. Oh, I'm not explaining it right, but it wasn't a break-up, trust me. I just pointed out to him that this situation isn't fair for me.'

'Well no, that's true, it wasn't really. So you initiated it?'

'Yes, sort of. I mean I got mad, over dinner, and told him it's not fair that I moved here and now have to live like a nun because he's in another country. He agreed, and said I should have the freedom to live my life here, and date other guys if I want to. This is about me though. He's not even going to see anyone else.'

'How do you know that?'

'I asked him before he left. He said he didn't plan to see other girls. You should have seen him, Chloe, he was nearly crying. He doesn't want me to see other people, obviously. So this is really something he agreed to do for me.'

'Bullshit.' That's Stacy, announcing her homecoming with profanity. 'Is that your mother?' She demands. 'He's a selfish twit, Missus Cumming! Talk some sense into your daughter. Lord knows I've tried.'

'It's not my mother. It's Chloe,' I hiss.

'Oh. What does *she* think?'

'Stace, I'll talk to you in a minute. When I'm off the phone. Sorry, Chloe, that was Stacy.'

'So I gathered. How is the wicked witch of the East?'

'She's, em, fine, thanks for asking. Stacy, Chloe says hello.'

I cover the phone, cutting off Chloe's colorful retort.

'Whatever,' Stacy calls over her shoulder on her way to her room.

'Stacy says hi back. Anyway, this all happened last weekend–'

'You poor thing! I'm so sorry I didn't call back till now. I was away with Barry till Sunday, and I got your message, but with the time difference… anyway, I'm sorry, Han, I should have called sooner.'

'No that's okay, really. I'm fine. Like I said, this isn't bad news at all. We haven't broken up and we've talked every day, just like usual. Really, I think this is just Sam's way of saying sorry for asking me to move here when he's not even here. Like a reward, so to speak, for taking the leap.'

'Your reward from your boyfriend is that you get to kiss other boys?' She sounds skeptical.

'Well, obviously he's hoping I won't be kissing any. But there's nothing saying I can't go on dates. In fact, I will.' This is Stacy's idea. She says I should be treating Hong Kong like a dim sum buffet, getting my hands on as many steamy buns as possible. That's why she's come home 'early' from work to take me out. 'I've got to run honey, we've got plans.'

'Now? It's nearly ten there, isn't it?'

'Yeah, Stacy had to work late. I'll call you over the

weekend, okay? Are you around?'

'I think so. Wait, no, I'm…' I can hear drawers slamming. 'I had my diary yesterday. Where is it? Anyway, I think I'm doing something. With someone. But I should be around. Sometimes. So call me, yes, please! Have fun tonight angel. Speak soon!' She puts the phone down muttering something about a wedding she may or may not have been invited to.

It might be because I'm still thinking about Chloe's potential wedding weekend that everyone seems to be in bridal veils when we arrive in Lan Kwai Fong half an hour later. Accessorized by improbably sized dildos and PVC dresses though, these brides are more likely to vomit in the gutter than walk down the aisle tonight. It's not Stacy's cultural milieu (she's more of an unpronounceable-vodka-in-your-martini girl), but based on how often she drinks in these crooked little streets late at night with her colleagues, she seems to like it. I always find it a little frightening. Many of the women are positively sinewy, prowling, and determined to turn back time in the face of gravity. I've seen them in the gym (as they pass by the juice bar). They are as dogged in romance as they are on their treadmills.

'All right,' says my best friend. 'Before Stuart and Brent get here, I want to talk to you about this whole Sam situation.'

'Stace, we've already talked about it, and you've made your views very clear. Do we really need to go over this again?'

'Yes. Han, you know I love you, and I want what's best for you. This isn't what's best for you.'

Sigh. 'Stace, I thought you wanted me to be free to date here. You've got your way. I'm free to date.' Try as

I might I can't take the petulance out of my statement. 'What more do you want?'

'I want you to see that Sam isn't doing this for your good. He's doing it for his. Han, no guy willingly lets his girlfriend go out with other men unless he's planning to see, or is already seeing other women. Guys are territorial. They're not going to let some stranger pee on their territory.'

'I'm not going to let anyone pee on me.' I do not want to have this conversation again. I regret even telling her about the weekend. She'd never have known if I hadn't mentioned it because everything is perfectly normal between Sam and me. Better than normal. He's being the most perfect, attentive boyfriend, calling all the time and sending cards. Well, a card. Très romantic. In fact, it's exactly like when he first moved away from London. There's no drama, no angst, no misunderstandings, just missing each other (in a good, I-can't-wait-to-see-you way), comfort, laughter, sweetness and anticipation. And I feel very in control, very sure of his feelings. I feel very cool. And I'm not moping, truly I'm not. 'If I'm comfortable with the arrangement, Stace, why can't that be enough for you?'

'Because you're deluding yourself. You won't acknowledge that this means he can date too. And I don't believe that you really plan to see other people.' She tops up our wine, daring me with a perfectly arched eyebrow to deny it. Stuart and Brent's well-timed arrival saves me from having to mount a defense.

'Hello, hello! Sorry we're late, Brent was too busy being chatted up by a teenager to tear himself away.'

'That's not true, Stu, and you know it. She was at least twenty-one. Hello girls.' Brent kisses each of us.

'Drinks?'

'You're not late,' says Stacy. 'If you want wine, just get a couple of glasses. We just got the bottle.' Her phone bdlllings with a text. 'Hmm.' She smiles.

'Who is it?'

'Hmm? Oh, just Pete, saying he enjoyed meeting… us the other night. We traded numbers before we left.'

'Why? He's such a jerk!'

'No he's not, he's actually very nice. I think you've misinterpreted him or something.'

'I doubt it. What are you going to do, go out with him?'

'Don't be ridiculous, we just enjoyed chatting, that's all. Why are you being so weird about it?'

'I'm not being weird,' I say, weirdly.

'I really am sorry we're late,' Stuart says as Brent goes for glasses. 'Especially since we've only got time for a quick hello. We've got to be at over on Kowloon at eleven. So, how's everyone doing?'

Stacy sighs dramatically. 'Hannah and Sam are *taking a break*.' She makes ditto fingers. 'But she won't date. Stuart, please talk some sense into her and tell her what men mean when they say you should see other people.'

'We mean you should see other people,' Stuart says reasonably. 'Stace, I'd love to say we're more complex than that but really, we aren't. We're easy to understand. Just feed us, give us drinks, some sport to play or at least watch, let us go out with our friends and have regular sex–' He smirks, anticipating the retort on the tip of my tongue. 'Not with the friends… and you've got us sorted. We're not like you women, always saying one thing and meaning another, and then wondering why we're confused.'

'You sound like you're speaking from experience,' I say.

'Hannah, I haven't understood women since puberty.'

'Last year then,' Brent quips, handing his brother a glass. 'What are we talking about?'

'Hannah is now free to date and she won't.'

Brent's face is the picture of concern. 'Hannah, I'm sorry, did you and Sam break up?'

'Thanks, but no we didn't. As I've explained to my dear friend here, Sam and I are still very much together. We're not on a break. It's just that while he's in Vietnam I can have dates if I want to.'

'But she won't,' Stacy interjects.

'I will too! I'm totally going to date. I came out with you tonight didn't I, specifically to let you throw me at random men?'

'Not to see us?' Stuart whimpers.

'Of course to see you… and also to talk to men. You're leaving anyway,' I note as they finish their wine. 'Psh. Some dates you are.' I mean that. I pity the women who try going out with them. Sure, it's exciting to be wined and dined nightly, but it must also get exhausting. An evening on the sofa never figures in their plans.

'Really sorry,' says Brent sheepishly. 'We just wanted to pop by and say hello. We'll see you this weekend though, right?'

'Absolutely, dim sum on Saturday,' I say, kissing them goodnight.

'Prove it,' challenges Stacy as our friends leave.

'Prove what?'

'Prove you mean what you say. That you'll really date other people.'

'What do you want me to do, Stace, drop on my knees in the bar?'

'If the mood takes you, I wouldn't judge,' she says, smirking.

'Fine, I will. Who's my victim? I *mean* to talk to. Dirty mind.'

She scans the bar. 'Those two over there. The blonde one's interesting. What do you think of the dark one?'

Stacy is far from one of life's coasters – she makes the rest of us look like slovenly layabouts. She's going to make me do this whether I want to or not. 'Fine, he's cute, let's go,' I say. I'm not afraid of her, and I'm not afraid to talk to that guy. He's not as cute as Sam – he's shorter, and more clean-cut, and his eyes are just a tiny bit too close together, making him look slightly like an Afghan hound. But, if I were single, I wouldn't say no to a date. Wait. What am I saying? I am technically single. In that case, come here, boy, there's a good fella. He smiles as we approach. This is easy.

The next morning, Mr. Chan stares suspiciously at my inseam. 'You grew,' he concludes.

'I did not grow, and besides those dresses are too big, not too small. You must have measured wrong.'

'I did not measure wrong, I never measure wrong! Your leg, it's bigger. Both. Bigger.' His look dares me to argue further.

It doesn't make any difference who's right. The fact is that these trousers are failing to fulfill their purpose in life, as tailored trousers. They don't fit.

Nothing fits properly. The dresses are either too big or too small, the jacket sleeves are too short and the trousers make my legs look like sausage links. I don't understand what's gone wrong. Mr. Chan spent so long measuring me, over and over, meticulously writing everything down. Clearly something was lost in translation. 'Look, Mr. Chan, I love the materials we've chosen and I'm sure you can just make some adjustments and everything will fit perfectly. Can we just do that please?' It's sweltering in this musty workshop. The closeness is making me feel a little ill, though that could be because I didn't go to bed until 3 a.m.

The tailor considers my request, weighing up my mortal insult against his desire to pursue his calling. 'Okay, stand still.'

'Thanks, Mr. Chan… can we hurry please, I need to be back at the offi– okay, okay, I'll just stand still.'

'Hannah, Josh wants to see you,' Winnie says just as I drop into my office chair nearly an hour later. The first thought to pop into my head (oh heady floaty thought) is that Sam has come to surprise me again. My second, stomach-clenching thought is that I feel guilty about flirting with the Afghan hound last night. Nothing happened, not really, so I have no reason for these pangs. He and his friend were certainly entertaining company, and their dancing skills were beyond reproach. Which is why we were out till the wee hours dancing to a Chinese cover band. I gave him my number, as I threatened I would. There was no kissing, only a few poorly aimed, easily deflected lunges. He probably won't call. So if I did nothing wrong, why do I feel guilty? Because there should be a statutory cooling-off period between flirting with a stranger and seeing your boyfriend. Still, I'm excited to see Sam! 'Oh really, Winnie? Whatever could Josh want? Give me a few minutes, I just need to freshen up.' Luckily I tipped most of the contents of my make-up drawer into my handbag this morning. On four hours of sleep, my face will only surrender to repeated attempts at repair.

'Seriously, Han, he didn't look pleased,' warns Winnie. 'I'd go in now if I were you.'

Oh she's a regular drama queen, she is. If I didn't know better I'd say she was really worried for me. 'Okay, okay, I'm going.'

'Josh?' I sing as I float through his door. 'You wanted to see me?' Sam's not there. Josh isn't smiling.

'Yes, Hannah, thanks. It's about the proposals. Did you send them?'

'Yep, a week ago Monday… Why?'

'I just had a call from one of the shops asking why we didn't put our offer in this round. Are you sure you sent them to everyone?'

'Positive, Josh. I faxed them all on Monday. Hang on, I've got all the paperwork. I'll get it.' This is bad. This is very bad. We're not the only ones pitching to the shops. Dozens of other exporters are in competition, all hoping that their clothes will be chosen for the next season. If they didn't get our proposals that means… that means that we have no chance of selling anything this season. This is very bad. But I did fax the proposals. It took me an hour to get them all sent. I know I sent them, the day after Sam left.

'Here, Josh, they're all there. Twenty-seven proposals, twenty-seven shops that you wanted me to send them to.' The sheaf of papers is quivering and it's not because we're having a earthquake.

'Do you have the fax confirmations?' Josh's voice is calm, but his face is uncharacteristically still. Normally the wrinkles, bags and creases are as animated as an undulating jellyfish. This is very bad.

'Fax confirmations? No. I don't know what those are. I'm sorry.'

'After the fax gets sent a page prints out listing all the sent pages,' he explains with incredible patience for a man who's realizing his hiring decision may have been a very expensive mistake. 'Maybe they're still near the fax?' He's trying to help me. I can tell he's not enjoying this conversation.

'Right, I'll just go check.' It's unladylike to run, and not altogether practical in these shoes, but time is of the essence if I'm to have any chance of halting Josh's free-falling opinion of me. There are no papers by the fax machine. Of course there aren't. Nazi Reese would have efficiently dispatched such a disorderly blight on her copy room. 'Mrs. Reese? Do you happen to keep the fax confirmations? I'm looking for the ones from a week ago Monday, when I sent all the proposals out. You remember, right? I asked you how to use the fax machine?'

'Yes, I remember,' she says. She hardly moves her mouth when she speaks. Imagine a fish talking to you. She is rather aquatic today, in her blue suit, with a face like a grouper. 'The fax confirmations are kept in the tray above the stationery supply for two weeks. You'll find them there. Hannah, do try not to put them out of order.'

All is not lost. I can prove I sent the faxes. The

shop's fax machine must have run out of paper or something. Not my fault, and not a disaster. There's an enormous pile of pages in the tray. In date order, of course, Mrs. Reese would have it no other way. Let's see, let's see, Friday, Thursday… Tuesday, Monday, Friday… Thursday, Wednesday, Tuesday, here we go, Monday. They're here. Disaster averted.

'Here you go.' I hand the pile to Josh. 'They're all there, all twenty-seven.'

He stares at the pile, slowly paging through it. 'Hannah? These are blank.'

'… No they're not. There's the information right at the top. See? Phone number, date, time, number of pages. It's all right there.'

'I mean they are blank. You've sent blank pages to these numbers.'

'How do you know that?' I can't have sent blank pages. Who would do that? I sent the proposals. The entire pile of proposals. They're right there.

'Because this is a printout of the first page of your fax, here below the status box. It's blank.' He looks sorry for me rather than mad. Though of course he's mad. I've just scuppered his business for next year.

'I don't know how I… It's not, I can't– I faxed them, Josh, I promise I did. I asked Mrs. Reese how to use the fax machine. She said to be sure to dial eight first, and the country code and number, and to wait till the fax did that long beep to make sure it went through. I did all that. I swear I did.' I don't want to cry but my tear ducts have other plans. Proof positive that waterproof mascara isn't just for swimming.

He sighs. 'Hannah, did you fax the pages upside down?'

What? No, I couldn't have. 'I… I asked Mrs. Reese how to do it,' I say in a voice choked off by rising panic. 'I don't think I fed them in upside down.' But the evidence is right there in Josh's hands, isn't it? I admit I was distracted by this whole Sam thing. Even though we are *not* broken up, I hadn't slept well on Sunday after he left. Is it possible that I fed more than 100 pages into a fax machine the wrong way up? Of course it is. Technology and I have never been firm friends. 'I guess it's possible. Well, yes, I must have done it. Otherwise you'd see the first page of the proposal on there. Josh, I am so sorry.' I will not tell him about Sam. My personal life is not his problem. 'I don't know what else to say. I'm just, sorry. Is there any way I can salvage this?'

He runs his hand through his hair, making it stand up even taller than usual. 'I don't know. If we know that none of the proposals went out then I guess we should split the list and call each shop, explain the situation and see if we can submit them now. It's probably not too late for all of them.' His face is animated again. It's not friendly, but at least that weird stillness has gone.

'Okay. Josh, again, I am so, so, so, so, so sorry. I'll do anything to make it up to you. I'm really not a screw up, I promise I'm not–'

He holds up his hand. 'Hannah, it's a mistake, that's all. It might be costly, but we don't know that yet. Let's see how many of these shops we can still send the proposal to. Okay?'

'Thanks, Josh.'

The man trusts me and what do I do? I prove myself incapable of using a fax machine.

'What happened?' Winnie wants to know when I slump back to my desk.

'Oh god, I'm an idiot. I faxed blank proposals to the shops. All of the orders, upside down. I can't believe I did that!'

'Oh my god. That's bad.'

'Thanks, Winnie.'

'I mean I'm really sorry for you. What are you going to do?'

'We're calling all the shops to see if it's not too late to submit the proposals. I've got to call all of these now.'

'Well here, give me some. I'll call too. Hang on, let me pick the ones that I'm friendly with. I've had relationships with some of these for years.'

'Really? Thanks. I'd better start calling.'

My stomach is churning as I dial the first number. Talk about penance. At least Winnie and Josh can blame a moron's failure to operate office equipment. I am that moron. 'Hello?' I croak. 'May I please speak to Mrs. Dermott?'

'This is she.'

'Oh, hi, this is Hannah Cumming, from Silk Road Exports. In Hong Kong.'

'Hello.'

'Hello. Em, I'm calling because there's been an error. You didn't receive our proposal, it was my error, really. I faxed the papers upside down.'

'I see.'

'And I hope it's not too late to send them through today?'

'I'm afraid it is Miss– Cumming? We've already chosen the lines for next season. I'm terribly sorry.'

I know for a fact that she's not terribly sorry. English people say this when they mean they don't want to do something. 'Well then–'

'Thank you for calling. Goodb–'

'Wait! Mrs. Dermott, please, isn't there any way you could even let me fax them through, just to have a look? The thing is, this was a huge mistake. I spent weeks putting the proposal together, and then messed up the fax. All the faxes actually. I've just started, and my boss is great but this is a humongous cock-up. Couldn't you at least have a look? If there's nothing in there that you'd like to stock then at least you've seen the best we have to offer. I know you've bought strongly off our recommendations in the past. Really, I think you'll want to at least have a look. Please?' I'm just barely resisting the urge to add 'pretty please with sugar on top'.

'I understand,' she says, with a little more warmth. 'Fax them through and I'll have a look.'

'Oh thank you, thank you, Mrs. Dermott, you're a lifesaver. And I'm sorry I screwed up. Next time I promise you'll get the proposal right side up.'

'I hope so, Miss Cumming. Goodbye.'

That woman just won herself a spot on my Christmas card list for life. I've got a second chance at least. That's something. On to the next groveling phone call…

My head is about to explode when Winnie sets a coffee on my desk two hours later. 'Here, I figured you'd need this. I've finished my calls. Only one said no because she already placed her orders. Here are the rest. You can fax them the proposals… Are you okay?'

'I think I might be having a stroke. It feels like my

head's about to lift off my shoulders.'

She makes the perfect oh-poor-lamb face. 'How'd your calls go?'

'Good. Two said no. The rest are letting me resend the proposals. And all of Josh's said yes. He doesn't seem too mad.'

'No, I'm sure he's not angry. He's one of the nicest bosses in the world. Don't be too hard on yourself, Hannah, it really could have happened to anyone. You should have seen some of your predecessors… I'll help you refax them if you want. We've got another machine near my desk. We'll finish faster that way. Then I will take you out for drinks. You need it.'

Do I ever.

Our arrival at Winnie's favorite bar reminds me again that outside of work we usually live in completely different worlds. Lan Kwai Fong is many things, but it's not Chinese. Here, though, I'm the only Westerner. It's an odd sensation to be so obviously different, but it's not uncomfortable. I'm clearly just a curiosity rather than an unwelcome guest.

'Winnie, was it strange when you first went to London to study?' Having London in common has made our friendship very easy, especially since she thinks of it as her home away from home too.

'What do you mean?' She waves hello to a group of women near the bar.

'Well, here everyone is Chinese. Was it weird moving somewhere where you're the minority?'

'I can ask you the same question. Do you find it weird living here?'

'I notice it, so yes, I guess so. Funny, isn't it? You never question things when you're the majority. I think everyone should have to live where they're a minority for a while. It'd make people more tolerant.'

She snorts. 'You overestimate us. Being singled out as a minority doesn't make us more tolerant. It makes us more sure that those singling us out are ignorant. Hannah, you're an idealist. Most people don't change their point of view just because they walk in someone else's shoes for a while. You're sweet to think they do though.' She smiles warmly.

Winnie is always telling me I'm sweet, or cute or naïve. To her I'm a first-class bumpkin, but she doesn't hold that against me. As someone who speaks half a dozen languages and has lived all over the world, she has to cut us mere mortals some slack. 'Well, it seems I've avoided being fired, which is good. There's no guarantee that we'll get the orders but at least most of the shops agreed to look at the proposals. I still can't believe I did that. I am such an idiot.'

'Hmm. I've been thinking about that.'

'That I'm an idiot? Thanks very much.'

She laughs. 'No. Although it wasn't very clever. I was thinking – are you sure you faxed the pages upside down?'

'Well, yes. You saw the printouts. I didn't fax blank pages, so I must have fed them in the wrong way.'

'What would you say if I told you this happened before? When Sandra worked here, she faxed a bunch of orders to the factories upside down.'

'I don't understand.'

'You asked Mrs. Reese how to use the fax, didn't you? Because Sandra said she did too but by that time everybody assumed she was clutching at straws because she'd screwed up so much already. In fact, this happened around the same time that she was caught stealing.'

'Stealing?!' With an act like that to follow, it's no wonder Josh was nonplussed. At least my mix-up didn't involve the police.

'Yeah, that's when she got fired. She took the petty cash from the office.'

'You really think Mrs. Reese sabotaged her, and me? Why would she do that? I haven't done anything to her.' Maybe I haven't always followed her tidying diktats, but that's hardly a reason to ruin someone's career.

'I have a theory. She's old guard, one of the Hong Kong hands. They're the gweilos whose families have been here for generations. I know she hates that the company started selling counterfeits, and that we stock cheaper lines now. She's never been shy about making her views known to everyone. She doesn't think Josh has honored his father's wishes, even though it was the old man who originally made the change to knock-offs. She was absolutely devoted to him. In fact… everyone also knows that old Mr. Bolton had an affair with her for years, decades.'

'You're kidding! I mean, I never knew the man but I can't imagine anyone having an affair with her. She's vile. And if it is true, why would Josh employ her? He must hate her.'

'Oh no, quite the opposite. She looked after his dad in the nineties, after his mum died. Though they never married. She was still legally married. Everyone knew about the affair, including her husband and Josh's mum. It sounds like they accepted the situation. Mrs. Reese was sort of the other wife. I'm sure that's why she still works with us. She sees herself as the overseer of Mr. Bolton's business, and his avenging angel.'

'So she doesn't dislike me per se?'

'Oh no, I'm sure she dislikes you. Sorry. She probably wants Josh to rely on her, not you. Maybe she's like the ghost that chases each set of new owners out of the house so she can live there like she's always done, without interference. Just watch yourself. She can be sneaky.'

'Thanks. I'll be sure to say no if she asks me to carry any unmarked packages across the border next week.'

'You're going to love that trip! I went a few times. You'll eat so well.' She gets the faraway look she always does when contemplating food. Winnie loves to eat. She says it's because of her culture. Chinese greet each other with the question: Have you eaten yet?

'I'm excited. It'll be my first time in proper China.'

'As opposed to improper China?'

'You know what I mean. Mainland China. I know Hong Kong is technically China too.'

'That's okay, we're different from proper Chinese,' she says, smirking.

'So you keep telling me. I just wish the trip wasn't next week. I was supposed to be with Sam in Ho Chi Minh for my birthday but I won't get back here till Saturday night. I can't exactly ask Josh to reschedule everyone, can I?'

'Aw, that's bad luck! And no, after today, it's probably best to be as accommodating as possible,' she agrees, reminding me that although the result wasn't catastrophic, it was still a major screw-up. So next Friday I go to China.

11

Mrs. Reese hasn't asked me to carry anything across the border but I'm still nervous. Unsmiling officials always make me nervous, and Chinese immigration officers are at the top of the unsmiling pecking order. So here I am, clutching a sheaf of papers and my passport, waiting to convince the man at the podium to let me cross the border. I make it sound like I'm standing at a dusty roadside with chicken-laden trucks and refugees. Actually we're in the airport, in a perfectly orderly line of other businesspeople and tourists. It's not exactly Baghdad. Still, my lunch is threatening an appearance.

The man gestures me forward. He stares at my passport, then my papers. He barks something to the fellow at the next podium. The next thing I know Josh is beside me. 'Don't worry, Hannah, just a little confusion.' He turns to the officer. 'We're guests of Mr. Chow at Fujian Apparel. See? Here.' His voice is uncharacteristically gruff. 'Miss Cumming is my employee. See? It's right here. She's been invited too. See? It's right here.' He keeps stabbing at the papers for emphasis.

'What's wrong?' I ask Josh.

'You're American,' he says. 'Oh, it's nothing

personal. The rules on visas change all the time. Different nationalities go in and out of favor. You are, unfortunately, out at the moment. Don't worry, we'll get it sorted.' He continues arguing with the officer, quietly now, while I wait to see whether I'll have to sleep in the airport until our return flight. But after a fraught ten minutes the officer stamps my passport. They're letting me loose in China!

Half an hour later and I wish I'd stayed in Hong Kong. Fujian is just a big, polluted city and we're sitting in a traffic jam. Where are the coolies in Chairman Mao pajamas? Where are the rickshaws, and men in conical hats balancing baskets from long poles? Where's the China I expect? It's bad enough that Hong Kong isn't the colonial outpost I'd imagined. *Et tu, Brute*? 'It's a city,' I say glumly to Josh.

'Well, yes. What did you think it would be?'

It's probably naïve to explain about the conical hats and the pajamas, so I say, 'I thought it'd be more Chinese.' Oh yes, Hannah, that's much better.

He laughs. 'I know what you mean. You thought it'd be more rural. My father used to take me on his trips when I was a child and that's exactly what it was like. It was a mysterious country to us. We saw Chinese of course, in Hong Kong, but the mainlanders were a world apart. Even twenty years ago the country would have seemed more like your imagined China. But that's all changed. They've torn down nearly everything from the past and put up skyscrapers. There's virtually nothing left of old Peking, the city my father knew as a child. They've razed the hutongs. Those are the traditional neighborhoods, the narrow lanes that were several hundred years old. They're wiping out their past. Though, ironically, what they do keep of their old architecture they renovate so that it looks new. You'd never recognize what's truly historic here.'

He sounds like he harks back to the good old days. 'Surely though, Josh, if the old buildings are falling down, it's better to start again with places that people can live in. They did that in parts of New York, areas that were ghettos, and now they're great, with loads of trendy shops, and restaurants and bars.'

He laughs. 'I sound like an old stick-in-the-mud, don't I? I'm not suggesting that progress is bad, just that it needs to be managed. Take New York. What happened to the people who lived in those ghettos?'

'Well, they moved somewhere else I guess.'

'Right. They probably went to another ghetto when they could no longer afford to live in their old neighborhood. So that destroyed a whole community and scattered the residents. The families that lived in the hutongs had been there for generations. Isn't it sad to displace them in the name of progress?'

'Why Josh, you sound like a conservationist.'

He looks shy. 'I am, in fact. I sit on the board of the Heritage Conservation Society in Hong Kong. My father was always very concerned about preserving Hong Kong's heritage… he meant its colonial heritage of course! Our projects are much wider than that now, and aren't all about saving the beautiful buildings. Do you know about Nga Tsin Wai?' He sighs deeply, shaking his head. 'It's a walled village in Kowloon, the oldest one remaining. Three families in the fourteenth century built it, originally near the harbor but development of the old airport meant that the residents lost their seaside view. It's not much to look at. It's a slum really, but it's very important historically. Unfortunately developers have bought it up and are tearing it down to make way for flats.'

'That's awful!' Suddenly I'm seized by the injustice. 'Isn't there anything we can do?'

He chuckles at my inclusion in his conservation work. 'Unfortunately not. Not for this one. We fought the plans for several years but the Urban Renewal Authority has won. They say they'll keep some of the more important buildings, like the gatehouse, the temple and ancestral hall, and incorporate them into a cultural park that they're planning. We'll see.'

I wonder what makes us want to hold on to our heritage and look backwards, when the Chinese want to look forward? Maybe it's opportunity. 'You really love Hong Kong, don't you?'

He looks surprised. 'Of course. It's my home, my heritage.'

'Yeah, I guess I think of you as English, because of your accent, and the fact that you're not Chinese. I'm sorry, that's probably obtuse of me.'

'I know what you mean. But no, I'm a Honker through and through.'

'An old Hong Kong hand?' I say, thinking of Mrs. Reese's ties to his family.

'Exactly. Ah, here we are.'

The taxi has finally reached our hotel, a nondescript concrete bunker of a building. If this is what progress looks like, I'd like the old buildings back please.

'We'll meet Mr. Chow at six-thirty so feel free to have a look around the area if you'd like. Although you saw the highlights of the city just now.' He chuckles. 'If we have time tomorrow before the airport we'll ask the driver to take us out to the countryside. There's something there I think you'll appreciate.'

'That sounds intriguing.' I smile. 'I'll just relax and read a bit, so I'll meet you in the lobby later. Oh, and is it okay if I call my boyfriend from the room?'

'Of course it is. I'll see you at six in the lobby.'

Josh really is the best boss a girl could have. Not only is he footing the bill for my travels to exotic lands, he hasn't held even the tiniest grudge for my having almost scuppered his business. We lost out on three of the orders, so I won't expect a Christmas bonus, but in my history of career snafus, it wasn't at the top. That honor remains with the first party I was allowed to plan in London. I don't know what my boss expected when she neglected to tell me that my 'death and rebirth' theme for the hostess's divorce party (still an excellent idea, circumstances notwithstanding) might not go down well considering that her ex-husband had cancer… and attended the party. Needless to say, the six-foot coffin cake wasn't a hit. But you know what they say: fool me once shame on you, fool me twice shame on me. I will not be duped again. Well, not since the fax incident anyway. I've been watching Mrs. Reese closely this week. I'll never prove that she gave me the wrong instructions but I'll always suspect that she did. Of course I won't say anything to her. It's safer for her to think she's getting away with it, and for me to know she can't be trusted. I do believe I'm finally learning.

'Bdllling!'

Hannah, Happy Birthday hony! Dad snd I hope you have a great day. We love you very much. Love mom and Dad

The first salutations of my twenty-eighth birthday.

It's a day early but I won't hold Mom's inability to calculate time differences against her. It's the sentiment that counts, and it fills me with loving parental thoughts. I can imagine them at home, probably at the kitchen table while Mom taps resolutely on the mobile, reading out each word as she types. Dad'll have the paper open, a cold cup of coffee at his elbow because he always gets too involved in what he's reading to remember to drink it. Mom will pop it into the microwave every half hour and set it beside him where it will remain untouched. No wait, that's the weekend routine. Today is Tuesday. Dad's at work. Mom probably texted in the car at a red light, on her way to meet her friends for lunch. It doesn't matter, the sentiment's the same.

I miss them. Funny how filial ties can ambush you like this. I remember one afternoon at my first job, walking into the elevator just as a woman exited. She wore my mother's perfume. It hit me with such force that I nearly followed her down the hall, sniffing in her wake. And Mom only lived twenty minutes up the road. It's probably a stretch of Josh's largesse to call the US, from a hotel room, at his company's expense. Airwave love will have to do.

Thanks Mom and Dad, I'll have a wonderful birthday! I'm in China now for work, so will celebrate here, then again in HK when I get back. I love you very much H

When I call Sam's office, his phone rings and rings. Finally, 'Hello, Sam's phone.'

'Uh, hi, this is Hannah. Is Sam there please?'

'Oh. Hi Hannah. No, he's not here. He's left early today. Can I tell him you called?'

'Yes please. Thanks.' The line rings off.

I definitely told him I had to be here in China today and tomorrow. I know I told him. He can't have flown to Hong Kong to surprise me for my birthday. Could he? That would be so romantic. But so bad! The idea that he's there, when I'm here, makes me queasy. The enormity of the missed opportunity is swelling in my gut. It's a heavy breathing, light-headed, panicky feeling. It's almost dread. It can't be healthy to feel such desperation for this man. What if he breaks up with me?

There, I said it. What if he breaks up with me? Because that's what this feeling is really about, isn't it? It's the fear of things going wrong in the future, even if they're right in the present. It's the fear that I won't be able to handle that.

Scared, I call his mobile. Panic dialing is almost always a bad idea, but I have to know where he is. This is a perfect case of my head warning me to calm down, and my heart telling it to shut up and mind its own business. 'Hi Sam?' Relief floods through me at the sound of his voice.

'Hi Hannah! How are you? How's China?' He sounds buoyant. I've been paranoid, overreacting, that's all. 'They let you in?'

'Ha, yes, after some arguing by Josh, they let me in. We're meeting in a little bit for the client dinner. It should be fun. I just hope I don't make any blunders... So you're taking the afternoon off? Doing something fun I hope?' There. That's breezy, casual, la la la la la. I'm such the cool girlfriend.

'Yeah, you know what kind of hours I've been working. I needed the break.'

'... Great. Where are you now?' Admittedly that's a

little less breezy.

'Oh, just wandering around, taking in some sights, you know, Reunification Palace, the museum. I haven't really had the chance, with the work and all.'

'Sounds like there are a lot of people there. Is it open late?' The V&A in London has late views on Wednesdays, and I went once. Maybe when I visit Sam we can go to the Vietnamese version.

'I'm not there anymore. I'm at a bar now. There's an outside area, so there are a lot of people walking by. What time do you have to meet Josh for dinner?'

'Fairly soon actually. I guess I'd better get in the shower. So will I talk to you tomorrow?' What's he doing in a bar alone? Granted, I've done it too, especially if there's a nice outdoor seating area. It feels like a treat, a decadent, slightly subversive flouting of the normal rules. He *has* taken the afternoon off to unwind.

'Of course I'll call!' He says. 'It's your birthday. Han, have a great time tonight at dinner, and good meetings tomorrow, and call me when you get back to your apartment, okay?'

'I will. Goodnight sweetheart, enjoy the rest of your relaxing evening. I'll talk to you tomorrow… I love you!' I blurt out, a split second before regretting the words. Oh God, it's like a fart has slipped out in the middle of sex.

'Okay, me too… Goodnight.'

'Goodnight. Bye.'

… Okay, me too. He said that, didn't he? I said 'I love you' and he said 'me too'. He loves me. Right? Unless he didn't hear me correctly. It wasn't exactly a heartfelt declaration. You'd think if your girlfriend says

'I love you' for the first time, you'd say something memorable back. So maybe he didn't hear me. It was noisy. Did he hear me or not?! I should call him and ask. I need clarification. But what if he didn't hear me? I'm going to have to repeat it. What if there's an awful silence as he struggles to say something that won't mortally wound me? This isn't the kind of conversation to have on the phone. So I shouldn't call him back. Unless he expected me to say something else. What kind of girlfriend doesn't acknowledge when her boyfriend says 'I love you' for the first time? Perhaps he's disappointed, and wondering why I didn't say anything else. So I should call him.

I redial. Ring, ring, ring… ring, click. Did his phone shut off or did the call fail? Shut off or fail? *Shut off or fail?*! Answer me, you damn universe.

See? This is why it's horrible being in love. I know I'm being insane. The question is whether Sam is making me feel like this or whether this is my natural state. There's no denying that my relationships in the past have suffered from an excess of paranoia. Some might say obsession (Stacy certainly has). Jake is the perfect case in point, but nearly all former boyfriends have, at some point, suggested that I might be overreacting, and over-thinking the situation. Are we all obsessive? If I'm alone then I'd rather know now, because, to date, I've assumed that I'm normal… well, in the normal range anyway. But if womankind is generally secure in relationships, enjoying them rather than spending large parts of the day analyzing them, then I am, in fact, a nut job. Isn't there some kind of test I can take to tell me where I fit on the crazy scale?

The taxi ride to the restaurant with Josh is a test of my willpower. I nearly blurted out the conversation, word for word, between Sam and me when he asked, 'How are you?' Can you imagine how inappropriate that would have been, how uncomfortable it would have made Josh? Then I'd be worried about him being uncomfortable, when I need all my concentration for this dinner. The last thing I want is a repeat of the client event in London last year, the very memory of which still makes me shudder with humiliation. It wasn't merely that I was dressed like a party favor when the rest of the room wore business suits, or that I was pressed into service at the last minute to fill an empty space at one of the tables of MPs. It was the speech I was asked to make. A terrible, misguided speech about immigration, given to a group that had all the warmth of a Gestapo convention in 1937. There will be no speeches tonight.

'All right?' Josh says as the driver pulls up in front of the restaurant. It looks exactly like a Chinese restaurant should, with red hanging lanterns and golden dragons at the entrance. 'Now, it's Mr. Chow, who's the owner of the factory, and his two top bosses Mr. Wang and Mr. Chung.'

'Wang Chung?'

He chuckles. 'Yes, I know, and Mr. Chow sometimes drops the Mr., which doesn't help matters. You'll know Mr. Chow immediately because the other two defer to him on everything. And it's easy to remember which is Mr. Wang and which Mr. Chung because Wang is fat and Chung is skinny. Just remember fat Wang, but obviously, don't say it out loud or you'll get me into trouble. I have to remember all my clients' staff using the same tricks. It's terrible really, but with so many people to keep track of, needs must.' He shrugs. 'They may ask a few polite questions. You probably won't be expected to say much. Though of course you can if you wish! But I also want you to feel free to just enjoy the dinner. We're really here to show Mr. Chow how much we value working with him. Okay?'

'Yep, I'm ready.' I smooth my very demure, chocolate brown skirt, take a deep breath, and open the door to face what I hope to be my first successful client event.

Halfway through dinner I decide that it isn't half bad. Our clients have pretty much ignored me, in the nicest possible way. Mr. Chow has been chatting non-stop to Josh about next season while Wang Chung nod in time to every statement. They're very nice. And hospitable. I'm stuffed to the gills but they keep feeding me. Every time I finish what's in my bowl, they take turns filling it again from the tasty morsels on the ingenious rotating tray in the middle of the table. I've just choked down my third helping and fear for my waistline. Even worse, every so often Mr. Chow gets in on the act, offering me the last bit from the serving plates. My mother taught me to clean my plate, but this is a fight to the death between my manners and my seams. Manners have the upper hand so far, but only just.

'Hannah.' Mr. Chow interrupts my bulimic fantasies. 'How have you enjoyed living in Hong Kong?'

'Oh, Mr. Chow, it's incredible! It's really a great city, with so much to learn about, and so much to explore. When I first arrived I only saw the modern buildings and thought it was like New York, but it's really very different. I feel like when I scratched the surface, I saw the real Hong Kong.'

'Hmm, yes, very interesting. And what is the real Hong Kong, do you think?'

Can I say what I'm thinking? It's not offensive is it? No, surely not. It's just my observation. 'It's very Chinese, Mr. Chow. I didn't expect that. I thought that because it was a colony for so long, it would be a little like London. But it's not at all. It's a Chinese city.'

A slow smile spreads across Mr. Chow's face, mirrored by Wang Chung. 'Yes, Hannah, it is a Chinese city. It's a great Chinese city. You are right. You are very right.'

When Josh smiles I know I've said the right thing. Who'd have thought it, considering how many of the wrong things I usually say? I've spent most of this night reminding myself not to mention the Dalai Lama or Taiwan (two subjects that Josh warned would win me no friends in China). But when the pressure was on, I said the right thing. Perhaps I, Hannah Jane Cumming, have finally turned over a whole new green tea leaf. On the cusp of my twenty-eighth birthday I may have ceased to be the village idiot and started being a fully-fledged adult who doesn't have to be shielded from polite society. This is quite a moment. Mr. Chung wants to celebrate it with another helping.

'Oh, no, thank you very much, Mr. Chung. This food is so delicious that I've eaten too much of it. I can't eat another bite. Thank you. And thank you, Mr. Chow, for hosting tonight. Everything has been perfect.'

Mr. Chung grins like I've just mistaken him for George Clooney, and Mr. Chow nods graciously. I've scored again.

As we make our way back through the hotel lobby after dinner, me trying not to waddle, Josh says, 'Thanks again, Hannah. That was a success.' He's grinning like a proud parent.

'No problem, it was fun… As you know, I've messed up a bit in my past jobs. I think you're a good boss for me. You never make me feel like I can't do something. That makes a difference.'

'Well, I'm very pleased that I hired you,' he says as we wait for the elevator. 'It's nice to know that my instincts were right…' He trails off, scanning the quiet lobby. 'I see a future for you, Hannah.'

How long have I waited to hear this? Only my entire adult life. Granted, I may not have always been very career-focused, so maybe I didn't consciously realize I wanted to hear praise from my boss. But there's no denying that this feels good, and it would have been nice to hear before now. This might actually mean I have a career, like grown-ups do. 'Thanks, Josh, you have no idea how good that is to hear. And–' I check my watch. 'Just minutes into my birthday too.'

He holds the elevator door open for me before pushing the button to our floor. 'It's your birthday? Why didn't you say something?' Consternation clouds his face. 'I hope this trip didn't scupper any birthday plans you had. You could have come along next time, you know. You should have said something.'

'No, no, it's fine, really. I didn't have any plans tonight. The celebration is tomorrow. It's just dinner with a few friends. If you wanted to come…'

The doors open. He looks a bit startled. Whether at the doors or my question, I'm not sure. 'Thank you, Hannah, I'd really like that.'

I shouldn't have asked him. Especially now, after a boozy dinner. I hope he doesn't get the wrong idea. Because I'm only asking to be nice, and because he's been so nice to me. Surely he understands that.

'Well, I'll see you tomorrow then. Eight-thirty for breakfast? Good,' he says as we reach our adjacent rooms. 'Sleep well.'

'Thanks, you too. Goodnight.'

He leans in and kisses me on the cheek. 'Happy birthday,' he says softly.

12

I think Josh has the wrong idea. Or else I'm being paranoid because the idea that he's got the wrong idea is lodged in my head. Or, possibly, the birthday drinks Stacy has already bought me have lodged in my head. I think it's one of the first two, though, based on mounting circumstantial evidence. First, when Josh and I met for breakfast at the hotel this morning, he toasted my birthday – with orange juice, it was 9 a.m. after all. Possibly that's just a friendly thing to do, but then, after meetings all day, he insisted on a sightseeing tour before we went to the airport for our flight back. He wanted to show me the Hakka houses he mentioned yesterday. He had the driver take us out of town to see them.

At first, glimpsing them from our mountain road, they looked like giant storage containers. It was only when we got closer that I saw the windows in the outer walls. They're essentially donut-shaped apartment buildings, ancient, vaguely coliseum-like, with families' apartments ringed around an open courtyard. It was very cool and otherworldly, a glimpse of old China. But that's not the point. Josh took us out of our way to show them to me. Again, that could be interpreted as a friendly gesture after I showed an interest in his conservation activities.

But now he's handed me a gaily wrapped package. In front of my friends. And Winnie, my colleague, his employee. 'It's just a little something. Go on, open it,' he urges.

'You shouldn't have, Josh! I didn't expect a gift, really. It's… Wow!' It's a key chain. With an orange and blue leather bowling shoe dangling from it. It never occurred to me that I gave off bowling vibes. 'Thanks very much.'

'What an ugly little thing!' Winnie accurately declares.

He laughs. 'I looked for a proper shoe but that's all they had in duty-free. I know you recently moved into your new flat, and I thought you could use it. It's just a token really.'

'Ah, I see. I like it, thanks!'

'That's very sweet of you, Josh,' Stacy purrs. 'Hannah never stops talking about how much she loves her job, you know.' She reaches for her phone as a text chimes.

'He knows, Stace, I tell him all the time,' I point out as she smiles at her message. 'I'm not exactly a poker face, am I?'

It's really rather embarrassing how grateful I am for my job. But after being treated like the gum on the bottom of my last boss's Blahnik, it's tremendous to feel appreciated.

'I think it's great,' Josh says. 'To have someone working with me who's as enthusiastic as Hannah. I told her when she interviewed that I was looking for a breath of fresh air for the company.' He gazes warmly at me. 'I definitely got that.'

That's not something a boss would normally say *in that tone*. I'm not being paranoid. Am I? I hate that I don't trust my own judgment. It's because of yesterday's phone call with Sam. I'm reading into everything now, and behaving like a spurned wife. Everything with him feels open to interpretation. I thought I was okay with our situation. When we first talked, I was sure I understood what was going on, and I was comfortable with it. I felt secure. I felt like I knew what Sam was thinking. Now I don't. Is it the distance that's doing it? Or is time making me forget the details of our talk that made me feel secure? My memory is shifting, slipping and leaving just tips exposed. I can't see what was underneath. And I still don't know whether he heard my declaration on the phone. When he called this morning to wish me happy birthday I chickened out. My heart dared my mouth to repeat those three all-important words but my brain scared it into keeping quiet. My brain's probably right. That's not the kind of conversation you have while rushing to meet your boss. It's going to have to wait until we see each other.

'That text was from Pete,' Stacy says, waving her phone at me. 'He says happy birthday and wonders what you're doing tonight… could I invite him along?'

'I don't know what you see in him.'

'Han, he's your boyfriend's best friend. You'd better get used to him, for your own good. I keep telling you that you just got off on the wrong foot. He's really nice. He thought to wish you happy birthday, didn't he?'

'I suppose.' I sigh. 'Fine, invite him if you want.' With everyone else here, I won't have to talk to him.

'Happy birthday, Hannah,' Brent and Stuart chorus on arrival. Of course they do. 'I got you a drink,' says Brent.

'We got you a drink,' Stuart corrects. 'We can't stay long, but wanted to wish you glad tidings and many happy returns.'

'Thank you.' I grin, accepting my champagne. 'Brent, Stuart, this is Winnie. We work together. And this is Josh, our boss.' Everybody shakes or kisses according to etiquette. 'You two must be the busiest men in Hong Kong. Do you ever have just one engagement in an evening?'

'That's for when we're old,' says Brent. 'Besides, I'm single. I've got to keep my hand in the game. Not like Stuart. He's one step away from a pipe and slippers, cooking dinners with his *girlfriend*.'

'I am not.'

'Are too. You may as well get married. You never come out anymore.'

Stuart gestures to himself and the bar as evidence of the flaw in his brother's statement. 'And we're going together to dinner, aren't we? Jesus, you sound like a nagging wife. I swear he becomes more like a girl every day.'

'Hey, watch it!' says Stacy. 'We're not all naggers.'

'Not you, I know, Stace. You're like a man with breasts.'

'Thanks. I think.'

Am I a nagger? I shouldn't have to think about this question on my birthday, but there it is, intruding on the party. Surely most of our unpleasant behavior when it comes to men is the direct result of said man. If he's not acting like a jerk then there's nothing for me to nag about. I haven't nagged Sam very much. Have I? Memories of uncomfortable conversations are now joining the nagging question at the party. Maybe I nag a little bit. Must try harder.

Stacy and Josh have become engrossed in conversation. 'The book was so much better!' Claims Josh.

'But Audrey Hepburn made the film. And I liked that there was a love story.'

'So you're a romantic.'

'God, no. I'm not, am I Han?' Her face says she'd rather be told she has BO.

'You are a bit, don't you think?' I say. 'You're very optimistic about the men you date, and I think you always hope for the best. That's romantic. But I agree with you, the film was way better than the book. Unlike *Gone with the Wind*.'

'Ah, a classic,' says Josh. 'Personally I never approved of the last half of the film. Too much war, war, war, and all the beautiful clothes disappeared.'

'Spoken like a fashion exporter,' I tease. 'Margaret Mitchell wrote such an incredible character in Scarlett, didn't she? I'd back her in a battle against any of the other famous literary heroines. She's scrappy.'

'It takes one to know one,' Josh says.

Okay, that's flirting by any standard. I don't have any response. Luckily, Brent returns from his shagability reconnaissance, grinning. 'See someone you like?' I ask.

'About half the bar,' he says, nodding.

'Go talk to someone then,' Stacy urges. Josh and

Brent trade looks. 'What? Have I said something wrong? Offended your sense of propriety?'

'No, no.' He puts his arm around my friend. 'Stacy, Stacy, Stacy, there are some things you should know about Hong Kong.' He looks like he's about to break the truth to her about the Tooth Fairy. 'Let me ask you this. How often have you been approached in a bar here?'

'I don't know.' She's blushing. 'A bit, I guess.'

'As much as back in the States?'

'Well, no. What's your point? Have I grown ugly here?'

'Not at all! You're definitely top one per cent.'

'So where's the problem?'

'The problem is, we've had it too good for too long. We live in a backwards bubble here. We don't have to do any chasing, so we don't. Am I right, Winnie?'

'You're right. We are very aggressive here. We approach the men.'

'White women too?' Stacy asks.

'Stacy!' I admonish.

'What? I can say white women, can't I? I am white – we are white. Everybody can see that.'

'Of course you can,' says Winnie. 'We know you're white. Don't worry about being too PC here. We're not. Yes, white women too. We're all in the same boat.'

'And because of that, men have devolved evolutionarily,' Brent continues. 'Really, ladies, you've not done yourselves, or us, any favors here. You've dulled our instincts with your kindness. We can no longer fend for ourselves like they did in caveman times. We've lost the ability to club women over the head and drag them back to our caves.'

'And that's a bad thing?' I ask.

'Not as long as we stay in Hong Kong. The women do the chasing here, so we don't have to. But if I went back to the UK I'd die alone in Stuart's spare room.'

Josh is nodding.

'Is this true?' I ask.

'I'm afraid it is. It's not very nice for the women who constantly have to be in pursuit, but it's great for us! We can be lazy, which is our essential nature anyway.'

'Great, thanks. Happy birthday to me.'

'Don't let it get you down, Han,' Stacy says. 'We'll chase men when we have to.'

'I'm not down, I don't need–' But I am down, aren't I? Because this dating realization has mixed with my Sam-uncertainty about as well as this champagne is mixing with the martini I had earlier. In just a few weeks I've gone from securely in love with my boyfriend to insecurely in love with my... what is he now? If you're going out with other people when you have a boyfriend, that's cheating. Surely, then, that means if your boyfriend says you can see other people, then you're not his girlfriend. You're his – bit of fun. Label-conscious I may be, but this is not one that I covet, thank you very much.

'We can, can't we?' Stacy is patting my arm. 'We've got no plans tomorrow, right?'

'I'm sorry? I... I wasn't listening.'

'Josh invited us to his club tomorrow, to go out on a junk.'

'I'd love for you to come out,' he says. 'We can

have lunch and then take the boat around the island… if you're free,' he finishes politely.

'Oh, oh yes, thanks, Josh, that'll be nice. It'll be cooler on the water,' I finish vaguely, still thinking about labels.

By the time Pete makes good on his threat to disrupt my birthday half an hour later, I just want to go home. 'Happy birthday,' he says, making no move to kiss. I'm grateful for this. No need to pretend social niceties that we don't feel. 'Have you had a nice day?'

'Yes, thanks,' I say formally. 'I've just come back from China, for work, so the celebration got delayed a bit.'

'I assume you've talked to Sam already?'

'Yes, of course I've talked to Sam. He called first thing this morning. After all, it's my birthday, and he's my boyfriend.'

'I guess that would be expected. Shame he couldn't be here this weekend, isn't it?'

Is he purposely trying to stir things up? 'Not really. I mean, I don't mean I don't want to see him. But I was supposed to be there this weekend, so it's not like he didn't plan to see me. The job thing only came up last minute, so I had to cancel.'

'I thought you were going to Phuket this weekend with Stacy. Did those plans change too? That's a shame.'

Stacy looks surprised to hear this, but doesn't blow my cover. 'If you must know, Sam asked me to go to Ho Chi Minh instead and… and Stacy and the guys understood. Like I said, it was only at the last minute that I had to cancel for work.'

He smiles, shaking his head. 'There's a lot of

uncertainty in long-distance relationships, huh? I couldn't do it. I'd miss the girl too much to be away from her like that. And I wouldn't take last-minute changes as well as Sam obviously does. Different arrangements work for different people, I guess.'

'Maybe you couldn't handle it because you'd be too insecure.'

'I guess so. I'm just saying that if I were Sam, I'd want to be here all the time.'

'What makes you think he doesn't want to be here all the time? Pete, he has to do this for work. It's not like he wants to be away.'

'Right, time for another drink,' Stacy neatly cuts me off. 'Han, come with me. Pete, what would you like?'

She drags me to the crowded bar. 'Hannah, you need to stop this. You're being very defensive when Pete isn't even being rude. Why do you have such a problem with him? He's Sam's best friend. Is that it? Are you jealous of him or something?'

'No, don't be ridiculous. I've told you. It's because he's rude to me.'

'Is he being rude now?'

'Why would he ask if I've talked to Sam if he wasn't trying to stir things up?'

'Er, because he's best friends with Sam and he's making polite conversation. Really, Hannah, I was standing next to you the whole time. He is not being rude.'

'I just don't like him.'

'Fine, then talk to Winnie and Josh when we go back to the group. I'll talk to Pete. But you should consider why you've got such a problem with him. If he's not being rude then maybe it's you who has the problem. And it's not going to end well if you hate your boyfriend's best friend. Just think about it.'

I didn't have to think much about it last night. Luckily Pete left after one drink. I just don't understand how he can seem so normal to everyone else. He's a subversive genius, always saying two things at once. Clearly he's unhappy about Sam and me. The question is, why? It must be jealousy. It can't be personal because I've never done anything to him, and he was rude from the first time we met. I guess he resents that Sam wants to spend time with me when he comes to Hong Kong. He should be happy for his best friend, instead of begrudging him his relationship.

I can't talk to Sam about it. What if Stacy's right? Then he'll think I'm paranoid. I don't want that clouding his view of me. We talked this morning and, once again, I'm confused. It wasn't that he was awkward or stand-offish. It was that he wasn't. He was wonderfully romantic and sweet and funny, exactly like he was when we were together in London. Exactly like every time we've seen each other here. I had the most secure, happy feeling when we hung up. He's coming next weekend. He's already planned the whole thing, without colleagues this time. And yet the fact remains: a boyfriend doesn't tell his girlfriend she can see other people. It doesn't matter that his behavior gives me absolutely no reason to feel insecure or sad or the least bit doubtful about our relationship. Something's not right about it.

Our walk to Josh's club gives me twenty sweaty minutes to ponder this uncomfortable fact. We should have taken a cab. Despite their drivers' universal inability to a) drive safely or b) understand me when I tell them where I'm going, there's something pleasant, if a little terrifying, about careening through the city's steep streets in the little red and white icons. Instead, we've walked in what feels like a city-sized steam room. The air clogs my lungs and the feeling of sweat popping out all over my skin, soaking my T-shirt, is about as pleasant as you'd imagine it would be. Stacy pointed out that sweat is good for hangovers. I bet a fried breakfast in an air-conditioned restaurant would be even better.

The guard at the club's entrance watches us curiously when we duck under the traffic arm. We have, after all, arrived at the parking lot with nothing to park. 'Morning,' I call. 'We're meeting one of your members inside.'

He waves us through with a careless shrug. Clearly his is a ceremonial post.

'Wow this is pretty, and right on the water!' Stacy says before snorting at the astuteness of her perception. We are at a boat club. An inland marina wouldn't have the same seafaring appeal. 'Please kick me under the table if I say stupid things like that later.' Ever the good friend, I promise to aim for her shins at the next gaff.

Josh is waiting for us in reception, looking relaxed and casual in a golf shirt and chinos. His hair is even more sticky-uppy than usual, and I notice he isn't wearing socks. Very boaty. 'Welcome!' he says, kissing us both on the cheeks. 'You found it all right? Good. We can have lunch any time, but if you're not hungry yet, why don't I give you a quick tour and then we can have a drink in the bar?'

Inside is colonial and charming, though the white concrete, curved exterior isn't what you'd imagine housing a hundred-year-old sailing club. It's designed a bit like a cruise ship, which I suppose gives it a nautical theme. Josh tells us it was built in the thirties but the club was around from the eighteen hundreds. 'The former headquarters is in Central now,' he explains.

'They moved the building?' Stacy asks incredulously.

'No,' he replies, laughing. 'They moved the land, which sounds even more incredible, doesn't it? The club was on the harbor front when it was first established of course. But the British decided they'd quite like more colony in their colony, so they simply expanded it. There was once water on the other side of Connaught Road, you know, where the Mandarin Hotel is?'

'I do know the Mandarin, great bar!' Stacy says. 'Do you remember when that was waterfront?'

'Stacy, I'm not that old. The planners filled it at the end of the nineteenth century. But I was around for the more recent projects. At the rate they're going, soon we'll be able to walk to Kowloon.'

The bar we enter is as yachty as I imagined it would be, with a dark wood-paneled ceiling and walls, and trophy cases displaying silver cups won in races around the world by the members. The long bar has been thoughtfully padded with leather at its edges, to keep the boatmen from bruising in their post-race enthusiasm. The top of the bar has at least a million layers of varnish on it, and looks like it's polished nightly by a cabin boy. Carved wooden seahorses grace the wall behind the bar. A ship's bell hangs from the wall, reminding me of the last orders bells in London's bars. Over the door hangs a lifeguard ring donated, it says, by the sailors on the HMS Vengeance. Plaques full of tiny flags, boats' insignias I think, cover one wall.

I've always loved the idea of sailing. It's one of those sexy skills that bring to mind safety and security, immense level-headedness, coordination and athleticism. None of which describes me, and is probably why I don't sail.

'Shall we take our drinks on to the veranda?' Josh proposes.

I don't object, since he's our host, but within thirty seconds I'm shiny. I can feel my thighs sweating. I should have asked for a frozen drink. I could have clasped it between my knees. 'Josh, how do you keep from melting in the heat?'

'It just takes getting used to. I was born here so I've had my whole life to acclimatize. My advice would be to stay in the air con as much as possible in the summer.'

'Easier said than done when we've got to get to our offices,' Stacy points out. 'I get sweaty just riding the escalator. I'm going to start wearing workout gear into work and changing when I'm there. I'm spending a fortune on dry cleaning.'

'Ah, speaking of which, you shouldn't keep things in the plastic bags when you get them back. They'll mildew. If you haven't got dehumidifiers for your flat, you might want to get some. Otherwise your shoes and handbags will go furry...' He grins. 'Isn't Hong Kong delightful?'

I roll my eyes, but I do still think it's delightful. Even with the whole Sam situation, I'm very glad I'm here.

'I'm guessing your family have been members here since the old days?' Stacy asks Josh. 'Are you a big sailing family?'

He nods. 'My grandfather came to Hong Kong when he was young and started the business just after the war. Grandmother was furious – life wasn't easy in London then, what with the rationing and everything, but she preferred bombsites and food shortages to a colonial outpost away from friends and family. Grandfather was determined though. He saw no way of making a success of himself in post-war Britain, so he put his foot down. Today she'd probably have stayed in London and let him chase his dreams here. They'd have just Skyped. But in those days a wife willingly staying behind, without children as an excuse, was unconventional. They were still Victorian enough to mind about those things. Besides, I think she loved Grandfather, and was grateful to have him back from the war. She didn't want to be separated from him again. So she packed up the house and moved them here. I remember her as a rather mean woman actually, but then I was only a child when she died… What was I talking about? Oh yes, the club. Grandfather joined when my father was a boy. My father sailed his whole life, so I grew up sailing too. You must be a sailor or rower to become a member. Goodness, I'm going on aren't I? Are you hungry?'

We shake our heads.

'I have a proposition then. Why don't I call Winnie now and see if she's ready? We can start the trip early and I'll have some food stocked in case we'd like to eat later. That way we can enjoy the day.' He gestures to the hazy scene before us. The harbor is choppy and full of ferries and boats. It reminds me of New York Harbor, a bit dirty and gritty. We're about to see what the rest of the island looks like from the water.

The 'junk' isn't what I expected at all. It's supposed to be an old-fashioned sailing boat, made of burnished dark wood. With sails. Instead, we're boarding a powerboat that would look more at home in Miami. I can see Stacy is thinking the same thing.

'Is this yours?' She says diplomatically, eyeing the cabin boys scurrying around as the captain barks orders. It's a rather big boat.

'No, they're very expensive to keep. Besides, I've got my sailboat. We hire them when we want. That way there's no fuss and we don't have to do any of the work.'

He hired a boat for us. That's impressive. Is it meant to be impressive? And who is he trying to impress? If it's me, this is very bad. Quite aside from the fact that I'm seeing Sam, Josh is my boss. I cannot have a fling with my boss again, not after London. And I don't want to. As nice as he is, and as smart and funny and I suppose all-right looking from some angles, I'm not attracted to him like that. I hope we'll be compatible colleagues for many years to come, but I've got no interest in being sexually compatible with him. Of course, maybe I'm just being paranoid. It does seem to be a common theme. I need a debrief with Stacy but I can't very well have a heart to heart while the subject for discussion is pouring us drinks.

'Sorry! Sorry I'm late!' Winnie hurries down the pier trying to hold on to her giant floppy hat while keeping her kitten heels from catching between the boards. Despite her rush she looks icebox-cool, and her floaty little dress is perfect for boating. Now I feel sweaty and underdressed in my T-shirt, white capris and ballet shoes. But I suppose Winnie always makes me feel like a fashion mutant. It may be a cultural difference that I'll have to get used to. Chinese women here are always meticulously turned out, and there's no such thing as too many labels. If Estée Lauder ever figures out how to get its moisturizer to spell its name out on a woman's forehead, I expect Winnie will be branded the next day.

I'm glad to see her, and not just because it makes Josh's generous rental seem less inappropriate. She's becoming my friend even though we usually only go out for lunch together. She hasn't invited me for drinks since the night after Missus Reese's sabotage (I'm convinced that's what it was). It makes me wonder about the cultural divide here – Chinese and expats don't seem to mix very much socially. Maybe it's a language barrier, though Winnie corrects my English often enough to make me suspect it's not that. I guess she's got her own life outside of work, with her own friends.

'You look great!' I tell her. 'Beautiful shoes! I mean beautiful *hai*.'

Winnie's hand flies to her mouth. 'Hannah, you mean haii. Like a long hi. At least I hope so.'

'That's what I said. *Hai*.'

'Stop saying that! It means… it's a very bad word. '

'I mean shoes. How bad?'

'The worst,' she confirms, pointing to her crotch. I've just complimented her vagina. No wonder she doesn't introduce me to her friends. 'Promise you won't say it around clients, okay?' she pleads. 'English is fine. Your *haii* are nice too. But that's – that's not your new dress…'

'No.' I sigh. 'Nothing's ready yet. I'll go back next week.' Despite Mr. Chan's rather gruff assertions that my ill-fitting clothes were the result of my indulgence rather than his tailoring, my clothes still didn't fit when I went back on Thursday. He knew better than to blame this on any weakness of mine, but it still means he's holding half my wardrobe hostage to his needle for another week. This time, he promised, we'd get it right. I hope so. I'm getting tired of letting him feel my inseam.

The harbor is crowded with other junks, and the captain negotiates the choppy water slowly. Then, a different Hong Kong starts to unfold. It's not that the skyscrapers are gone. All along the shoreline, clusters of buildings perch close to the water, as if bullied from behind by the imposing dark green mountains. But instead of housing law firms and banks as they do in Central, they house Hong Kongers, stacked on top of each other for fifty stories or more. Balconies on every apartment make the buildings look like upended air filters. It's a vision of contrasts. All I have to do is look over the opposite rail and I see steep, foliage-carpeted islands jutting from the water, and boats bobbing on whitecaps. As we motor further from the harbor, the high-rises peter out. A nature reserve, and then a wide beach.

'This is wonderful!' I say, with some feeling.

'I'm glad you like it!' Josh shouts back above the wind. 'Shall we stop for a swim?'

'I didn't bring a swimsuit.' And I certainly don't

plan to bare my thighs to my boss.

'Oh, okay, another time then. We can continue round to Repulse Bay. It's a big beach and quite built up. After that we'll come to Stanley. There're a few nice restaurants at an old colonial building on the waterfront there... What is it? Is something wrong?'

My face has given me away. 'Well, I just wondered. Is all of Hong Kong so Western? I mean, I expected it to be more Chinese.' I shoot a glance at Winnie. 'No offence. I don't mean that you're not Western. I mean-'

'Don't worry,' she says. 'I know what you mean. Gweilos are always surprised that it isn't an old colony and we don't all run around with rice paper hats and chopsticks.'

'I didn't mean to offend you,' I say quietly.

'No, I'm not offended! I'm just not saying it right. What I mean is that most white people think we're hiding the "real" Hong Kong, that our traditional houses are all hidden away from Westerners. But Chinese want modern things. We don't like old buildings or old ways.'

'That's why it's so hard to be a conservationist in China,' Josh affirms. 'I know what you mean, Hannah. You expected to see some of the traditional Hong Kong here. It is there... it's just tucked away. Behind a façade.' He elbows Winnie. 'Shall we show her, Winnie?'

'You're the boss.' She smiles.

'You don't have to be anywhere soon, do you?' Josh wonders.

'Erm...' Stacy looks sheepish. 'I've got plans at six.'

'What plans?' I ask.

Her sheepishness deepens. 'I'm meeting Pete.'

'Why? Does he have some puppies he'd like you to help him kick? Planning to knock a few old ladies over in the street?'

'It sounds like you really like Pete,' Josh teases.

'He's Sam's friend,' Stacy explains. 'And he's very nice. He and Hannah just got off on the wrong foot, that's all. It was a misunderstanding.'

Somehow I still doubt that.

Josh doesn't say another word about where we're going. He goes to speak to the captain and a few minutes later the boat turns back towards Central.

'What is this place?' Stacy asks an hour later as we pass several battered fishing boats anchored in the mouth of what looks like a river.

'Tai O,' Winnie says. 'Here's your traditional Hong Kong. Though even back in the old days most people didn't live like this.'

'It's an isolated community,' Josh explains. 'They're called Tanka and the village has been here for centuries. The people have always lived in these houses on stilts. They feel safer living on the water.'

We're motoring slowly through the somewhat narrow waterway, between rows of mostly single-story buildings raised at least six feet from the water on stilts. They're a motley collection, and colorful in their extreme decay. Corrugated iron roofs have drawn rusty stains down the outside walls, some of which were painted once, now faded. Almost all have covered porches, although some are boarded up with a ragtag assortment of weather-beaten plywood and tarpaulin. The owners' boats are tied to rickety ladders leading from the brownish-yellow water to the porches. Yellow or blue flags flutter atop many of the houses, and nets and other fishing accoutrements hang from the porch's edge.

'Is this more your idea of Hong Kong?' Winnie asks.

'Definitely. But surely not everyone was as poor and isolated as this. Were they?'

'Of course not,' Winnie says. 'But until the last few decades most people lived in places you'd consider poor. The housing starts to look old very quickly here, because of the heat and rainy season, and crowding. It's a crowded city. There isn't enough money for everyone to be rich. But we'd all like to be!' She grins. 'And who knows? It's a new China now!'

It's nearing sunset when we motor back to the marina. Stacy shrugs when I point out that she'll be late for Pete. 'This is worth it,' she says, hugging my shoulder. 'We're so lucky.'

'I know. Josh is–'

'I don't mean this, today. I mean we're lucky to be here. Han, think of everything that brought us here. You getting fired, seeing that billboard, deciding to move to London, getting the job there, meeting Sam, finding Josh's company. You're very lucky. We're very lucky.'

Squeezing my friend back, I think about my fortune cookie. *Following your heart will pay off in the near future.* I suppose maybe it will.

13

It's not every Friday night that a girl gets to snub her boss and a table full of important clients. So it must be my unlucky night. I don't know how tardiness is viewed in Hong Kong but judging by their looks I'm guessing that when it's combined with my favorite clubbing outfit, it's not favorable.

'I'm so sorry I'm late,' I say again to Josh. 'I thought we were meeting at eight-thirty.' Because that's what Missus Reese told me. I don't even have a jacket to put over my shoulders. I feel like a Christmas ornament.

'I'm glad nothing happened to you, I was getting worried when you didn't answer your phone.'

I note that he hasn't said 'that's okay'. Because clearly it isn't. Everyone smiles as we are introduced, but I know I've screwed up.

When Josh asked me to this dinner, he went to great lengths to emphasize that it was an important one. Twice a year he hosts his best suppliers by flying them to Hong Kong to wine and dine. And dance. Or so I was told. To be specific, Missus Reese explained that these were hospitality events and that the men invited (because there are only men around the table with me now) see the trip as one almighty boondoggle. I was led to believe that dinner was merely a vehicle to line the stomach before we hit the town for a night of dancing and debauchery. Hence my outfit.

But we're in a very staid, very Chinese, very covered-up restaurant. Nobody looks like they're going dancing. Some don't even look like they walked in here without assistance. The few women at other tables are all wearing suits or dresses with demure jackets. Hermès scarves protect necklines. No knees dare show themselves. And then there's me. Pewter sequined tank top with contrasting black strappy bra that stubbornly makes an appearance every time I lean forward. Black skinny jeans and my favorite taxi shoes – five-inch platforms that make my toes go numb but are so worth it. 'I'm sorry,' I whisper again to Josh, unhelpfully punctuating my apology by flashing my bra.

That work permit isn't getting any more likely.

At least the waiters quickly descend to fill the awkward silence with dumplings. Thanks to Stacy, now I know, mostly, how to eat. I don't stick my chopsticks in my rice (it means death) or cross them (bad luck), never take the last morsel, or eat the last bit on my plate (sorry Mom, I know, all the starving people in China… well, it's their rule so I follow it), and always use serving chopsticks instead of my own when taking more. Her bank signed her up for a cultural course, so she doesn't mortally offend anyone accidentally. In her line of work, mortal offence should only be done on purpose.

Over the delicious dumplings I watch Josh working the table, trying to make amends for me. Like those buskers who spin plates on sticks, he manages to keep everyone chatting. Some people have such a knack for putting others at ease and making them think they're the center of attention. It comes so naturally to him that he probably doesn't even know he does it… which makes me realize that I've been stupid. And paranoid. He's just a nice man. *That's why* he bought me the ugly shoe key chain, and invited Stacy and me on the boat. I couldn't be fuller of myself. Not everyone wants to sleep with me.

Josh's attention turns to me while I'm chasing a dumpling around my plate. 'A lot of our buying choices were down to Hannah this year, gentlemen. She's got quite a knack for spotting future trends. She nailed the restraint that women are showing in their fashion decisions. We've had record orders from the shops for next season.' I blush at his compliment.

'Yes, we were very happy with your orders from us,' says the man across the table. 'Tell me, Hannah, what's in store for the future then? What will women want after the next season?'

Suddenly the table is quiet, waiting for me to answer. How am I supposed to know? I can't say the same thing I said to Josh about next season. But I'd better say something. 'Well. Erm.' Think, think. What have I seen lately? Only too-tiny clothes that I can't wear, which is no help. And it's not like Mr. Chan has come through for me. Gosh, it's been a long time since I've had anything new to wear. Wait a minute. Wait. A. Minute. I think Chloe is the answer.

'Well, I have this friend,' I start, wondering myself where it's going. 'She's a little scatty, and often buys the same thing twice by accident. Which I guess is a vote of confidence for the item of clothing, right, if it appeals so much even after you've bought it? Anyway, we were talking the other day – she lives in London, where I lived last year. That's how we met. We were talking and she mentioned that she was taking some things back to the stores for refunds. Finally! I've been telling her to do this for ages. She needs to go through her closets at least once a month and look for duplicates. You'd be surprised how many she has. We, her friends, have benefitted from her forgetfulness since she gives the extras away, but she's not made of money. She's a recruiter. Well, Josh, you remember, I told you about her when you asked about next year's trend. Jeez, here she is again. Maybe she's my muse… Anyway, the point is that she should be returning these things instead to get the refund. Some are quite expensive. So I was happy when she told me she'd taken a bunch of stuff back. But the clerks wouldn't give her a refund, only credit. When I was in London I used to return things for her – it's easier for an American I think. We're not afraid to argue. But Chloe could only spend the credit in the store, and she had to find things that she liked, but hadn't bought before. As I said, this isn't always easy. To minimize the risk, she went to the one section where she shops less often: lingerie. She bought the loveliest under things, and she said she felt indulgent but a little guilty. Then she said, "But nobody can see them so they're my little secret." It seems to me that that's how women are starting to feel – like we're in this recession and opulence is frowned on, but we still love beautiful things. So we'll look for opulence that's a bit hidden. It might be fantastic underwear, or a beautiful flash of colored lining in a jacket, a purse with a gorgeous pattern inside or unbelievably soft leather on our shoes.'

Not *hai*, do not *say soft leather on our vaginas* to the clients.

'We want opulence, we just don't want everyone to be able to see it.'

The whole table has either gone to sleep or didn't understand a word I just said. Great, Hannah, babbling to a table full of Chinese men whose first language isn't English. Well done.

'That's very interesting,' says the man to my right. I gather that he's the most senior of the exporters. I gather this because the fish head is pointed at him. Dead animal heads may not be your usual sign of respect in the West. It certainly wasn't the case in *The Godfather*. But in China the guest of honor gets to stare his dinner in the face.

Suddenly everyone at the table is nodding and smiling. Josh grins at me. 'See? I told you she knows trends. Excellent, Hannah. We know what we'll be looking for from our friends next season, don't we?'

I am glowing with pride. I did it. I really did it, didn't I? I've impressed my boss and made an important contribution to our business. That means my pitch last month wasn't a fluke. It was no lucky guess that won us record business (record business!). Maybe I really am cut out for this job. It wasn't just wishful thinking that made me apply to thirty-eight exporters in the hope of being given a chance. I really can do this! Take that, Missus Reese, you old crone. I will not let you win.

'Thank you, Josh, for giving me a chance,' I murmur.

'No, thank you, Hannah, for finding us.'

I can't wait to tell Sam about my triumph at dinner when he arrives the next morning. We're walking hand in hand, ducking down narrow passages, through a Hong Kong that is no longer shiny glass and exhaust fumes.

'So then I said, "We want opulence, we just don't want everyone to be able to see it."'

He stops walking so he can hold my face, look into my eyes and kiss me. 'That's wonderful, Hannah, I am so proud of you. I've always known you'd do well… Do you remember when you got mad at me for saying you were better than your job at M&G? I was right. You've got the ability to go very far. You're talented in fashion, Han. I know I've made fun of it in the past, but that's just because I'm a man. I don't want you to think I'm making fun of you. Because I think you are remarkable.'

Oh, am I now? If I'm so remarkable, why is he fine about us seeing other people? I kiss him back, still wondering.

I know he suggested the walk to try to make everything seem as normal as possible but the fact remains, it's not normal. Not when I had to kiss him good morning at the airport early this morning, instead of just rolling over. Even so, my heart skips every time he looks at me. I love being with him. No matter what the circumstances, I am in love with him. Heaven help me.

Tiny shrines dot the pavement. Some look like upended shoeboxes painted red, gaily decorated with gold Chinese characters and ribbons. Others are more firmly built into the shop's outer wall, filled with little statues and plates of food. Most have incense sticks that perfume the air.

We turn down another alley, now aware that it's a game of how-lost-can-we-get. All along the street are little shop-front temples, like garages, with wide roll-up doors. This is a locals' street, nothing in English and no white faces.

We hover uncertainly outside one, peering into its dim interior. Eventually the old woman near the entrance smiles toothlessly and beckons us inside. It's close and warm, the summer's humidity mingling with smoke wafting from large incense coils that hang overhead, waiting to drop live ash on the faithful. Sam squeezes my hand as we stare into a murky glass display case filled with hundreds of small statues. It's tatty and intriguing and wonderful. Being with Sam is wonderful.

A little further along, another alley drops us in the middle of a street market. Unlike London, where markets usually means fashion, bric-a-brac or East End traders selling fruit and veg, this market stocks fresh food. I wouldn't mind if we were talking about plums or tomatoes. These aren't plums or tomatoes. Hanging from hooks in the oppressive heat is an array of animal carcasses. They remind me of an exhibition I once saw, of skinned animals and humans in surprisingly lifelike poses. Those hanging here in the heat aren't meant to be anatomy lessons, they're meant to be dinner. 'Is that…? It's a tail!' I gasp. 'A skinned tail. What animal do you think it came from?'

'Ox,' Sam says definitively.

'Oh? Do you see a lot of those in Wyoming to be such an expert?'

'Oxtail, Han, as in soup?'

'Oh. I thought that was just an expression. That's

actually an ox's tail in my soup?' I'll stick to chicken noodle.

Further into the market is the seafood aisle. There's not a fish finger in sight (or a freezer, for that matter). Instead, there are whole fish in red plastic bowls. They're not on ice, they're in water... 'They aren't alive, are they?' I ask Sam, who's staring as uncertainly as I am.

'No. At least, not most of them. They are fresh though, aren't they? In some parts of China they eat live fish. You know, while they're alive. Japan too, I think.'

'I feel a bit ill just thinking about it.'

'Do you want to go?' He tucks a lock of hair behind my ear. It's such a comforting gesture.

'Yes please. I don't see myself shopping for meat here. This is all a little too close to nature for me. How about if we go to Stanley? Josh suggested it when we were on the junk a few weeks ago. He mentioned it again last night when I said you were coming. Hopefully by the time we get there, the memory will wear off enough to be hungry for lunch.' Knowing my stomach, I'm sure it will.

An hour later, we're on a London double-decker bus, which shouldn't be driven around Piccadilly too fast, let alone down Hong Kong's narrow mountain roads. We've just passed a point at the top of the mountain pass, where, looking down the rollercoaster drop ahead, I was tempted to raise my arms and scream. I don't, but that's only because I've got Sam's hand in a death grip and I'm not letting go until our starters are served in the restaurant. He looks like he might take a nap. 'Does nothing faze you?' If I didn't know his anti-drug views I'd suspect he was stoned.

'Your boss was right. This is a great view – look at that!' He cranes his neck to look down the side of the bus, and down the side of the mountain.

'I'm surprised you didn't do this when you first arrived,' I say, realizing immediately that this sounds accusatory.

'Pete and I planned to go once but were out too late the night before. I'm glad I waited.' He smiles and kisses me while I wonder who else was on his late-night jolly. Li Ming?

What is wrong with me? Maybe I have a medical condition that prevents me from enjoying myself with Sam. It shouldn't be this way, should it? It's supposed to be easy, at least at the beginning. We're still in the honeymoon stage. So why do I feel like we're heading for divorce? Stacy says I should just relax. That advice is about as easy to take in this situation as it is when spoken by your gynecologist in the exam room.

I need to talk to Sam about us. I want to know what he's thinking. But I'm afraid to know what he's thinking. But it's better to know. If it's bad then we can deal with it. And if it's good there's no reason for me to feel so angsty. But what if it's bad and we can't deal with it? I don't want to break up. I want to go back to the way things were before. But I can't find the rewind button.

'Do you want to check out the market first?' he asks as we gratefully leave the bus in one piece.

'Will it have tails?'

'I can't make any promises but I don't think so.'

We enter the market, really just a tangle of narrow streets lined with stalls. There are no tails, only cheap clothes. I deal with cheap clothes every day. It's about as exotic as Walmart. Overhead, tarpaulins stretch between the buildings in an attempt to keep out the sun. Deeper into the market we see a random selection of gaily painted paper lanterns, figurines, dazzling arrays of lighters, dolls, beach balls and more cheap clothes. 'Lunch?' Sam asks as we turn a corner into a seemingly identical aisle.

'Yes please.' My stomach is churning, and it's not hunger. Maybe it's because I know I have to talk to Sam. Maybe it's because today isn't all I hoped it would be. I expected the worry to be swept away once he arrived. Instead, it's intensifying with each moment that passes. I've got to talk to him.

The restaurant isn't far away, housed in a beautiful two-story colonial building with wide verandas on Stanley's bay front. Mounting the stone stairs to the black and white tiled veranda feels like walking into the nineteenth century.

'How's your family, by the way?' Sam asks once we've ordered. 'Your mom?'

Sam never asks me about my family. It's not a thoughtless oversight, but a thoughtful one. He knows how much she drives me crazy about living here. 'She's fine, thanks. Why do you ask?'

'Oh no reason really, I talked to my mom last night, that's all.'

'Is yours okay?'

'Yep, she's fine.'

'I mean about your move. I've never asked, have I? Does she mind that you're here? In Vietnam, I mean?'

'Nah, I don't think so. She knows it comes with the territory when your family are all academics. Is your mom any more comfortable with your move?'

'No.' Plus, she refuses to accept that I might actually like living in Hong Kong. No matter how many emails I send describing how great it is here, how much fun I'm having with my friends, she thinks I'll run back to the US if Sam and I break up. Which is definitely not true. 'I don't think I'll ever win that battle.' It's an unwelcome line of thinking. 'So what else is there to see around here?'

'I'm not sure. I think it's just the market and the beach.'

'I'm not really up for the beach. Besides, I don't trust those shark nets.' Hong Kong's beaches are cordoned off to keep the predators from picking off the tourists.

'You don't have to worry. They're very strong nets.'

'That's not the point. I don't like the idea that they have to have nets. It's like drinking gallons of water and popping aspirin before a night out to stave off a hangover. Isn't it just better not to drink too much in the first place?'

'You can't seriously be equating a hangover with man-eaters!'

'Right, exactly my point. Why would I risk being eaten by a shark when I don't even usually risk a hangover?' I'm pleased to have made my point.

'Right...' Sam looks unconvinced. 'Anyway, we won't swim today— 'scuse me a sec,' he says as his phone rings. 'Hello? Hi. That's okay, what's up? You're kidding! You are kidding. That's great. No, it's super. Of course. Fantastic. Absolutely. Thanks, no, thanks for calling. I'll see you Monday. Bye.'

I wait to hear what's so great-super-fantastic.

'That was Li Ming – we got the grant!' He beams.

'Wonderful! What grant?'

'I'm sure I mentioned it. She, we, she really, applied to the World Bank for funding for a two-year-long project. And we got it! Isn't that great?'

'Super, fantastic… Where is the project?'

'It's here, Han, in Hong Kong.' Now he's grinning even more.

Gaahh! 'That's so wonderful, Sam! That means you'll be back here? Soon?'

'As soon as this project finishes, yep, I'll be back in Hong Kong for the duration of the next project. Han, I told you this wouldn't be forever.'

Forever. That's what I hear. Forever. Sam is coming back. I'm dizzy with relief. This is going to be okay. *Following your heart will pay off in the near future.* The near future.

Call me his girlfriend or call me something else. The label doesn't matter. It's what's inside the can that counts.

14

Hong Kong sparkles these days, maybe because I know that Sam is definitely coming back. It's certainly not because the weather is improving. The sky turns from pale blue to near black in minutes, and stepping from air-conditioned buildings is always like being hit in the face with a warm wet washcloth. It's raining nearly every day now, in short but startling bursts. A monsoon's worth of rain can fall from the sky in less time than it takes to duck for cover. The pavements run with water and the streets fill within minutes. Short of a jet pack it's impossible to keep my feet dry, so at some point in the day they're going to look like I've fallen asleep in the bath. Also, this season makes everyone smell of laundry that's been left in the washing machine overnight.

Even so, I love it. I love the shining new buildings and the sleek rooftop bars and the crush of people and dangerous taxis and even the street markets. What a difference a day makes. Or a week, in my case. Sam's announcement turned out to be that reset button I was searching for, making me realize that he probably wasn't acting differently at all. My perception was making me view our relationship differently. What mind games we play with ourselves sometimes.

'Almost ready?' I ask Stacy, who's applying another coat of mascara (waterproof, given the forecast). 'We've got to meet Josh at the pier in half an hour.'

'Ready,' she sings, clearly far from it. 'Oh, Chloe called while you were in the shower.'

She's always doing this. 'Why didn't you tell me when I got out of the shower, two hours ago? Now I haven't got time to call.'

'I forgot,' she says, shrugging.

'You did not. Stacy, why do you still have such a problem with Chloe? Get over it. You don't like her. I get it. But I do like her, so please be an adult. I don't keep your messages from you.'

'Only because nobody calls me on the home phone. Besides, pot, you're one to call this kettle black. You're not exactly nice about Pete.'

'Pete again, really? You don't see why I dislike someone who was rude to me? Who clearly doesn't think I'm good enough for his friend, and said as much when we first met? He's a dick, Stace. I don't know why you're bothering to spend time with him, because he's a dick.'

She stares at me. 'So you have that little faith in me. You think I'd be friends with a dick? And what about Sam? I thought they were supposed to be best friends? Long-time and best friends. His judgment is obviously wrong too then. It must be, or they wouldn't be friends. Or roommates.'

Well, she's got a point there. Here is my best friend, and my boyfriend, and both think this guy is worth spending time with. But then again, don't we all have friends that others don't get along with? Chloe is a perfect example. I know she's an excellent friend and a good person. Stacy can't stand her. That doesn't mean she's a bad person, only that she rubs Stacy the wrong way. So that proves my point. Wait a minute. No it doesn't, it proves Stacy's point.

'All right,' I say. 'If I'm prepared to give Pete another chance, will you promise to be nicer about Chloe? It's not like she's coming to live here, or that you'll probably ever even see her again. You can afford to be gracious.'

She sighs, actually looking contrite. 'That's fair. I'm sorry I didn't tell you she called. I won't do it again.'

'Thanks. And I won't say anything bad about Pete.' I can't promise I won't think it though.

'You can do better than that,' she says, slyly. 'We're meeting up tonight. Want to come?'

I do not. I definitely do not. 'Sure.'

Josh has rented an even bigger boat today, and it's rammed with people. 'Hello, welcome aboard!' He calls when he sees us peering uncertainly at the mayhem. 'You're just in time. The margaritas are ready!'

It's 10.30 a.m. We accept our drinks, kissing our host hello and bracing for a very long day. 'We'll leave in a few minutes to get a good spot,' he says. 'You're going to love this.'

A wave of excitement washes through the boat as its engines start and we pull away from the pier. I jumped at Josh's invitation today. Brent and Stuart rave about the dragon boat races, and we get to see them by boat! That's the holy grail of the day, apparently. I'm not sure why yet, but I feel lucky already. We're not the only ones with the idea though. Dozens of boats are motoring alongside us towards Stanley's bay. Most look like they're on their way to do a swimsuit shoot. Perfectly formed bikini-clad Chinese women are draped across most flat surfaces. Normally this would cause me a bit of competitive angst, but I felt about ten pounds lighter after Li Ming called Sam with her news. Metaphorically, I mean. Even ten pounds lighter I wouldn't look like those Chinese women. But I'm not jealous of them. And I should never have been jealous of Li Ming. Clearly she's just a good boss. What generosity of spirit I'm showing! Every insecurity flew out the window when Sam announced he was coming back to Hong Kong. Or… nearly every insecurity. There is one teeny tiny thing that's been bothering me. It's hardly even worth mentioning. Which is why I haven't told anyone, even Stacy.

Sam and I had a virtually perfect weekend together. Pete was out of town, thankfully, so we cooked dinner at his apartment. It's not somewhere I'd willingly spend a lot of time, but it could be made livable with a woman's touch. And a deep clean. We drank a lot of wine and cuddled on the sofa. Until he fell asleep. Playfully I stroked him. He smiled and shifted position on the sofa, but didn't wake up to put a happy ending on our evening. So I did what any normal girl would do. I shoved him awake, then pretended I hadn't. 'Hi,' I'd said.

'Hmm? Time for bed?' he asked. Definitely! We brushed our teeth, snuggled under the sheets and started kissing. For about a minute. Then he said, 'Sleep well darlin'.' And he went back to sleep. So we had no sex last weekend. I don't think it's a big deal, because sometimes couples just want to cuddle. At most, it's a tiny deal.

We maneuver into position in Stanley Bay. It'll be a miracle if we don't witness a drowning today. Imagine the first day of the Selfridges sale, or opening doors on Black Friday. Then put that chaos into long, narrow rowing boats, in a choppy bay, and add dozens of pleasure craft vying for the best position closest to the racecourse buoys. 'This is insane!'

'I know. It's great, isn't it?' Josh grins. 'It's even more fun to row.'

'You've done this?'

'Sure, for a few years. It's not as hard as it looks. Well, it's hard to see from here. You should be closer to watch… I'll just be back in a mo'.' He trots off to the bow.

'This is incredible!' Stacy gushes. 'Stuart was absolutely green when I told him we were coming today. The bank cancelled the boats they usually hire. Apparently because there's a recession at home we're not allowed to have any fun out here.' She makes a face.

'I guess they'll be over on the shore then.' I can make out the crush of people on the shore. Poor landlocked suckers.

Josh returns, grinning. 'All right, ladies, let's wander over to another boat. You can bring your drinks.'

'Sorry, Josh,' Stacy interjects. 'Wander over to another boat? What are we, Jesus?'

He chuckles, leading us to the rail to wave over an approaching boat. 'My friends are on another boat, over there. This man can ferry us over. Ready? Just step down.' The rickety little craft that I'm aiming for sits at least four feet below ours, bucking in the choppy water. 'Here, I'll hold– You'll have to let go of the rail. No, just–' He sighs. 'Hannah, hold still.'

Eventually the captain grabs my arm and yanks me into his boat to join two couples already aboard.

'Very smooth, Han,' says Stacy, swinging herself into the boat with acrobatic precision.

Slowly we chug between the yachts, picking up and dropping off passengers until finally, Josh stands. 'Here we go.'

The boat we board is even bigger than ours. It's also more crowded, as you'd expect for its position right beside the orange and grey pontoons marking the course's edge. It's overcrowding like this that makes news items ending with 'rescuers are still searching for survivors'.

Josh wrestles a few people aside, in the nicest way possible, and installs us along the bow's rail. 'I'm just going to say hello to my friends. Don't lose your spots – this is prime real estate. I'll be right back, okay?' We assure him we're fine.

'I wonder how many of these people actually know each other?' Stacy muses. 'It looks like one of those house parties we went to in college.'

She's right. Back in school, news of parties spread within hours. Hundreds of students turned up at the bashes, hosted by complete strangers. I was always struck by the generosity, and stupidity, of the renters who willingly risked their security deposits. The level of destruction made a Category 5 hurricane look like a stiff breeze. I haven't been to a party like that in years.

Inside the boat, I begin to hear chants of 'drink, drink, drink, drink' getting louder. I spoke too soon.

I'm at a party like that. I just hope they'll get their security deposit back.

Drumbeats start to float across the water, slow and rhythmic. 'Just in time.' Josh appears at my shoulder, pointing. 'They're getting ready for the next heat.'

Six laden boats make their way from the faraway shore. As they get closer I spot something odd. Each boat comes equipped with a giant kettledrum, wedged between the knees of a girl sitting at the bow. She faces the crew, keeping time for the nine pairs of rowers packed closely together. The boat is no wider than the rowers, and sits dangerously low in the water. At each stern a man stands, steering with what looks like a gondola paddle. 'How does he not fall in?' Stacy wonders. He looks perfectly comfortable despite being on a boat that's bouncing along the waves.

'Sometimes he does,' Josh says. 'And sometimes the boats capsize, but people rarely get hurt. It's an occupational hazard given the choppy water and pumping adrenalin. Look, they're about to start.'

A rather unconvincing air horn sounds, spurring the boats to life. The water churns white as the rowers dig deep with each quick stroke. Everyone is shouting. It's thrilling, but lasts just a minute. The horn sounds again as the first boat crosses the finish line and everyone cheers. It's a bit like having sex with an overexcited man.

'Our friends are in the next heat,' Josh says.

'You weren't tempted to race?' Stacy asks.

'Nah. That's fun but it's more fun to boat-hop and party. As you'll probably have noticed, we Hong Kongers love our traditions when they involve parties.'

I'd noticed. Josh is so lucky to have grown up here.

What a life he must have led, and he's not even forty yet. I can tell Stacy feels the same way. She hasn't stopped grinning since we met the boat…

Wait just a minute. I know that grin. Her thoughts are not on the rowers today. I pounce on her as soon as Josh goes for more drinks. 'Stacy, is there something you'd like to share with the class?'

'Hmm? What do you mean?' she says, watching the boats.

''Fess up, Stace. You like my boss.'

'Well, of course, what's not to like? He's charming and nice and smart, engaging and not at all as ugly as you claimed. In fact, he's downright handsome.'

'He is not!'

'All right, not handsome exactly. But interesting looking.'

'So you really like him? Do you think he likes you back?' I'd love it if they went out, because this man hiatus is not natural for her.

She looks anguished. 'I don't know if he does! This is killing me. You know I don't usually like someone who doesn't like me back.'

'You don't know he doesn't like you,' I point out. 'Maybe he's just waiting to be sure you're interested before he asks you out. I wouldn't worry. You always get your man.' My smile takes any malice out of this (very true) statement. As we watch the next heat I try to remember if an object of Stacy's desire was ever not interested. Except for William, The Hopeless Crush, there hasn't been one. Josh must like my friend. What's not to like? Except that she's a workaholic, she's perfect.

'Oh shit!' Someone shouts, pointing to the water as

others gasp. Debris is strewn wide. Oars and people bob in the waves. I don't want to watch in case someone is hurt, but I can't stop myself. Orange inflatable dinghies are already at the scene. It doesn't look like anyone is hurt and they're hauling the rowers into the other boats. I wonder if the drum has sunk.

'I don't think anyone's hurt,' Stacy says, squinting at an approaching boat. 'Aside from their pride. Are they coming here?'

'Those are our friends.' Josh shakes his head. 'Bad luck.'

The rowers climb aboard to laughter and jeers, assuring them that their near-death experience amused their friends. Everyone looks very sporty in matching green and black Lycra catsuits. It's almost tempting to learn how to row, but I suppose my aversion to the gym, and exercise in general, tempers that idea.

Josh introduces us to a stunning blonde Lycra-bound Australian woman called Jackie. They look cozy enough together to give Stacy quiet conniptions beside me. I don't think she needs to worry. Living with Aussies in London taught me that Australian women are this nice to everybody. 'Aw yeah,' she's saying. 'I don't know what happened, mate. One second we're in the boat, the next we're in the drink. Speaking of drinks…'

'Bar's in the saloon, Jackie, help yourself.'

'Thanks,' she says, chucking him on the shoulder. 'I will.'

'Would you like another drink as well?' Josh offers. 'I can just go get–'

'No thanks, not for me,' I say as Stacy shakes her head. My sea legs aren't wholly due to the waves. 'So how do you know Jackie?' I ask, saving Stacy the trouble.

'Oh, we were at uni together.' I wait for more details but none are forthcoming.

'… And she moved here after uni with you?' I prompt.

'No, not with me, but about six months later. So what do you think of the boats?'

Why are men unable to have a normal conversation? By normal, I mean a conversation that actually provides the information we seek. Do they do this on purpose? 'The boats are gorgeous,' I tell him. 'I had no idea that they were actually *dragon* boats.' Some of the boats are brightly painted with green, red, blue or white scales, making them startlingly vivid against the greenish-grey water. The variety of carved wooden dragon heads at the boats' bows are remarkable. Big, small, and all colors, they've got bulbous eyes and open mouths showing impressive teeth. Some have long wispy beards that dangle towards the water.

'It's a long tradition,' Josh tells us. 'More than two thousand years old. The Lycra is a new addition. It pays tribute to the dragon, the Chinese symbol for water, to bring luck and rain to the farmers' fields. Then a legend got mixed up with it, about a great Chinese poet who drowned himself after his kingdom was defeated. The villagers took their boats out to try to find the poet, whom they loved. To keep the fish away from his body they beat drums. And today the drum symbolizes the dragon's beating heart… but mostly it's a national holiday off for drinking.' He clinks our glasses.

Sam would love this. Next year I'm going to make sure we get to go together. I wouldn't even mind being on the shore. Well, I'd mind a little. But the important thing is that we'll be together. I let my mind drift to all the experiences on our horizon. We'll finally get to take our relationship out of this holding pattern, and build a life with each other. For the first time I can dare to anticipate that, instead of just wishing for it. It feels a bit like I've been under the cloud of a touch-and-go illness. Now, after months of letting it dominate my life, poof! The treatment is finally working and the symptoms are lessening. It looks like a brand new beginning from where I'm standing.

If only that brand new beginning feeling had lasted into the evening. Instead I've got the same old feeling, trying very hard to understand what Stacy sees in Pete. He insisted on taking us to Lan Kwai Fong, to a bar that's a dive even when you're drunk. It's nearly condemned when you're sober. 'Why do you like this place?' I ask him.

'The booze is cheap and the women are easy.'

'Charming.'

'Lighten up, Han, he's kidding. You are kidding, right?'

He laughs. 'Yeah… the drinks are pricey. Want another?' I nod. 'Good, it's your round. I'll have the same, thanks.'

Believe it or not, this is him being marginally nicer. That doesn't make him likeable, only less loathsome. He and Stacy do seem to get along famously though, which I can only attribute to their mutual understanding of obscure financial products and economic theories. Not that they've been talking about those things tonight, thank goodness. I suppose he is interesting, if you can overlook his grating personality. He's a geek at heart, like Sam, having spent most of his adult life under teacher supervision. I suppose that means he's smart. He certainly thinks he is. In fact, he's the kind of man who lives for those one-liners that are sometimes funny but usually tedious. I just don't get the attraction.

'So, Sam's coming back on Friday,' I offer, to fill the silence as Pete and I stare at each other.

'Yeah, he mentioned that. He's coming back for the meeting on the next project.'

'And to see me.'

'Right.'

In the ensuing silence I've got plenty of time for my insecurities to settle back in comfortably.

'You're very cool about this you know,' he says.

Is that admiration in his eyes? 'Cool about what?' I must come across as a real prude if he thinks I'd be uncool about the bar. I mean openly, to his face.

'About your whole dating situation. He said you were, but I thought… but you really are okay with it.' He shakes his head.

My, my, my, it is admiration. Despite my dislike for this man, I'm pleased to be judged as cool by him. Maybe he doesn't dislike me so much after all. Or maybe he just assumed I wasn't cool (what are we, sixteen years old?) and therefore not worthy of his friend. Well, clearly I am. I think I've handled the long-distance relationship really well, considering.

'So, your boss. Are you seeing him then?' Pete enquires.

'Hmm? No, of course not! Stace– No, of course not. I certainly wouldn't date my boss!' I scoff like I've never done *that* before. 'Why would you think that?'

'Oh, well I guess just because Stacy mentioned that you were out with him today, and at his club before. I just assumed, what's good for the gander is good for the goose.'

He's watching me intently. Is he trying to goad me in to saying I'm cheating on Sam? I take it all back. He is a dick. And he can't even get the stupid expression right. 'What's good for the *goose* is good for the gander,' I correct.

'Except the goose isn't dating anyone else, is she?'

It takes a moment for his meaning to sink in.

'Hannah,' he continues. 'Do you think you're making it too easy for him? I mean, he's my friend, and I'm not telling you to kick his ass. Bros before hos and all that. But you seem like a nice person, and from everything Stacy says, you came out here in good faith to be with him. He's got no control over his job, that's true, but if he asked you to be here, then it makes sense to either commit or break up.' He sighs while I sit here with my mouth open. 'This halfway bullshit is, well, bullshit. I've talked to him about it, a lot, so he knows my feelings on the subject. I'm not going behind his back or anything by talking to you. It's just not fair. It's not fair to you but frankly, my main concern is Sam, since he's my best friend. I think that if he won't shit or get off the pot, then you need to.'

He turns to Stacy, who has clearly not heard this before. 'I'm sorry. I've been going back and forth for a long time about whether to say anything. I can't get through to Sam. He's pissed at me for trying. Should I have kept quiet? I mean, come on, he's my best friend. And she's yours. This situation isn't right.'

'You definitely should have said something, Pete. You're right. I've been telling Hannah that for months.' How nice that they're bonding over this little conversation as if I'm not sitting here. 'What, exactly, is he doing?' she asks, voicing the question that's making me feel woozy.

'Don't make it sound like he's doing something to Hannah,' he snaps. 'They're allowed to see other people. He's not doing anything wrong. It's the situation that's wrong. That's what I'm saying. And Sam's too close to it to see that it's not good for him. Hannah, I guess I hoped that you'd understand what I'm saying. It's got to be one way or the other. Limbo sucks. Make him commit or let him go so he can find someone else.'

I feel like the ceiling just caved in. Was it just a few hours ago that everything seemed so bright?

'It sounds like he's already found someone else,' Stacy accuses.

'No, it's not serious.'

'Well, if it's just a bit of fun,' she says, shooting me a warning look. 'It'll come to an end when he comes back to Hong Kong anyway, right? So what's the big deal? Though I guess she'll be here too. That might be a bit awkward.'

Oh God. It's Li Ming. Of course it is.

'Nooo, I don't think so.' He looks confused. 'Her assignment is in Cambodia. She wouldn't move here, unless they suddenly need to clear landmines in Central.'

Now I'm confused. They got the funding for the project here, not in Cambodia. And what does Li Ming know about clearing landmines? She's a hard-headed economist, not some airy-fairy save-the-world type who parachutes into war-torn countries to clear landmines and build schools, like some Teva-wearing Mother Theresa… Tevas. Landmines. Mother Theresa.

My blood runs cold as I struggle to speak. 'Well, it won't be long now till Sam's back,' I manage. 'Just a few weeks, when his assignment is finished! Then we'll see. Is it hot in here?' I'm babbling while my world crumbles. 'Stace, I'm wiped out – too much sun today. I'm going to head back. Stay if you want, I'll just text you in twenty minutes or so when I get back to the apartment.'

'Nah, that's okay. Do you mind, Pete? I'm a little tired too. I'll head back with Hannah.'

'Yeah, sure. Hannah, are you okay?'

'Oh yeah, fine thanks, Pete. Just tired that's all. Listen, thanks for your concern. You're a good friend to Sam.'

The second we round the corner, out of Pete's line of sight, Stacy grabs me and hugs me hard. 'Honey, I'm so sorry. I didn't have any idea, I swear. But when Pete said that, I knew I could get him to give us the details. Was I wrong to do it?'

'No, you weren't wrong. But it's worse than you think.' I sob into my best friend's shoulder. 'I can't believe I've been so stupid.'

15

My boyfriend has been going out with Lara Croft. The Groom Raider. For how long, I have no idea. For all I know they got together while we were still in Laos. Clearly they bonded while I was ankle-deep in mud. They probably had sex while I had my head in the toilet. Uff. I feel like I've eaten bad pork again, except there's a searing sensation in my belly to add to the nausea.

I took to my bed as soon as we got home after Pete's little bombshell, and called in sick to work yesterday and today. I am sick. I'm also a bit smelly. My hair is turning a bit Rastafarianism. I've managed to clean my teeth only because the taste of morning breath and desolation was too much to bear.

There seems to be a hole in the middle of my soul. When I dare to peer inside, I see what I had with Sam. Every time I look, a dizzying chill sweeps over me, pushing more tears out. My eyes couldn't be more swollen if they'd just undergone lid surgery. My world is collapsing and I don't know how I'm ever going to feel better. Maybe I'm not. Maybe the rest of my life will be spent under the duvet in my tiny maid's room, forcing down the food that Stacy keeps hopefully bringing back to the apartment. 'You've got to eat,' she says. Why? Why do I have to eat? Every mouthful is dry and tasteless.

I'd trade physical pain for emotional pain any day. At least I could dope myself if I'd merely broken a leg or accidentally lopped off a hand. It's absolutely impossible to take away these feelings though.

I'm having thoughts, scary thoughts, the kind of thoughts that are dangerous, of the, 'Well, if I'm never going to feel better in my whole life, then…' variety. Luckily they're fleeting, and there does seem to be some sense in my head because every time one pops up, another thought says, 'Yes but you're not crying as much as you were yesterday, are you?' So it appears that I'm schizophrenic, not suicidal.

When Stacy comes back from work she tries to feed me again. 'Thanks, I'm really just not hungry.'

'But I cooked!'

'You what?' There's little she could say that would make the prospect of eating less appealing. 'You don't cook.' I know she didn't cook. I live in a doorway off the kitchen. Even in this state I'd have noticed activity in there.

'You're right. I assembled. Look, all your favorites. Spaghetti lobster from Grissini's, avocado and crab maki roll from Zuma, and Ben & Jerry's Phish Food. Won't you try a little something?'

'Grissini's does takeaway?'

'I convinced them it's an emergency. Zuma too. They were really very nice. Come on, just a little bit?' She's laid out a feast on the dinner tray and is a short step away from playing choo-choo train with a forkful of lobster.

'Thanks, Stace. I appreciate that you're trying to make me feel better. I just don't think anyone can do that right now. It's me. It's in my head. I have to get over this. I'll try to eat something.'

Dipping the maki roll in the soy sauce, an odd thing happens. My mouth starts to water. I'm not hungry and yet I'm salivating like Pavlov's pooch. It does taste good. It tastes really good. And the spaghetti has just the right blend of chili and garlic. Mmm, what sweet lobster.

Stacy sits on the narrow bed and rubs my back, wrinkling her nose at bit. It's definitely time for a shower. 'Feeling better? With the food I mean.'

'Yes, a bit. This is really delicious, thanks. And thanks for going all over to get it. Grissini's was way out of your way.'

'Don't give it a thought. I just popped over on the way home. Besides, what's a little walk when you get this?' She grabs a chunk of lobster from the plate. 'I'm just glad to see you eat. This diet of despair is out of character.'

'It must be serious then, eh?' I chuckle without mirth. 'How can this be happening? I just never thought…'

'Well, I've been thinking about this and, I don't want to give you false hope, because you know my feelings about Sam. I still think you're better off without him, at least if he won't commit. But, really… technically… he's done nothing wrong, has he? I know,' she says to my are-you-kidding-me expression. 'I know it's shitty for him to date what's her name. But technically you're both able to see other people. Technically he did nothing wrong. Now, from a human being's perspective he's a complete shit who deserves to die.'

'So I can forgive him or kill him? Isn't there any middle ground?'

'Sure there is. You can stay in limbo like you are, ignoring his calls and emails while you wallow in hurt and anger, never resolving the issue. But it needs to be resolved, don't you think? One way or the other, whether you like that or not. Pete's right.'

'I know he is. But what am I going to do?' Just thinking about definitively ending it is making me snuffle. 'I don't want to break up with Sam. I love him!' There I go again, shooting for gold in the snot Olympics. The really shitty thing is that Sam doesn't even know that I know, so while I'm single-handedly driving up the share price of Kleenex, he's not suffering in the least. I haven't been able to face talking to him. Okay, I've been afraid to talk to him. I know I'll confront him if we speak. That's not a good idea on the phone. He's coming on Friday (Lara must be busy building another school for deaf children or donating her bone marrow). I know Pete won't give him any warning. He went behind his friend's back to talk to me. Besides, I don't think he caught on to the fact that the conversation shocked me. Sam must know something's wrong though. I'll have to talk to him before Friday, if only to put his mind at ease so I can ambush him in person. 'And all this time I thought Pete didn't like me, or that he was jealous. I'm sorry I misjudged him.'

'I know. Who'd have thought that he was just trying to make Sam talk to you about it? It's sweet really. You don't think about guys being romantic like that.'

'What would you do, Stace?'

She gazes at me with pity. Despite her feelings about Sam I know she won't say anything psychologically damaging right now. I want her to tell me what to do because my head and my heart are giving very different orders. She sighs. 'Let's start with you. What do you want?'

'I want everything to be back to normal with Sam.'

'But what's normal with Sam? Do you mean what you've had? Because that's what you've got now, isn't it? You're living in different cities, able to see other people. That's not what you really want. Is it?'

'No.' I sigh. 'I want it to be the way it was when we were in London, at the beginning. We were so happy. Everything looked shiny and exciting. We had a future.'

She takes my hand. 'But you can't turn back time. You've moved on from those first, new-relationship days. You've had experiences, both of you, together and apart, and you've had conversations and you've had feelings that make things different now. I'm sorry, honey. I wish I could put you in a time machine. If it were that easy everybody would do it. You've got to look at where you are now. What you know now, about each other, and… maybe more importantly, about yourself. Because you've changed. Hannah, don't you think? Your move here has changed you, just like your move to London changed you. It showed you that you can stand on your own two feet. You can move halfway across the world, find a great job and build a life for yourself. That's amazing. You should be proud. I'm proud of you. So while you may love Sam, you don't need him the same way you did six months ago. I know it feels like you do. But you don't really. So if you don't need him, then you should have him in your life because you want him, right? And I know you do want him. But see if you can try to say what you want in a man in general. Try not to think of Sam as you say it. Tell me what your ideal is.'

I'm not sure I've got the mental capacity right now for this kind of thing. I want what all women want. 'I want someone that I'm in love with, and who loves me back. Someone who's supportive and open and caring. And funny and smart and sexy.'

'And local?'

'Well, yes, in an ideal world. But we can't have everything.'

'Why not?'

'Hmm?'

'Why can't we have everything? Don't you deserve all those things? I think you do. I know I do. So why do we settle for less than what we want? I think we're brainwashed into shrugging our shoulders and saying, "Oh well, can't have it all", when really, if we can give it all, why shouldn't we get it? Aren't you supportive and caring and funny and smart and loving?'

'And sexy?'

'And sexy.' She smiles. 'Yes, aren't you all of those things?' I nod. 'Then you don't deserve someone who is less. I'm sorry, Han, you really don't.'

'But I want him!' This is where my heart's petulance wins over my head's common sense. 'It doesn't matter that he's not perfect. Nobody's perfect.'

Stacy laughs. 'Honey, sometimes I want to shake you. Listen to yourself. He's not perfect? Hannah, he's dating someone else. He's not fully committed to you.

Has he said he's in love with you? No, I didn't think I missed that memo. Wouldn't you say those are pretty big flaws? You're right, nobody's perfect. But in the right relationship, you're going to be perfect for each other. Because you tick each other's boxes in the things that matter to you. So you can overlook his snoring, or he can ignore your aversion to exercise, or whatever it is that doesn't exactly align, as long as you each fulfil the big things, the important ones. I'm afraid your differences are just too much. You want a commitment. He isn't giving you that.'

Maybe she's right. Maybe I've been short-changing myself, accepting less than I deserve. Have I betrayed me?

'I love you, you know,' she says, hugging me. 'I'm going to help you through this, whatever you decide to do. And I'm going to support whatever you do, okay? You have to make the decisions, not me. I'm your best friend. We're in this together.'

I'm sobbing as I hug her. This is what a relationship should be – total support and commitment, the assuredness of unshakeable love. Stacy's right. I do deserve more.

'All right,' she says. 'I love you, Hannah, but you are rank. Please go shower. Then let's go over to Stuart's. He's invited us for drinks if you're up to it. He thinks you need to get out of the house, and I agree.'

'But what if I start blubbering all over them? Thanks, Stace, but I'm not fit for polite society.'

'That's all right, we're not polite. If you don't get some normalcy back soon, how are you going to face Sam this weekend? You need an intervention before you become a danger to yourself. Come on, trust me, you'll feel better after you shower. I know I will.' She waves her hand in front of her nose.

It's a short walk to Stuart and Brent's apartment, just along Robinson Road, but the fresh air does wonders. When I say fresh air I mean the hot, humid air in which the pollution is custard-thick, with only the slightest whisper of a breeze. Still, it beats the staleness of heartbreak in my bed.

They're in one of the swankier buildings, just where you'd imagine a successful banker and an architect would live. It's nice walking into a friend's apartment building. I guess that's the high water mark that tells me a place is home. And Hong Kong does feel like home, despite everything that's happened. My best friend is here. My job is here. And this is where I feel like I'm growing up.

'Come in!' Stuart hugs us at the door. 'Brent's just in the living room and I'm in charge of drinks. Hannah, fancy a glass of something?'

I can see the concern in his eyes and nod. I'd like some courage, please. Make it a double. 'Red, please.'

'Coming right up me lover! Stacy, the same?' He leads us to the living room where Brent is staring at Central's twinkling panorama below. 'Hello!' He kisses us. 'It's a beautiful sky tonight.' Hundreds of skyscrapers pulse and glow in the lilac twilight, their stairwell lights running up them like excavated dinosaurs' spines. The dark pool of the harbor beyond the buildings reflects back at us, deceptively calm. And Kowloon blankets the far shore, stretching into the distance. I don't think I'll ever take these views for granted. I hope not.

'How are you feeling?' Brent murmurs, rubbing my arm.

'Not great, but better for coming out. Thanks for inviting us. I'll be all right in time. It's just a shock, you know?'

'Oh I know, believe me. I went out with a woman for four years and then found out she was having an affair… not that Sam is having an affair!' he exclaims.

'Brent!' Stuart chastises, sighing dramatically. 'I told you not to bring it up unless she does. Jesus, you're hopeless.'

Brent looks sheepish. 'I'm sorry, Hannah, we don't have to talk about it at all if you don't want to.'

'No, that's all right, I'd really like your opinions. Stacy's given me her view. How much do you know?'

Brent's sheepishness deepens, and this time Stuart joins him in pink-cheeked embarrassment. 'Quite a lot, actually. Oh, it's not like we've been gossiping about you or anything but obviously, with you so upset, Stacy mentioned what happened, and Stuart told me.'

'That's okay, really I don't mind,' I assure them. 'Four heads are better than one on this one, don't you think? So… what *do* you think?' I've never had a close male friend to talk to before. I guess Stacy and I have always made a comfortably self-contained unit. Perhaps we'd have made fewer romantic mistakes if we'd had boys as informants.

They stare at each other for a moment, deciding who's going to go first. It's like waiting for the doctor to tell you you're terminal. 'Let's double-check all the facts first, all right?' Stuart starts diplomatically. 'As I understand things, when you moved out here, you weren't seeing anybody else, right?' I shake my head.

'Was that because you'd agreed not to? Did you have the talk? I'm only asking so we know whether there was a verbal contract.'

'A verbal contract?' Stuart scoffs at his brother. 'What's she going to do, sue him?'

'Does that make a difference?' Stacy asks. 'In a guy's mind, I mean?'

'Sometimes,' Brent says. 'Come on, Stu, you know it does. If you've not explicitly told a girl you're not going to sleep with anyone else, and then you do, it's a get-out clause. I'm sorry, but it is. If it's not been agreed, then in our minds it's not a promise. It's more of an intention. And despite the best of intentions, sometimes…'

'God, men can be dicks,' Stacy exclaims, turning to me. 'So did you have the talk?'

We did. We were meandering hand in hand through Covent Garden's narrow streets when I asked him. Are we exclusive? He'd looked surprised. 'I am. I don't want to see anyone else… Do you?' No, I'd told him, with feeling. I didn't want anyone but Sam. 'There was a verbal contract.' I smile at Brent. 'We only mentioned seeing other people when he was here one weekend, after a fight. So we did agree we could do it, technically. I just didn't think he would. And I didn't think he'd do it with that woman! He must have stayed in touch with her all along, right? Otherwise how would he have been able to start seeing her after the weekend we talked? That's why I'm so upset. He's been in touch with her all along. It's a betrayal, no matter whether he's technically done anything wrong or not.'

Stuart reaches out and pulls me to him. 'It is a betrayal,' he murmurs over my shoulder as my tears flow. 'He had no reason to stay in touch with her. If he was just her friend, he would have told you about it. You're not wrong, Hannah. He is.'

Stacy joins our hugathon. 'I know it hurts, Han, but you've got to stand strong on this when you see him this weekend. As much as you want to make everything all right, you've got to remember that he's at fault here. He hasn't treated you fairly.'

'Stacy's right, Han,' Stuart continues. 'You've done nothing wrong. He has, and he's not treating you right. So you can't be weak. You have to stand up for yourself.'

'Hah!' Brent exclaims, startling us. 'That's rich advice coming from you, Stuart! He's right, Han, you've got to stand strong. But really, Stuart, take a dose of your own medicine. You've been led around by the nose for months now. You could learn a thing or two from Hannah.'

'Brent is right, Stu,' Stacy agrees. 'You don't deserve to be treated like shit by that woman any more than Hannah does by Sam.'

When the conversation shifts to Stuart I can relax. I appreciate their words but there's really nothing new in them. They're simply telling me what my head has been saying for days. It's my heart that needs a good talking-to.

That's easier said than done. Look at Stuart. His yellow fever infatuation has led him to worship his colleague, the one Stacy christened the Ice Queen. She sounds like an extremely bad choice of girlfriend. He may talk with more bravado than Brent but he's just as nice. Deep down he wants a girlfriend as much as his brother. And the Ice Queen must know this. Anyone can see that she's stringing him along. One minute she accepts his dinner invitations and sleeps with him, the next she ignores his phone calls. She always has some excuse, and Stuart accepts them. Brent is right. I'm not the only one who needs to be strong these days.

I'm full of wine, good advice and strength when we get home a little later. 'Hello Sam? It's me,' I murmur into the phone, my heart skipping. 'I'm sorry I didn't call back. I've been… busy. But I'm really looking forward to seeing you this weekend.' I feel strangely calm as I tell him this. And, as much as I'd like it to be different, I'm not lying.

16

'You're quiet,' Sam observes as we walk hand in hand through Kowloon on Saturday.

'I'm taking this all in,' I tell him truthfully. I mean the sights, sounds and smells bombarding us. Hong Kong continues to reveal her small wonders to me. It's not an obvious city in that way. New York wears her charms proudly for all to see, and London overwhelms with her voluminous architectural wonders and history at every turn. But Hong Kong enthralls in a million little ways. I was right to suspect that the sleek façade was just that. Mixed cultural metaphors aside, Hong Kong reminds me of a geisha. The external perfection and stylized appearance are actually the least interesting things about her.

The flower market is crowded when we get there. We see it as we turn a corner off Prince Edward Road, but its aroma spreads beyond the stalls themselves. Like Sheung Wan, most of the shops are converted garages, and they're just as visually intense. Uncountable buckets are filled with every color flower imaginable, from humble freesias and carnations to soaring lilies and birds of paradise. Mostly women, mostly Chinese, clutch their blooms, haggling with the vendors. Some stalls sell potted flowers and plants. I'd buy one but it would mean sending a plant to certain death.

'How lovely,' says Sam, squeezing my hand and making my heart hiccup. It's been a hard morning. He's got no idea that I know about the Groom Raider, so he's acting just like he always does when we're together – fun, attentive and kind. I, however, am starring in the most challenging role imaginable. I know I have to talk to him, but oh, how I wish I didn't. In a way I hoped that Pete would tell him after all, but there's no sign that he knows I know.

'It's amazing. Hong Kong is amazing. I'm grateful every day for being here,' I say. 'It's such a city of contrasts. And secrets…'

'What secrets?'

'… Things often look like one thing, but are actually another… I don't know if I'll ever know exactly where I stand.'

'But that comes with time, doesn't it? As you get to know a place you learn what's genuine and what isn't.'

'But you wouldn't if you're not exposed to the genuine side. If you only have sporadic exposure, or you only see one side, then you're never going to feel totally comfortable, are you?'

'That's why you have to keep exploring, and getting out there to experience everything,' he says.

My attempt to introduce the conversation isn't working.

We find the nearby bird market by sound rather than sight. A cacophony of chirps, whistles, screeches and hoots fill the air. There's a wide walkway lined with flowers and trees running alongside it, where several men are meandering through carrying bird cages. Others have hung their cages next to each other along bars under the eaves of the bird market buildings. The men sit and chat, their birds catching up with each other on the previous days' events. 'Wow,' I say. 'I read about this but didn't think it could be true. I figured it was like the Wishing Tree, something that happened in the past.'

'You've seen the noodle shops, right? Where the men hang their cages on the rails over the tables?'

'I suppose it's nice for the birds to get out of their apartments. And it's probably exciting for them to come here within earshot of all their cousins to hear the gossip.' As I ponder what bird gossip might be, an old man totters up the walk, but elects not to join the others under the eaves. Instead he brings his birdcage to a tree branch quite close to us, and stands alone. I wonder what he's done to be ostracized from the others. 'Do you think they're all friends?' I ask Sam.

'Nah, I'm sure they fight. Someone is getting above himself with his shiny new cage, or this one said that one's bird is ugly. We humans aren't built to live happily ever after.'

My heart goes out to the lone man, until I notice a younger man calling to him as he approaches. The old man smiles broadly, clapping him on the back as he hangs his bird's cage. I bet their birds are good friends too. Maybe sometimes we do live happily ever after.

The bird market itself is almost overwhelming in the number and variety of birds for sale. Most are tiny and colorful, and all are noisy. A few of the stalls sell bird food, but it's not the kind you'd find in PetSmart. It's the kind you'd find crawling around your garden. Crickets, grubs, grasshoppers – it's a bird banquet. Some of the cages are utilitarian but many are delicately woven bamboo confections, beautiful, and tempting to buy even without a bird.

As we continue down the row I notice one non-bird-related stall nestled in the midst of the hubbub. A seamstress sits behind her ancient heavy black Singer sewing machine, stitching away. And she's singing, beautifully voiced and powerfully, joining the birds in their melodies. She looks so strong and assured, deftly turning her cloth and singing to herself. She looks content, and at peace. I want desperately to be like that.

'Sam,' I whisper, welling up. 'We need to talk.'

He freezes, searching my face. 'Let's sit down.' He leads me to a low wall. 'What is it, Han? Are you okay?'

'No. And we're not okay.' I take a deep breath. 'Sam, I know about… her. I know you've been seeing someone else. Pete mentioned it. He didn't mean it as a betrayal or anything I'm sure.' I feel I should defend Pete now that I know he never had it in for me. 'You'd told him about our talk, that we could see other people, so his comment was innocent. Sam, how long has it been going on, with her? And remember, I can ask Pete.' I could keep talking but my vocal chords have seized up.

'Aw, Han, I don't want you to be upset.' He grabs my hand. I let him. 'It's not what you think. We traded details way back when we met. We're in similar fields and, oh I don't know, it was innocent.'

'What do you mean you traded details? When? In the jungle? I was with you the whole time.'

'When you asked me to go out and take photos, remember when you were ill? I ran into her, in that cafe across from the school.'

Of course. I assumed he'd asked a stranger to take his photo in front of all the landmarks. Lara was the photographer.

'I didn't think anything of it,' he says urgently. 'That's why I didn't tell you. We just had a coffee and wandered around for an hour. It wasn't even worth mentioning. I forgot all about it to be honest, then, *months later*, I randomly got an email. I answered because there was no reason not to. Han, I can see by your face that you think it's more than that, but it's not. She's got a few friends in Ho Chi Minh and put me in touch. They're two guys, really nice guys, who've set up a business there. You know I've been working late, and on weekends, and it was nice to be able to go out every so often for drinks. I felt like I was able to enjoy being there a bit, not just working all the time… then I saw her once when she visited them for the weekend. Nothing happened, I promise you! But then you said you didn't want a long-distance relationship and we agreed that we could have dates with other people. So the next time she visited we went out. It's not serious with her, Hannah, I promise. You don't have anything to worry about. It's just a bit of fun, she's not even in Ho Chi Minh and I hardly ever see her.'

My ears hear everything he's just said. Yet my mind registers just one thing. It's not serious. 'Do you think that makes a difference, that it's not serious? Sam, you're my boyfriend, and you're fucking another woman. I assume you are fucking.' He flinches. 'Yes, I thought so. Are you saying you're willing to throw us away for *a bit of fun?*'

'No! I'm not throwing us away. Han, I care very much for you. I want us to be together in Hong Kong. And we will be, very soon. We agreed we could see other people while we're apart. Didn't we? Am I missing something?'

'Yes, you are. You're missing the fact that you shouldn't want to see other people if you like me as much as you say you do. And yet you are. That means one thing to me. That you don't *care for me*, to use your words, as much as you say you do. Or at least you don't care for me enough not to want to be with someone else. The thing is, Sam, I don't want to be with anyone else. That's what makes us different. And I don't think we can reconcile that.'

'But we can be together, just us! If you don't want to see other people then I won't either. Like I said, it's not serious with Svetlana.' Svetlana. I hate hearing her name. Now she's a person, not a computer-generated boyfriend-stealer. 'I'll call her tonight,' he promises. 'I'll call her right now and tell her. Han, I don't want to lose you.'

'I'm sorry, Sam.' I can't believe I'm about to say this. My throat threatens to choke off my words, but they are determined to come. 'You lost me when you chose to see somebody else. Technicalities don't matter – whether you legally could or not. I want someone – no, I deserve someone – who's as committed to me as I am to him. You're not that person. So I'm sorry, you've already lost me.'

He stares at me, dumbfounded, as I sob. 'Hannah, can't we talk more about this?'

'There's nothing – what could you possibly say that

takes away the last few months, Sam? Can you make anything you've – hiccup – said not true?'

'No,' he says quietly.

'I've loved you, Sam. I didn't deserve this. And you know that. Don't you?'

'I feel terrible.'

'Well, I don't feel like whistling a tune myself.'

'I mean I feel terrible about what I've done.'

'You should.' I stand on shaky legs. 'You fucked this up, not me.'

'I've been such an asshole.' He shakes his head, clenching his fists. 'You've been nothing but wonderful and supportive and kind. You moved out here for me and I'm not even in the country! You did move for me, didn't you?'

'Yes,' I whisper.

'And I knew that. Even back in London I knew you were doing it for me. Even when I was telling you I didn't want you to, I knew you were. And I let you. Even though it scared me that you'd make that kind of leap, I let you because it didn't feel like a big step. What I mean is, it felt natural. It felt like the right thing to do. I didn't feel scared by it. I felt good, and excited and positive about our future. Even when I found out I had to be away, it didn't seem like the end of the world because I knew I wanted to be with you. Hannah, what I'm saying is that I love you. God, what an idiot I've been. Why didn't I just say it before now?'

'Maybe you didn't feel it before. I don't know, Sam, maybe you don't even really feel it now. You're scared of losing me. Why wouldn't you be? You've had this entire relationship your way. Of course you don't want to lose that. Maybe that's all you feel.'

He's crying now. 'It's not. I do feel it, Hannah. How can I convince you?'

'I don't know, Sam. I don't know how you'd do that. Just because you say it doesn't mean I'll believe it. Your actions speak louder than your words. You've said all you can say. I've heard you, Sam, I really have. But I want to go back by myself now.'

'Can I call you later to make sure you're okay?'

'No, it's best if you don't.'

With nothing left to say, without a kiss or a hug goodbye, I leave him sitting on the low wall. As I walk back through the bird garden, attracting curious stares from the men, I find my phone in my bag. 'Stacy? I need you.'

'Hang in there, Han, I'm leaving the apartment right now. Where are you?'

It was a slow journey back to our apartment, what with me sobbing into Stacy's shoulder every five yards. Now I know why nineteenth-century heroines took to their beds when they got bad news. How I'd love to take a sabbatical to wallow in heartbreak. But no, we are twenty-first-century women. We can juggle all the balls, even when one of them is a razor-studded orb of poo. And I suppose it might be a tad unhealthy to let a break-up give me bedsores. Stacy certainly thinks so. She's been merciless in her attempt to get me over this Sam-sized bump in the road. I appreciate her monumental efforts, though they seem to mainly involve grooming. She's had me cut and colored, and plucked, but I drew the line at a bikini wax. The irony of adding insult to injury was too much to bear. I have, however, acquiesced to a pedicure, which Stacy insists will be relaxing. I'm sure it would be, if not for my deep-seated aversion to emery boards. I think she's tired of hearing me repeat the Sam conversation and figures I'll keep quiet if I'm clenching my teeth in fear.

We've found a place near the escalators, pushing a nondescript buzzer that unlocked a steel-reinforced door. Black leather loungers ring the bare-walled, strip-lit room where half a dozen Chinese technicians fondle their clients' feet. It's the chicken assembly line of foot care. The women confer briefly among themselves to decide who's going to work on Stacy and me. Five minutes later my feet are soaking in hot water and the woman in front of me is sharpening her tools on a leather strap. Or it seems that way.

She starts gently with some sort of scissors, which don't hurt, though I'm flinching as if slapped each time the blade touches my skin. I can see her patience wearing thin. By the time she graduates to a file that's used to shave down lopsided doors, I'm shooting her pointed looks that say, 'I will not hesitate to knock your teeth out if you hurt me.' Through the miracle of non-verbal communication, she understands perfectly, and stops grinding away quite so enthusiastically.

Meanwhile Stacy is chatting away like she's not losing important bits of her foot. 'If it's not raining let's go to The Backyard tonight,' she says. 'We'll sip cocktails, show off our feet and soak up the atmosphere.'

What she means is that I'll be distracted from thoughts of Sam. Any relief is welcome, and I do love The Backyard, but comfy rattan sofas amidst Mong Kok's skyscrapers aren't going to make me forget what I've done. I vacillate between certainty that it was the right thing and certainty that it was the painful thing. Neither assures me it was the best thing.

My mind constantly flicks to Sam, where he is and what (who) he's doing. Did he wait until he got back to Ho Chi Minh to call Svetlana, or was he on his mobile to her as he left the bird market? It's none of my business. I broke up with him. Of course, I'm desperate to know.

When the technician drags an emery board across my big toenail, I squeal to tell her how much I'm enjoying the experience. She stops abruptly.

'Please,' I gasp. 'No emery board.'

'Just a little?' She asks.

Not unless you want to go to the hospital. 'No, none. Please.'

'You not let me work!' she cries, like Picasso being relieved of his brushes. She's jealously eyeing Stacy's feet, being whittled away, no doubt wishing she'd made a different choice of customer. To prove her mettle, she chooses a gleaming instrument and begins running it across the bottom of my foot. Bits of foot flake off on to the towel.

'What's that?' I cry.

'It's a razor,' says Stacy. 'She's shaving the calluses off your foot.'

'But don't I need those?'

'For what?'

I'm not sure, but I've got to think that if my body sees fit to make a callus, there must be a good reason.

'Trust her, Hannah, she knows what she's doing. Just try to enjoy it. This is supposed to be taking your mind of things.'

It is. Now I'm obsessing about physical rather than

emotional scarring. Job done, thanks, Stace.

Of course, falling out of love isn't as easy as slicing off a callus. If it were, then women the world over would have perfect feet and intact self-esteem. More than two weeks after my talk with Sam and my feet and nerves remain in tatters. Unfortunately I have to rely on both today.

'My god, this is huge!' I exclaim to Josh. Exhibition stalls stuffed with clothes run off into the distance of the huge AsiaWorld-Expo building. 'How many manufacturers are here?'

'It seems to be all of them, doesn't it? But it's only a fraction of those that are actually in China. Lots of the hopeful newcomers come to these shows for exposure to the exporters. It's a beauty parade of sorts, with each firm showcasing their best work. We get to wander around and be made a fuss over. Watch carefully and you can see them puckering up. Your bottom is about to be kissed.' He reddens as he says this, probably aware that mentioning an employee's bottom could be misinterpreted. I've never told him the details about my old boss, Mark. If I had, he'd probably be less afraid to offend me.

I sigh. 'I could use some adoration at the moment.'

'Stacy told me about you and Sam. I'm sorry, Hannah, that's a very hard thing to have to go through. But for what it's worth, you probably did the right thing.'

'Thanks, Josh. It doesn't feel very right at the moment… Are you and Stacy in touch?' I had no idea. But then again she could have set her hair on fire lately and I probably wouldn't have noticed. Yet another downside to heartbreak: you turn into a crappy friend.

'Yes, we chat occasionally,' he says shyly. 'She's a very nice woman, and interesting, but then you know that already, don't you?'

'Are you… an item, Josh?' I tease, hoping I'm not overstepping my bounds. I'll get all the details from Stacy when I get home, but that's hours from now.

'Has she not mentioned anything?' He looks disappointed. 'We went for drinks on Monday. I assumed she'd have told you. That's not a problem, is it?'

'Oh no, not at all! I think you're great, and she's great, so it'd be… great if you liked each other.'

'Well, it is still early days, just one date, but I'd like to see her again.'

'Great,' I contribute lamely as we stare at each other in this suddenly awkward silence. 'So, uh, what would you like me to do today? How can I help?'

Pleased to be off the great subject of his love life, he says, 'Generally at these things I try to get round to as many stands as I can, taking notes on any that look promising. Why don't I start at that end and you start at this, and we'll see what we come up with? Let's meet at the front, where the bar is, at noon?'

'Sounds good. I'll listen for the gun.' I smile. The noonday gun is an institution here. Each day the artillery gun booms over Causeway Bay. 'I'll check my phone too.' Because modern technology also has its place.

I feel self-conscious as I enter the manufacturers' stands. I know I've got the right to be here – I'm *supposed* to be fondling these frocks – but sometimes it still feels unreal. I'm an exporter's assistant! This makes me smile every time I think it. What a long way I've come, from Felicity's reign of terror to Josh's tutelage. It's amazing, really, to be here today. Oh I say, that is a nice jacket! The vendor smiles broadly as I take it from its rail for a better look. Yes, it's quality all right. Taking a card from his table I make a note of the exhibition number, and wonder briefly if they sell their wares to overly enthusiastic exporter's assistants.

The morning slides by while I peruse the stalls, but my head is killing me by the time the gun signals my return to the bar to meet Josh. 'Well? How'd it go then?' He asks. 'Would you like a drink?'

'Yes please, a coke. I found a few things, and wrote down the stall numbers. Here are their cards.'

'Tell me then,' he says, handing me my drink. 'What did you look for when you were assessing the clothes?'

'Well, honestly, Josh, I'm a sucker for looks. So that's what always attracts me. My mom called me a magpie when I was a kid because I always went for shiny things – wrapping paper, women's rings, anything sparkly caught my eye. Which of course meant that sparkle won out over quality, and I'd be the first to think a piece of tin foil was valuable. That made leftovers priceless in our house! But when I started buying my own clothes I learned the hard way that all that glitters is not gold. I bought trendy and cheap, and my clothes fell apart. Which was really gutting because that meant my favorite clothes disintegrated. I once had a military jacket that I literally wore to threadbare rags. It was only because I hated to lose my favorite clothes that I started to watch for certain things. Because I realized that lots of designers copy each other, with varying quality. I started looking at things like seams. Obviously the fabric's got to be cut on the grain and anything with a pattern has to be sewn straight, so the patterns match up. Even then, you'd be amazed how shoddy some jackets are on the inside. I've passed over so many beautiful jackets because their linings weren't sewn properly. If the seams aren't straight, which you can plainly see, they probably haven't taken much care with the parts of the jacket you can't see. And the lining's got to be thick enough because places like shoulders get a workout, especially if you go dancing, and you don't want the fabric to give way. I hate those Frankenstein scars at the seams. Better to give up the jacket before you buy it than have it fall apart a month later. Also, in things like leather bags I always look for the edges to be sealed. Those raw edges are a dead giveaway. And I once had a teal handbag that rubbed all over my white jeans… It was a disaster. Yes, I know, white jeans, ugh, but I meant the handbag! So now, unless I know the designer already I always do the rub test on handbags. The clerks think I'm insane but I scrub them with a white hankie. If even a smidge of color comes off I walk away. Things like buttons are too obvious to mention, right? I always check those. You may say that a loose button can always be sewn on but to me it's a sign. Today a loose button, tomorrow your trouser seam rips open to show everyone you're wearing your thong. I say no thanks.'

Josh is shaking his head.

'Sorry, was I rambling?'

'Yes, but I'm used to it now. I know I'll never get a short answer from you when it comes to fashion but, amazingly, your stories do always come around to their points eventually. And you're right, once again. The other things I look for are colors that don't blend very well – say there's a red top with ochre trim, and the trim is just a little too bright. That says to me that the designer had the right idea but the fabric that the manufacturer sourced was poorly dyed, so it may run when it's cleaned. And you mentioned buttons. I also always try the zip. It should move smoothly. I know you can rub it with a pencil to loosen it up, but I don't want our customers to have to. Thank you, Hannah.' He clinks my glass with his. 'Shall we have a good look at the ones we've chosen? I think we may find a few new manufacturers to work with today.'

Surely my grin can be seen from space. As Rachel, that flaky rock whisperer, might have said, my career is clearly on the ascendant even if my love life is in retrograde.

17

Even I'm tired of hearing me obsess now. It's been more than a month. Is getting over someone really just a war of attrition? Do we bore everyone within earshot and then turn the tedium on ourselves until sanity makes us move on? Because I'm at risk of OCD, so often have I read his text.

I know you said not to get in touch but I hope you're good. I'm back in Hong Kong. Hannah, pls let me know you're okay. OK? :-)

It came a week ago today, in that in-between time between teeth brushing and bed. I heard the bdllling, told myself it was Mom, or Chloe. Because they're the only ones who text me now. Even so, every text makes me jump, and wonder. I've started playing a little game with myself. When I hear the chime, my heart quickens, prompting a stern talking-to. It's not him, I tell myself. You were strong. You told him what you want, and what you don't. He's out of your life. It's not his text. I've been very persuasive, in the text charade if not the amount of headspace he still occupies. I'd almost convinced myself that what I was saying was true. Then, it was him. Asking for… what? A way to assuage his guilt, perhaps? Maybe another chance? Or, as the text says, simply to know that I'm okay.

It's incredible that I get bored of the newspaper by the time I finish the front page, yet I can spend hours reading into a single sentence when it's from him. It isn't just the reading into, of course. It's the entire line of thinking that goes along with every possible interpretation. It goes something like this, accompanied by a healthy dose of self-righteousness. Say it is an innocent question born of his concern for me. Then shouldn't he have shown such concern when deciding to have a relationship with another woman? Surely it would have been more courteous not to hurt me in the first place. And what if he's texting in the hope that my answer will let him sleep at night? Well, my brain thinks huffily, see first response.

And then this morning:

Hi, wondering if you got my text? Han, please, I'd love to talk. Is that at all possible? Any sign will do. :-)

What if he still believes he's made a huge mistake, and that he loves me? The fact remains that words are cheap. How will I ever know what he's really feeling, and why? But am I really strong enough not to entertain the possibility of another chance? That's the hope I've been clinging to all this time. It's what my heart wants. But my head says it's a self-betrayal to let him back in after standing up for what I deserve in a relationship. And what if I let him back in, and he changes his mind once he's got me hooked? Head or heart. Heart or head. Head, head (shut up heart) … head. My fingers move before I can change my mind. Edit, select text… delete. And again. In dubious tribute to the late Amy Winehouse, I say, 'No, no, no.'

I don't know what I'd have done without Stacy. Every day she calls and texts while we're at work. Every evening she makes herself available as my sounding-board-cum-entertainer. It's getting better. The longer I can go without tears the more certain I am that I was right to stand up for myself. I was right to take control of my relationship. I can look back now and see that when 'we' decided we could see other people (did we really decide that? My memory plays tricks), I got angsty. As if some low-grade annoyance moved in, always there. I ignored it for the most part but it played on my mind, nevertheless. And now that angst is gone, poof, blown away by our final conversation. Equilibrium is returning, slowly. I can look ahead now and feel, if not joy, then at least not angst. The sadness is still there, and probably will be for a long time. But I'm more peaceful now, more me. I know the joy will come.

'It fits,' declares Mr. Chan, nodding in satisfaction as we stand in his sweltering workshop. Yes, it's in small moments like this that normalcy returns. Even better, joy returns.

After the better part of a year, I'm wearing my handmade dress, grinning at my reflection. The deep blue shantung silk drapes perfectly, molding to my body in all the right places. It feels lovely. I feel lovely. 'Thank you, Mr. Chan, it's beautiful. They're all beautiful.'

'Good. Take off now. You sweaty.' Mr. Chan must certainly think I have a glandular problem. Every time I arrive for our appointment I look like I've just finished a half marathon. I will never get used to wading through this 95°F humidity soup. But at least now I'll get to sweat in handmade clothes.

'Thanks again, Mr. Chan. I'm going to tell everyone about you!'

'You are welcome,' he says solemnly. 'You fit nicely now,' he says as he hands over my credit card receipt.

He's right, I think, smiling as I hurry back to the office, I do indeed fit nicely now.

Josh is due back later this afternoon but Mrs. Reese trains her beady eye on me as I float back to my desk. She makes a show of consulting the old-fashioned gold watch she keeps pinned upside down on her jacket. I don't care. Not even her disapproval can dent my mood today. *Winnie*, I instant message, *come over when you get a minute, I've got something to show you!*

She's at my desk in fifteen seconds, clearly as loath to work today as I am. 'Show me!'

'My clothes finally fit!' I unfurl them from the gym bag. The silks whisper against each other, forming a rainbow of jewel tones across my desktop. 'I've got two suits too, but look, they've got these great linings, and the pattern is subtle but makes them very funky, don't you think? I'll mainly wear the dresses to work, or out, though. I love them!'

'They're beautiful, Hannah, well done,' she says, expertly eyeing their design. Winnie knows quality when she sees it. 'It took a long time to get it right, but it was worth it, wasn't it? Now you've got the patterns. You've got it sussed. We should go out tonight to celebrate.'

'Absolutely, great idea. I'll call Stacy and see if she can join us.'

'Hannah,' Mrs. Reese announces, suddenly appearing by my desk. I hate when she does that. 'These gentlemen would like a word with you.'

'I'll talk to you later,' Winnie says, frowning at the Chinese men standing patiently beside Mrs. Reese.

'You may be more comfortable in Josh's office,' she says. 'He's not due back for another hour.' With a smile she walks away.

'Uh, hello, I'm Hannah Cumming. I'm sorry, did we have an appointment today? If you'll come this way, we can use Josh's office.' I'm sure my diary was clear. I checked when I made Mr. Chan's appointment. Plus, no client has ever had a meeting with me. That's the kind of thing I'd remember.

As we settle ourselves at the little round table in the office, both men take out business cards, formally presenting them to me. Dizzily I read them. Immigration Department. 'Miss Cumming, we are here to discuss your working in Hong Kong,' Man One says pleasantly.

I'm not fooled by his smile. 'Of course,' I say, trying to keep the panic from my voice. 'How can I help you?' I wonder if they'll let me get my things on the way to the airport. I remember the story my Aussie housemates told back in London, about their friend who got caught without a visa. It didn't sound like Immigration wasted any time getting him on a flight back to South Africa. I might not even be able to tell Stacy what happened. She'll think I've been kidnapped.

'We will also want to talk to Mr. Josh Bolton,' Man Two explains. 'We are interested to know about your work situation. You are employed by Mr. Bolton?'

It's a trick question. Saying yes gets me deported

and Josh probably fined or even thrown in jail. Saying no is an outright lie, and given that we're here, at my place of employment, it's one I'm unlikely to get away with.

'I'm so sorry, how rude of me. May I get you some tea?' I stand up, startling them. They both smile their acquiescence.

On shaking legs I make my way to Winnie's desk. 'Winnie,' I whisper. 'They're from Immigration. What am I going to do? I've stalled them, said I'd make tea.' I could make a run for it but in these shoes I wouldn't get very far. Foiled by footwear.

'What do you mean, what are you going to do? Hannah, don't you have a work permit to be here?'

'Winnie, now is not the time to judge me. No, I don't. Josh hired me without one. I'm going to be deported, aren't I?'

'Let me think. Take your time with the tea. Good thinking, by the way. Chinese are too polite to refuse tea. I'll call Josh right now and get him back here.' Her eyes are wide as she shakes her head. 'Oh Hannah, this is terrible. But stay calm and stall them. Josh will know what to do.' She doesn't look too sure.

Stay calm and stall, she says. Easier said than done. Oh god, oh god, oh god, I'm going to be deported! That might even involve being arrested. Am I about to do time in a Chinese prison? My mind flashes to *Midnight Express*, which my sister made me watch years ago. It was dire, and that was just a film. I don't even know a lawyer, or whether I get to make a phone call. Should I call Stacy? I can't. I left my phone at my desk. Which they can plainly see from Josh's office. I don't even know her number by heart. I don't know anyone's number, come to think of it. I make a terribly inept fugitive. My hands shake as I boil the kettle and find matching teacups. They'll be wondering where I've gone now. Taking a raggedy deep breath, I steel myself for the performance of a lifetime.

'Here we go,' I say smoothly as I set the tray before my inquisitors. 'I quite like it strong, I hope that's okay.'

'Thank you, Ms. Cumming,' Man One says. 'Now, would you mind–'

'Sugar?'

'No, thank you. If you'd just–'

'Sugar for you, sir?' I smile at Man Two, who nods. 'One or two?'

'Just one. Ms.–'

'Milk for you both? Would you prefer full-fat? I can just go get–'

'No thank you, really, this is fine. Thank you. Ms. Cumming, we've been alerted that there may be some, irregularity, in your work situation. At the Immigration Department we take all such notices seriously, and we're here today to resolve these questions. So could you please tell us: does Mr. Bolton currently employ you?'

'Well yes, he does. Clearly.'

'And when did your employment begin?'

'Oh goodness, I don't have that date to hand.'

'Approximately. Please.'

'Well, it's not very clear you see. I'm sorry, I probably sound obstructive, it's just that the date of my actual employment, if by employment you mean paid work, isn't very clear.' I wonder how many ways I can repeat this sentence before they start shouting. 'I'd better explain. You see, I came from London, where I was employed. Not by Josh, Mr. Bolton, though. I didn't know him in London, although his family is from the UK. Well, of course there are lots of British families here. His grandfather started the business. But you probably know that already. Josh was born and raised here but he went to school in the UK. That was in Cambridge, before I was there. In London, I mean. Do you need those dates?' They shake their heads.

'Because I remember those clearly. I arrived on January 2nd, I flew overnight on New Year's Day. Not the best idea given my hangover. Anyway, as I mentioned, I was employed in London, though not in fashion. I worked as an events planner, so it was completely unrelated.' Probably best not to mention that I wasn't on Immigration's books there either. 'It was all right but I've always believed that fashion was my natural calling. And there were some issues at the end with my job in London, well, I needn't bore you with those. Unless you're interested?'

They shake their heads again. 'Ms. Cumming, if we could just—'

'Right, stick to the relevant facts, of course. Where was I? Oh right, my job in London.' Man Two stifles a sigh. 'So I was an events planner, and before that I worked in PR, but as I said I had this dream of working in fashion. I can't think now why I didn't pursue that earlier, like, when I was in London.' I shrug. 'Circumstances often stop one, I guess. Besides, it's sort of a pipe dream, isn't it? Lots of people would love to do it, and that's what makes it so hard to get into. Well, then I decided to visit here. And Hong Kong is a fashion capital. Any place that produces Vivienne Tam has to be cutting edge, right? Ha ha, you don't look like you know who Vivienne Tam is... East meets West? No? Well, anyway she's an icon in the fashion world... Where was I? Oh right, a job in fashion. Well you know, my mother said I didn't stand a chance, what with no background in the industry, and not even a related degree. But I was just looking for a chance to learn something about the industry, so I persevered, and I did my homework. Of course nobody, anywhere in the world, would hire me without experience. So I got in touch with some of the exporters and offered to help out on an, uh, informal basis, just to learn the ropes. I figured it wouldn't cost them anything and I'd get to learn about the business and, well, it seemed like a good idea.' I'm really warming to my theme now. 'Naturally, most of the exporters ignored me. I guess they get that kind of offer all the time. There must be thousands of people trying to break into the business, so I understand completely. More tea? Oh dear, it's too stewed now, I'm so sorry. Won't be a moment, I'll make a fresh pot.'

I jump up, snatching the tray against their gentle objections. Winnie meets me in the kitchen. 'How's it going?' she asks, flipping on the kettle as I dig around for fresh teabags.

'Ugh, I can't tell. I'm not letting them get a word in but I don't know, Winnie, it feels like a lost cause. I mean, I do work here. No matter how long I talk they're not going to forget why they've come.'

'No, no, no, Hannah, you must stay positive. Josh will be here soon and he says to just keep talking. He says he knows you can do that. And then he laughed... Hannah, you know who's behind this, don't you?'

'I have no doubt whatsoever,' I say grimly.

The Immigration officers look more determined when I return nearly a quarter of an hour later with fresh tea. That's not good. They must know that I'm stalling. 'By the way,' I tell them conversationally as I pour. 'Josh, Mr. Bolton, will be here soon. In fact, perhaps I should just get an extra cup in case–'

'Ms. Cumming, please. Will you please answer our question? Are you employed by Mr. Bolton?'

'Oh, of course. I mean, of course I'll answer your question. I was answering it, actually, before you interrupted just now. As I was saying, I emailed several companies and only Josh got back to me. He was very sweet right from the start. We had a chat on the phone first and he completely understood my conundrum. Chicken-and-egg, you know… can't get work without experience, can't get experience without working. He suggested I might like to come to the office to see how they operate and ask any questions I might have. So I did. It was fascinating. I mean, here I was, inside a fashion company! Josh answered all my questions and we talked about the market, you know, how the problems in Europe are affecting his business. Is the recession affecting your business? No, I suppose it wouldn't. It's not too bad here either, because we– Josh has such good relationships with his clients. Then he… he invited me back… and here I am. Time has just flown, it's–'

There's a commotion in the foyer and my heart leaps as I see Josh striding past Mrs. Reese towards the office. 'Hello, I'm Josh Bolton.' He smiles, extending his hand as if visits from Immigration are an everyday occurrence. 'Hi Hannah, everything okay while I was out?' Solemnly he takes the men's business cards, examining each one, before extending his own. 'I'm sorry, I didn't know you were coming or I'd have cut my meeting short.' He's opening and shutting drawers, stuffing papers from his briefcase into them. 'Now, how may I help you gentlemen?'

Man One clears his throat. 'We're here about Ms. Cumming's work status. We understand that she is in your employ, but we don't seem to have any record of a valid work permit. I'm sure you can clear up the confusion.'

'Oh. Oh, of course. Really? No record? Are you sure?'

'Quite sure, sir. So if you could confirm Ms. Cumming's employment status…'

'Well certainly, but I'll need to check our records, for accuracy you understand. It may take a few minutes. If you'd rather, I'm happy to fax–'

'Yes, sir. We'll wait.'

'All right. Just a moment, please. I'll ask our accountant.'

'So Ms. Cumming is being paid by you?'

'Of course she is. Why else would she be here?'

Man Two shoots me a look.

Josh punches his speed dial, spinning his chair away from us and speaking in a low voice. 'Thank you,' he says as he hangs up. 'The twenty-first of June this year. That's when Hannah started. She may be a recent hire but already she's proving her mettle.'

No, no, no, I want to scream, I don't want him to lie. I've been here since February. He's in enough trouble for letting me work without a visa. He shouldn't compound it by lying. They might put him in jail. He could lose his company! We need to come clean and take our chances that it won't be too bad. 'Josh,' I say quietly. 'I think–'

Man One interrupts, possibly not realizing that I've spoken. 'Do you have your records, sir, showing Ms. Cumming's visa?'

The moment of truth. Josh might be an amazing boss but even he can't conjure a visa out of thin air. As my mother would say, the jig is up. Oh God, my mother. First Sam, now this. It's won't be easy to dispute her claim to righteousness now.

'Of course, it's right here.' Josh reaches into his drawer and withdraws a stapled pack of papers. Abracadabra. 'I'm happy to make copies for you, if you'd like.' They nod, scrutinizing the papers.

'Fine. Mrs. Reese?' he calls. 'Mrs. Reese?'

She appears in the doorway. 'Yes, Josh?'

'Will you please make two copies of these papers for me? Thank you.'

I watch her carefully as she takes the papers. Her expression doesn't change, but the stillness in her face tells me her thoughts. 'Now,' he says. 'If there's nothing else I can help you with…'

'Thank you, Mr. Bolton. We'll just need to see Ms. Cumming's passport.'

He looks at me. 'I'm sure Hannah doesn't have her passport with her. Can we fax a copy to you tomorrow? Or come over with it?'

The officials agree that we should go to their offices, and stand to leave. 'Thank you, Ms. Cumming,' says Man One as we shake hands at the stairwell, as if this was all just a silly old misunderstanding. 'That was a very interesting story.'

As soon as they're safely down the stairs Josh motions me to his office. He closes the door.

'Josh, I'm so sorr–'

'Hannah, I don't know what to say except sorr–'

We stare at each other. 'Why are you apologizing?' I ask him.

'I should have sorted your visa months ago. I kept meaning to but then with one thing or another, I put it off. It was stupid. You could have been in serious trouble.'

'I thought I was dead! But Josh, how did I have a visa?'

'You didn't,' he says simply. 'At least, you didn't until about an hour ago. When Winnie called I knew I had to sort something quickly. I called in a lot of favors, friends of friends and so on, and got the papers done up. Luckily I was near Wan Chai to pick them up or you'd have had to talk for a lot longer! They're not quite legitimate but only insofar as the Immigration men were right. They're the real thing. A real visa, I mean. They just weren't in the records. Well, they will be now, filed away as if they've been there all along. We need to get your visa stamp first thing tomorrow. Don't ask. You're legal now, that's all that matters.' He grins.

'Josh, you're amazing. Okay, I don't need to know the details. In fact, it's better if I don't, in case I ever have to testify against you,' I say, beaming. 'But I do need to talk to you about something. Do you know who called Immigration on me?'

He nods, and sighs. 'Yes, it occurred to me as I was running around.'

'There's more.' I tell him everything, watching his expression get sadder and sadder. 'I'm sorry,' I say when I'm done. 'I know she's a long-time family friend.'

'A real friend wouldn't do those things. Nor would she jeopardize this company. Leave it with me, okay?'

As I leave to tell Winnie all that's happened, I hear him call for Mrs. Reese. He called her Camilla.

'A toast,' says Josh, raising his glass beneath the fairy-lit mango trees. Red lanterns glow overhead, making it easy to forget that our sofa under the stars (well, under the light pollution) is nestling between Mong Kok's skyscrapers. The Backyard just might be my favorite Hong Kong bar, I think as I raise the last of my grapefruitini. 'To work permits!' Stacy grins at him, lightly stroking his hand. 'I was afraid we'd lost you today, Hannah. I'm very glad we didn't.' Everyone clinks glasses.

'And to Hannah's promotion! Congratulations, sweetie!' Stacy adds. 'It is a promotion, right Josh?'

'Absolutely. It's a promotion.'

'To Hannah's promotion!' Winnie grins. 'And to second chances. I didn't think you were going to get a break there, Han. I should have known Josh would figure something out. Here's to second chances. I'm so glad you got one!'

Me too. This day couldn't have worked out better. For me, at least. Despite everything Mrs. Reese has put me through I still felt a little sick thinking about what Josh must have said to her.

They were in his office for a long time, and when she emerged she went straight to her desk, got her handbag and left. Josh appeared in the doorway, ran his hand through his mad hair, and called me in. 'Mrs.

Reese is taking a few weeks off, before deciding what she'd like to do. Hannah, why didn't you say anything earlier? I feel like a fool, that I didn't see what she was doing before this. Not just with you, I mean. When I think of your predecessors… I feel like a fool.' He held up his hand to my protest. 'It doesn't matter now. What's done is done. The important thing is that we go forward, and that I've got a team I can trust, and rely on. You've done a very good job for me, and I expect that'll continue long into the future. I hope this whole business hasn't put you off of us.' I shook my head. 'Good. Then I'd like to discuss your future…'

So here I am, gainfully employed in a job I love, with a boss who, for the first time in my life, believes in me as much as I believe in myself. This feels good. It feels really good. I may not know exactly where I'm going, or what the future holds for me, but I know I'll make the most of it. I've proven that to myself. 'I'll get the next round,' I say, grabbing my bag, which bdlllings in response. My heart skips as I dig out my phone.

Just got your emaik honey, Dad and I are so proud of you. Congratultions. We lovyou. xx Mom

Now will you come home for Christmas?

Yes, Mom, I'll go home for Christmas. I know my own mind now, and I'm strong enough to withstand any convincing she might wish to do. After these past few months, I'm strong enough to withstand anything. Opening my wallet to check for cash, the tattered fortune catches my eye. *Following your heart will pay off in the near future.* Maybe it will after all, I think as I pay for our drinks… 'I'll grab them in a sec,' I tell the bartender. 'I've just got a couple of texts to send first.' I take out my phone, thinking about second chances, and text Sam.

I'll make no promises. I know what I want, and more importantly, I know what I deserve. It's what my heart, and my head, demands.

The End

If you enjoyed *Misfortune Cookie*, please take a moment to write a review on your favorite book website.

THE SINGLE IN THE CITY SERIES

Single in the City (Book One)

Take one twenty six year old American, add to a two thousand year old city, add a big dose of culture clash and stir

Misfortune Cookie (Book Two)

Would you move 6,000 miles to be with the love of your life?

MICHELE GORMAN

The Twelve Days to Christmas (Book Three)
What if his proposal had an expiration date?

ABOUT THE AUTHOR

Michele writes books packed with heart and humour, best friends and girl power under her own name, and writes cosy romcoms under the pen-name Lilly Bartlett. Lilly's books are full of warmth, romance, quirky characters and guaranteed happily-ever-afters.

She is both a *USA Today* and *Sunday Times* bestselling author, raised in the US and now living with her husband in London.

www.michelegorman.co.uk
www.michelegormanwriter.blogspot.co.uk
Instagram: @MicheleGormanUK
Twitter: @MicheleGormanUK
Facebook:
www.facebook.com/MicheleGormanBooks

MISFORTUNE COOKIE

MICHELE GORMAN

MISFORTUNE COOKIE

Printed in Great Britain
by Amazon